THE
SECRETS
OF THE
BASTIDE
BLANCHE

Center Point
Large Print

Also by M. L. Longworth and available from Center Point Large Print:

The Curse of La Fontaine

THE
SECRETS
OF THE
BASTIDE
BLANCHE

A PROVENÇALE MYSTERY

M. L. LONGWORTH

CENTER POINT LARGE PRINT
THORNDIKE, MAINE

For Kathy, Bev, and Sue

Je te tiens, tu me tiens, par la barbichette;
le premier de nous deux qui rira aura une
tapette!
(I have you, you have me, by the little beard;
the first one of us who laughs will get a
smack!)
> —French children's game sung by two
> children who stand face-to-face,
> holding each other by the chin

When night makes a weird sound of its
own stillness.
> —Percy Bysshe Shelley,
> "Alastor; or, The Spirit of Solitude"

Chapter One

New York City,
September 22, 2010

Justin Wong grew up in New York City, but he had never walked its streets as quickly, nor with such intent, as he did that afternoon. He felt like he could fly. It had only been seven years since he graduated from the Liberal Studies department of NYU, and here he was, working at a major publishing house—even if he was a lowly associate editor—and about to meet one of the most famous authors in the world. Prix Goncourt 1982. Voted into France's Légion d'honneur in 1986. Short-listed for a Nobel in 1987. Millions of sales and translated into forty-two languages. Justin stopped to catch his breath, with his hands on his hips and bending over slightly. *Don't blow it,* he told himself. *You have to get this deal tonight. Maybe then Mom and Dad will forgive you for not studying medicine.*

He straightened up and looked at his reflection in a design shop's window. Average height, slim, jet-black hair freshly cut, and new clothes purchased specially for that evening (chinos, a pressed white cotton shirt, and for added flair a blue-and-green-checkered waistcoat and blue brogues that were too expensive even on sale). Ready.

He turned at the Flatiron, and then slowed down as he got closer to East Twentieth Street. He knew this neighborhood well; he and a few buddies used to go to a cheap jazz club nearby. Not only his boss but also the publisher had met with Justin to decide on the evening's venue. They chose a restaurant famous for its food and extensive French wine cellar. The writer was known for his love of wines and cigars. Justin liked both, but that wasn't why he had been chosen for this meeting. The editor in chief or publisher could have easily gone instead. Justin had been singled out by the great writer himself, whose lawyer had written a letter to New York on very old-fashioned embossed letterhead. Justin walked slowly now—he was early—with a huge smile plastered on his face as he recalled part of the letter for the millionth time: "My client, Valère Barbier, would like to meet with Mr. Justin Wong, an employee of your esteemed publishing house. M Barbier will be in New York for three days in September. *Merci beaucoup.* Maître Guillaume Matton, 15 avenue Hoche, 75008, Paris."

The letter surprised Justin as much as it did the publisher, who immediately called Justin into her office (They had never met; it was a big company). "Did you call Barbier's lawyer, this Maître Matton person?" she hollered, pacing the room. "How did he get your name? You can't just contact world-renowned authors without your boss's consent!" She was red in the face, almost as red as the Chanel jacket she wore. Justin looked at the floor, hiding his grin. He always laughed when he was terrified. He sat down in a leather chair, resting his sweating palms on his thighs. There had to be an explanation. *Think.* What connected him to this French writer? He had spent a year at NYU's Paris campus, but he never even read Valère Barbier's works while he was there. He had been too busy chasing French girls. Besides, Barbier had switched genres by then, infuriating his critics but gaining even more readers.

Clothilde had thought it a wild joke. "It looks so good on us!" she laughed over beers in the Latin Quarter. "We French are such snobs! And Valère Barbier has shoved it back in our Gallic faces!" She reached over and rubbed Justin's cheek— that part he remembered vividly. "You are such a cute little New Yorker!" she said. "So cute I am going to take you back to my flat tonight!"

"Clothilde," he said aloud.

"What?" the publisher asked. "Who is Clothilde?"

"Clothilde is a French girl I met while studying

9

in Paris," Justin began to explain. It was the only connection he could think of. "She was writing a thesis on Barbier."

"So what?" the published lashed out. "A lot of people have—at least until Barbier went off the rails."

"Clothilde actually met him and did some secretarial work for him. And she sent me a weird e-mail a few days ago. I didn't understand—"

"Read it to me."

Justin pulled out his cell phone and scrolled down until he found the e-mail. He began reading, omitting the sexual banter at the beginning. " 'Justin, *chéri*, you will soon need to brush up on your knowledge of French wine. Your career may depend upon it. *Bisous*!' "

The publisher stopped pacing. "That's Barbier all right. He once quizzed three separate publishers about wine before deciding which one to go with." She looked at her young editor. "Do you know French wines? I don't drink."

Justin nodded.

She looked at her watch. "It's evening now in Paris. Text or e-mail this Clothilde person. Ask her what's going on." Justin ran through his contact list, amazed that he still had Clothilde's cell number. He sent her a text, and while they waited, he cruised his Facebook page and saw that he and Clothilde were friends. She could have easily seen his employment status. She rarely posted photos or news, nor did he, but he read her latest status. She now worked for Canal Plus, one of the big French television and film companies. That didn't surprise him.

In minutes his cell phone beeped. The publisher, who had been looking out at the Hudson River from her eleventh-floor window, swung around. Justin read Clothilde's text, again omitting the sexual innuendo: " 'I'm still in contact with Valère Barbier, *cher* Justin. Ran into him the other day at work, and we had some mojitos together. Imagine! Mojitos *avec* Barbier! Sounds like a film title, *n'est-ce pas*? He told me he is unhappy with his publisher—a big competitor of yours—and I gave him your name. He wants to write another book, an autobiography! Voilà! I told him you love France.' " Justin paused and said, "True . . . and I love his new books," then looked at the publisher and shook his head, grimacing. He silently finished reading the text: "*La vie est belle*. Ciao, darling! *Trop cuuute!*" The publisher meanwhile sat down and folded her hands on her desk. "Well, that's that," she said. "Who's to argue with the Great Man?" To Justin's delight, she gave him permission to proceed. He got up and shook her hand, thanking her.

She returned his handshake and smiled. "I was silly as an undergraduate."

Justin looked at her, perplexed.

"I, too, did a year in Paris, but I didn't have a love affair."

Justin was still grinning when he got to the restaurant. He looked at his watch—ten minutes early—opened the heavy glass door, and walked in. His publisher had booked the quietest table possible. Justin introduced himself to the hostess and followed her long legs as she led him through the nearly empty restaurant, to a table in its own snug room. The walls were painted a golden hue, the lighting was subdued, and wine bottles in wooden niches ran, floor to ceiling, around three sides of the room. It bothered Justin that the room wasn't climate controlled, but perhaps these were cheap wines or bottles that sold easily. "There's a curtain, if you need more privacy," the hostess said, pulling lightly at the beige velvet drapes on either side of the room's entrance.

"Thank you," Justin said. "We'll leave them open until my, um, acquaintance arrives." He had almost called Valère Barbier his friend. Too much hyperactive Clothilde influence. *Trop cuuute!* "He's elderly, kind of. Sixtysomething. With thick white hair and a French accent."

The hostess nodded. "Would you like to drink something while you're waiting?"

"Water, please." Justin coughed, realizing how nervous he was. "Sparkling." *May as well go all out,* he thought. *It's my first expense-account dinner.*

"Forget the sparkling water," an accented voice sounded from behind the hostess. "Bring two glasses of your house champagne."

Justin quickly stood up, and the hostess coolly nodded to the Frenchman and walked away.

"The house champagne will be good, *non*?" Valère Barbier asked in perfect but accented English.

"*Oui*," Justin said, coughing again. "*Il est très bon.*"

"We can speak English," Barbier said. "I lived in New York for five years, to escape the French press after my infamous genre switch." He smiled. "How do you know that the house champagne is good?"

"I looked up the wine list before coming. It's Drappier."

"Excellent!" Valère said. "You've done your . . . *devoirs*!"

"Homework. Yes, I hope so. Please, have a seat."

Valère Barbier sat down across from the editor. He was taken aback by his youth, but, then, Clothilde had said Justin Wong was a friend, so of course they must be roughly the same age. Almost thirty. Valère realized that he himself had done much by that age. "I like people over eighty and under thirty. One of my best friends in Aix-en-Provence is eleven years old. The ages in between are full of *la merde*! How old are you?"

"I'm twenty-nine," Justin said. "One year away from becoming *une merde*."

Valère slapped the table. "*Énorme! Quel garçon!*"

Justin smiled, wondering if the author had been drinking before he came. But it didn't matter. The hostess returned with two flutes of champagne. Valère reached over and swiftly plucked them from the platter. "*Merci beaucoup!*"

"Tell me, which of my books is your favorite?" Valère asked, lifting his flute to Justin's and giving it a strong tap. "*Santé!*"

"Well," Justin began. "When I found out we were going to meet, I started reading *An Honorable Man*."

Valère leaned forward. "And are you finished?"

"Halfway."

"*Énorme, ce garçon.* You won't lie and say that you love all my books?"

"No," Justin replied.

Valère took a big gulp of champagne. "So why did you start with that one?"

"It was your first, and you wrote it when you were my age. Twenty-nine. Before you—"

"Before I became a shithead!" Valère yelled.

Justin smiled awkwardly; that wasn't the way he had intended to finish the sentence. "Let's get down to business," he said.

"*Négociations? Déjà?*"

14

Justin laughed. "No, M Barbier. Let's look at tonight's menu and wine list."

Justin was careful not to argue too much about the wine. He was there to try to sign Valère Barbier as an author, not to show off his own knowledge. He had asked for the market list instead of the impressively thick reserve list, not wanting to spend all of the publishing house's money. That was the way he had been raised. But he also surmised that one should be able to find a great wine at a reasonable price in such a good restaurant. He shared this second line of reasoning with Barbier, who was impressed and agreed. Valère silently thought that any other editor would have chosen from the reserve list. They agreed on a burgundy, a few years old, from Puligny-Montrachet.

"We're showing off," Valère said. "Even if the price is good, eh?"

"I know," Justin agreed. "But I've never had it."

Valère laughed. The waiter, a young man with freckles and dark-red hair, walked in and announced the amuse-bouche, "Peekytoe crab in a cucumber roll," placing dishes in front of each diner, "with smoked corn chowder and a yellow-tomato sorbet with balsamic vinegar."

"*Merci*," Valère said as the waiter left. He

leaned over to Justin and asked, "What is this peekytoe crab?"

"It's all the rage in New York right now. It's just an Atlantic crab whose legs curve inward."

Valère raised an eyebrow and said, "You seem to know a lot about food and wine. When I was your age, my books were selling, but I was still counting my *centimes*."

Justin smiled. "I like to read foodie magazines. But always on a full stomach."

Valère laughed, selected a spoon, and dipped it into the tomato sorbet. "*Bon appétit.*"

"Same to you," Justin said. "I love the look of this sorbet. It's like egg yolk."

"I was just thinking the same thing," Valère said. "It could almost be zabaglione. Very imaginative . . ."

Justin set down his spoon when he had finished and looked at Barbier. "I've read a lot about your life, but I have questions."

Valère set his own cutlery down and looked at the young man. "Go on."

Justin saw something in the writer's eyes change. Up to now he had been a bon vivant, a man without a worry in the world. All of a sudden he looked older and more pensive. His large brown eyes narrowed, and a few wrinkles appeared on his forehead.

Justin said, "This château you bought in Aix-en-Provence—"

16

"*Bastide,*" Valère corrected. "La Bastide Blanche."

"Right. I've read a few articles about the fire and everything that happened this summer. I became a little obsessed by it."

"Tell me what you know," Valère said.

"Well, that the *bastide* burned down, and, no offense, that some people accused you—though that was never proven."

"No, it wasn't proven."

"But you were there when it happened."

Valère nodded and began eating. "I can't remember much from that night," he said. "They tell me I was yelling something about Agathe—"

"Your late wife."

"Right," Valère replied. "There was a time when Agathe was more famous than me. But only very briefly. Do you know anything about her?"

"Well," Justin began, "I know she was an artist, that you guys were married a long time, and that she died in 1988." He resisted using the word "mysteriously" after "died."

Valère smiled and picked up his wineglass. "Do you believe in ghosts, Justin?"

Was Barbier talking about Agathe? Justin rested his chin on his folded hands and tried to think of an honest reply that would also get Barbier talking. He now remembered reading that Barbier claimed the house was haunted on the night of the fire. "Yes. Yes I do," he answered. "I believe the dead prance around old buildings at night because they think they are still living there. When I was in high school we had to memorize a poem. I chose Shelley. All I can remember now is 'When night makes a weird sound of its own stillness.' "

"Night's weird sounds . . . I couldn't sleep at La Bastide," Valère said, sighing. "It was their busy time."

Justin asked, "Their busy time?"

"It's a long story," Valère said, draining his champagne. "But we have all night. If I'm going to write one last book, my potential editor needs to hear, and believe in, my story. Are you up for it?"

"*Oui, monsieur.*"

Chapter Two

New York City, September 22, 2010

Valère Begins His Story

As its name implies, La Bastide Blanche had a stucco facade, painted white but cracked and peeling by the time I bought it. The house was perfectly symmetrical, as *bastides* usually are: a wooden front door—three feet across—in the center, flanked on each side by two tall windows. Above that were two windows in the same configuration, and over the front door another window, bigger than the others, with a Juliet balcony. A large *B* was woven into the balcony's wrought-iron railing. The third story, not as tall as the other two, allowed room for five bull's-eye windows, ovals set on their side rather than vertically. The red-tiled roof—obligatory in Provence—was a patchwork of new and old tiles, replaced over the centuries, each one a different shade of red, orange, and even yellow. Sometime in the future, I imagined, I would restucco the crumbling facade and paint it yellow;

the shutters, a faded red, would be olive green.

When I bought La Bastide Blanche last winter, I was prepared for Provence's hot and dry summers. We had vacationed in the South often enough that I could remember the early morning ritual of closing the shutters and windows in every room and opening them up again late in the evening. Agathe used to be quite insistent on getting the houses we'd rented closed up by 7:00 a.m. I am by nature lazy and enjoy my morning sleep-ins. Among my most cherished memories of Agathe is her standing over our bed, hands on hips, telling me it's time to get up. *"Les volets! Les fenêtres!"* she would say, reaching down and tickling my toes under the cotton sheet. I would try to argue, *"Je suis en vacances!"* and pull up the sheets. But the truth of the matter was that Agathe was a harder worker than I have ever been. She was physically stronger too. She was a potter—or I should say, a *ceramist*. But you know that.

One of my first memories of La Bastide Blanche was on the fourth of July—when all the trouble started—opening the windows, then the shutters, and yelling, "Turn it off!" I had remembered the heat but forgotten about the *cigales*. I can see you look confused. Cicadas. It was nine o'clock in the morning, and they were screeching. I stuck my head out one of the three enormous bedroom windows and unlatched the weathered shutters. More *cigales* joined in, their song sounding like dozens of Parisian car alarms or thousands of tiny chainsaws. I yelled out once more, for theatrical effect, "I said, turn it off!" and closed the shutters and then the ancient single-paned window with a purposeful loud bang. I felt like Agathe was watching me, annoyed that it was already nine o'clock. I raced across the tiled floor, which felt cool on the soles of my feet, and closed the shutters and windows of the two south-facing windows.

When we'd vacationed in Provence, I'd found the *cigales* charming—a symbol of the South, of summer, of friends and rosé wine, of endless lunches, siestas, aperitifs, and dinners. We'd been on holiday then, not working. That night I had worked until three and fell asleep around four.

And it was not a restful sleep. But more about that later.

Just before closing the last shutter, I looked at the landscape, trying to remind myself why I'd bought this grand house. Just below the garden lay a pebbled terrace, which I had furnished with expensive wrought-iron furniture bought from a pretentious antiques dealer in L'Isle-sur-la-Sorgue. The terrace was edged by a single row of lavender, which at the time my story begins was in full bloom. Below the terrace was a silvery-green olive orchard that I had intended to cultivate on my own. How hard could it be to pick olives every winter? And beyond that, the rolling vineyards, some of which belonged to me and the rest to a neighbor whose golden-stone farmhouse showed, at the edge of the vines, its newly painted white shutters. The village of Puyloubier sat at the edge of the vineyard, for centuries poised firmly on its bed of white rock. It's only a fifteen-minute drive to Aix, a fact that attracted me to the house. I can't think of many towns as small as Aix—what does it have, 150,000 people?—that have the same beauty, serenity, and culture. And so it's ironic that that summer I hardly ever got into town.

That morning I carefully made my bed, resisting the temptation to crawl back in. Looking around the vast room, I sighed at the work ahead of me. Cardboard boxes were stacked against the walls, waiting to be unpacked. Books mostly. Suitcases of varying sizes, from when we used to travel. Surely those could go in an outbuilding? Or in the attic? My clothes were heaped beside the bed in a crumpled mess. I bent down, picked them up, then walked across the room and threw them into the wicker laundry hamper.

I then remembered that I had—very uncharacteristically, I might add—invited the neighbors over for tea that afternoon. I had met them at the foot of the drive the day before—our mailboxes were side by side. I knew that Hélène made wine—I recognized her name and face from the better wine magazines. Her husband was a big brute of a fellow, with a bald head but brown puppy-dog eyes with long, dark lashes; their daughter, who looked to be about ten or so, was, well, completely charming. She was why I invited them over, spur of the moment. Kids have never moved me one way or another. And when Agathe and I found out that I shot blanks—excuse the expression—she didn't seem upset. She already had a son—an oaf who will make an appearance later in my story. But this girl, Léa, was bright, and original.

The winemaker, Hélène, was clearly nervous when she shook my hand—I was used to that. Her husband feigned indifference, and I was also used to that. But their daughter jumped out of the car to look at the grapes hanging in big fat bunches from their gnarled, ancient limbs. She took no notice of me or the scorching dry heat. "Léa, come meet our new neighbor," Hélène said, taking her daughter by the hand and bringing her over. Léa smiled, and I bent down so that she could give me the *bise*. "I'm very pleased to meet you," she said, kissing my cheeks. "It's nice here, isn't it?"

"Extraordinary," I replied. I felt her chubby cheek and could smell fresh air, dust, and something else. Apples.

"The grapes are green but will soon turn red," Léa continued. "You'll see."

"Come for tea," I said, before I could stop myself or change my mind. I'd been on my own at the new house for a little over a week and was lonely. "Tomorrow afternoon, around four. There's no electricity yet, but I have a gas stove and can at least make tea."

"Thank you. I'll bring cake," Hélène offered. "The *boulangerie* in the village is quite good, and they make a few cakes. We're lucky."

The big guy smiled and put his arm around his wife. "Tomorrow, then," I said. I fumbled while trying to get my mail out of the box as quickly as I could. Hélène and her husband pretended not to notice, but Léa watched me. She saw my embarrassment. Since Agathe died, I have had a hard time looking happy couples in the face.

So that morning as I made my way down the wide stone staircase, still in my pajamas, to the kitchen, I said aloud, to no one, "What a ridiculous house." The mid-eighteenth-century fresco in the stairwell needed repair. Two white-wigged ladies and three gents peered out at me, pretending to push aside a heavy red velvet curtain, as if they were on stage. Behind them was a Provençal landscape, much like the one I had just seen through the bedroom window. The painter had been an amateur: in the foreground, the slender cypress trees were as tall as the noble men and women, and the buildings in the distance looked more Venetian than French.

But the figures were charming, especially the tall woman dressed in pale pink chiffon, in the middle of the group, who appeared to be about to leap over a stone balcony and onto my staircase.

Matton, my lawyer, almost fainted when he first saw the out-of-focus photographs of the *bastide*, minutes before the auction began. He said, "If you don't buy it, Barbier, I will." Matton has been my lawyer for decades, and we've always, like schoolboys, called each other by our surnames. I've only just realized that now.

The auction photographs hadn't lied—the house came complete with wall and ceiling paintings, centuries-old tiles on the floors, multipaned windows, and marble mantelpieces in most of the rooms. But the photographs also revealed broken windowpanes, a family of doves that had proudly taken over the salon, and the beer bottles and fire pit that had been left in the middle of the dining room by village teenagers. One of them had even tagged the faux-marbled walls: "*Dylan et Maéva toujours!*" "What ridiculous names," I complained to Matton.

When the auction was over—we somehow outbid a fashion designer and a Chinese billionaire—Matton congratulated me, and leaned over and whispered, "Don't worry. I have a niece who lives near Puyloubier who can have the house cleaned for your arrival. My gift." *Gift?* Maître Matton was handsomely paid to accompany me to the auction, his presence required by French law. Still, this was something. In all the years I'd known him, he'd never been a generous man, which, come to think of it, was why I wanted him as my lawyer.

I had to admit that Matton's niece had done a good job with the cleaning. I began making coffee on the stove top. She had left a short note on the kitchen counter, signed *Sandrine Matton*, that said I should call her if I needed more help. *There is still much to be done,* she added, after her telephone number. There was a spelling mistake, but Sandrine was obviously organized, and I knew that I should call her. I had lived among cardboard boxes for too long, and the EDF was giving me trouble about the ancient wiring, so I still didn't have electricity. Sandrine had even gone to IKEA to buy all the necessary things she correctly thought I might not bring from Paris: brooms and dustpans, kitchen utensils, a set of perfectly adequate white plates and bowls, bath towels and tea towels, and white linen sheets. *Uncle Guillaume must have paid you well and given you some money up front,* I thought. Linen sheets were expensive, even at IKEA. I looked over at the dish set's box, which now sat empty on the floor. The label read, in that black blocklike font that IKEA always uses, "Starter Kit." I smiled. Yes, at sixty-eight years of age, it was a little bit like starting over. Or just starting.

I didn't get much done that morning, except for calling Sandrine Matton and leaving a message asking her to come as soon as she could. Hours later I heard a knock at the front door and had to shake myself awake. I had fallen asleep on the black leather Mies van der Rohe daybed. We'd bought it as newlyweds—when we were both making names for ourselves and fancied ourselves young cultured urbanites. I stumbled to the door and quickly looked in the hall's gilt mirror, patting my thick white hair and briskly rubbing my face. When I was younger, I easily tanned and had a look that Agathe called "rugged." I no longer tan—doctor's orders.

I could hear them chatting on the front steps. "*Je suis ici!*" I called out, thankful that I had changed into a clean white shirt and linen pants before my unplanned *sieste*. I unlatched one half of the wooden door and the noise of the *cigales* filled the hallway. "Please, come in, come in," I said, motioning with my hand, "and get away from those noisy insects."

I saw that Hélène had a box in her hands and remembered her offer. "Thank you for the cake, Hélène," I said.

"If this is a bad time . . . ," her husband said. I saw the look on his face—he didn't want to be here, and he thought that I had forgotten about the visit.

"No no," I said. "It's perfect. I'll just take the

cake into the kitchen and put it on a plate, and then start the water boiling. Or is it too hot for tea?"

"Not in here," Hélène said. "These old houses have their problems, but they stay mercifully cool in summer."

"In winter too," her husband joked.

"I'm sorry, I've forgotten your—" I began.

"Bruno. Bruno Paulik," he answered. He put his arm around his daughter. "And this is Léa."

I had forgotten her name as well. I looked at the girl, who was mesmerized by the fresco in the stairway. "Léa, go look at the painting if you like," I said.

She nodded and slowly walked up the worn stone steps, holding on to the wrought-iron banister. "We'll be in the big salon," I told her. "The room on your left when you come down the stairs."

"*D'accord*," she called down.

I liked her. She wasn't a chatterbox, nor did she speak out of turn or dominate the conversation, as some children do—or are permitted to do. She was clever, I could see it in her eyes and furrowed brow. And she was talented, but I wasn't yet sure what that talent was. Horse riding perhaps. Or drawing.

"I'm sorry," I said, gesturing around the room, "I'm still moving in." Although furnished, the salon still had boxes stacked against its walls, no curtains, and no light fixtures—they had been stolen long ago, during the years the house lay vacant. "Please, make yourselves comfortable, and I'll be back in a few minutes."

"Thank you," Hélène said. "And be sure to call if you need a hand carrying things out."

I gave her my winning smile—my Jean-Paul Belmondo smile, Agathe used to tease—and left. I hurried to the kitchen, hoping that Sandrine Matton had bought some kind of soft drink or juice. I opened the fridge and sighed with relief when I saw orange juice. I wasn't very familiar with children, but I was quite sure ten-year-olds do not drink tea.

I could hear Hélène and Bruno walking around the vast living room. The shutters were closed to the heat, and the air was musty, with a touch of lemon wood polish or floor cleaner. They were whispering, no doubt about me. They stopped whispering, and Hélène said in a normal voice, "The fireplace is like ours."

Bruno answered, "Orange-and-yellow marble from Sainte-Victoire. No need to go far."

"It's garish," I said, walking into the room and carrying a tray laden with mugs, a teapot, and Léa's orange juice. "The other fireplaces are all white marble." I realized I was sounding snobbish, especially since Bruno had just said they had the same kind of fireplace.

Bruno shrugged. "I've always liked it."

"Can I help you, M Barbier?" Hélène asked me.

"No, but thank you. I'll just put this down and go get the cake." As I began to turn around, Léa ran into the room, out of breath. Her face was red and she went straight to Bruno and hugged him. I stared at her, unable to move. The tray began to wobble in my hands.

"*Chérie? Ça va?*" Hélène asked.

Léa took a few deep breaths and turned her head to look at her mother, her hands still wrapped around Bruno's torso. Hélène walked over and felt her daughter's forehead. "You're burning up," she said.

"I'm okay," Léa replied, catching her breath.

Hélène looked over at me, and I could feel the blood drain from my face.

"You look like you saw a ghost," Bruno said to Léa, with a laugh.

I looked at the girl's expression and thought she was trying to decide how to answer her father. She said slowly, "I didn't exactly see one . . ."

"I think you should lie down," Hélène said. "You feel feverish to me."

"*Mais ça va, Maman!*"

Hélène went on, "It's this heat."

"We can delay our tea for another time," I suggested. I set the tray down on a very old and ornate wooden table, one of many that had been trucked down from Paris. *Not the little girl too,* I thought. I suddenly felt very tired.

"I'm afraid we may have to reschedule, M Barbier," Bruno said. "We should get this girl home."

"What happened to Léa?" Justin asked. He set down his wineglass, realizing he was gripping it with both hands. He suddenly became aware of noises in the restaurant—cutlery, hushed voices. He had forgotten where he was.

"I was panic-stricken when she came into the room," Valère replied. "How irresponsible of me to have allowed her to wander around on her own."

"But what did she see?"

Valère shrugged. "What did she see? I don't know. Whatever she saw—or felt—it was clear she was keeping it to herself."

"It didn't frighten her?"

"Correct," Valère said. "But it scared the hell out of me."

"Please go on," Justin said. "I interrupted you."

That evening for dinner I ate about a third of Hélène's cake, washed down with whiskey. It's surprising how well a good single malt goes with a sugary cake. I wandered around the grounds; it was still warm and light out, and I didn't feel like being in the house. I was stalling. I sat down on one of the fancy chaises longues and lit a Cuban cigar and thought about Agathe.

Maybe it was the move, and unpacking, but I found myself thinking of our early years together, in the seventies in Paris. We were poor, but when Agathe got a contract with *Le Bon Marché* to produce a line of dinnerware, it allowed me to quit *Le Monde* and write full-time. Now you can find some of Agathe's *Bon Marché* dishes on eBay for sale at astronomical prices. My books began getting good reviews, and sales crept up, and after a particularly glowing review in *Le Figaro* I found myself being wined and dined by publishers, journalists, and famous writers. Agathe sometimes came to these parties, sometimes not. She found them silly and pretentious. *Red Earth*, which was published in 1975, was made into an artsy short film, but when my next novel, *The Receptionist*, was made into a feature film and won the Palme d'Or, I became more famous than Agathe. Have you seen *The Receptionist*, Justin? You should. It starred Alain Denis, who was killed a few years ago on the Île Sordou, off the coast of Marseille. I wrote more books, won lots of awards, each time feeling more and more unworthy. A fraud.

My trip down memory lane in the *bastide*'s garden ended with my cell phone ringing. I had been keeping it charged with a gadget hooked up to the cigarette lighter in my Mercedes. The caller was Sandrine Matton, saying she would come the next day. I liked her voice—she had a thick Provençal accent. She would bring some *paing*, instead of *pain*, in the morning, and did I need anything else? Coffee? Milk? Words just flew out of her mouth. I was relieved to have someone coming to help.

I thanked her and hung up, noticing that it was finally quiet. The *cigales* had stopped. I relit my Cuban cigar and sat in the dark. I could see the Pauliks' old stone house lit up and tried to imagine what they were doing. Did Hélène do paperwork in the evenings while her vines slept? Did Bruno help her? I realized I had no idea what M Paulik did for a living.

It was quiet without the buzzing *cigales*, so the unexpected sound of branches snapping and crunching coming from the olive grove caused me to drop my cigar. After I picked it up and set it in the ashtray, I straightened my back and leaned forward to listen. A few more crackles, and quite possibly a grunt or two, convinced me to go back inside before the wild boar, or whatever it was, decided to get closer. Anyway, I was feeling tired—but calm and a little bit buzzed and happy from the whiskey and cigar.

I cursed EDF for not coming that week to rewire the electricity, but I had a basket of candles in the entryway. I shoved one in an empty wine bottle and lit it, then walked around and opened up the downstairs windows and shutters. Thieves have easy access to any house in Provence in the summer. Perhaps that's why so many people put those huge, obnoxious gates at the foot of their drives. I preferred no gate, and noticed that the Pauliks did as well.

Halfway up the staircase, I paused. The woman in pink was smiling at me, and I could swear that her painted face was flushed by the light of my candle. I wished her a *bonne nuit*, purposely speaking aloud, trying to make my voice as light and happy as possible. I walked around, opening the shutters to get a breeze circulating. But even at ten o'clock it was still hot, especially upstairs. The rooms felt thick with stale heat and smelled of dust. I'd have Sandrine mop every room.

I saved my room for last, as I usually did, and as I slowly opened the door I could feel the lady in pink watching me from the stairway, smirking. I thought of little Léa and what might have happened earlier that day. Do you remember me mentioning the wrought-iron *B* on the first floor's balcony? It's a coincidence—strange, I know—that my name begins with the same letter. I bought the place on a whim and assumed that the *B* stood for Bastide Blanche. But after I signed the check for a ridiculous amount of money and the house was legally mine, Matton began looking into its past. He seemed obsessed and delighted in informing me that the original owners were the *famille* de Besse. Hence the *B*. It seems generations of fat, lazy, inbred de Besses inhabited the *bastide* until, early in the twentieth century, a notary bought it from the last of the lustrous nobles, who had drained the family fortune. Matton began calling me at all hours, each time he found a new tidbit, but the crème was what he discovered about Hugues de Besse, son of the first owner. Hugues was born in 1688 and unfortunately lived until 1760, which gave him decades to torment the *bastide*'s other occupants. I'll tell you more about that swine later.

I held up the candle and swung it around the room. I didn't think I'd actually *see* anything, but I had to reassure myself that I was alone. I shone the candle at the far end of the room and then on the bed. You'll remember, Justin, that the bed had been carefully made—by me. Hospital corners are my specialty. It used to drive Agathe mad. She was tall and complained that when I made the bed her feet felt like they were bound. Anyway, that night I saw that my side of the bed was perfect, with the coverlet pulled up tightly over the pillow. But someone had been lying on top of the coverlet beside it—as they had been every night since I moved in. A head had sunk into the pillow, and the coverlet was indented where the shoulders and hips had been. This visitor was tall, like Agathe. I set the candle on the bedside table and shook my head. Agathe used to tease me when I'd fret about not deserving my awards:

"Valère, you *do* have a brilliant imagination," she would say. But was it my imagination, Justin, when that same night I was awoken by someone tugging on the bedsheets beside me?

Chapter Three

Aix-en-Provence, Sunday, July 4, 2010

I'm sorry I'm late," Antoine Verlaque said, kissing Marine Bonnet. He pulled out a café chair and sat down across from her. It was just after 7:00 p.m. and the square, surrounded by honey-colored stone buildings, including Aix's massive town hall, was full of people. Tables and chairs spread in a circle around the central fountain, and the *cigales* made their sawing noises in the ancient plane trees.

"No worries," Marine said. "I have a good book."

Verlaque reached over and looked at the title. "The new Claude Petitjean! May I read it next?"

"It's Sylvie's. But I'll ask her."

"What's it about? In a nutshell."

"In a nutshell, it's the story of two friends, a boy and a girl, growing up in Paris in the fifties—neighbors, from the 13th arrondissement. They move away for university, and both go on to have distinguished careers, then meet up again in their seventies."

The waiter came, and Verlaque pointed to Marine's pastis. *"Le même,"* he said.

"I love women who drink pastis," the waiter said. "They are a rare breed."

"I agree," Verlaque answered, smiling. The waiter left, and Verlaque turned back to Marine. *"Le Monde* said it was as good as Valère Barbier's early books."

Marine nodded. "I agree. It has the same humor mixed with wisdom and a dash of Barbier-like melancholy and sarcasm."

Verlaque laughed and then sat back and looked around the square. That morning it had been full of flowers and plants for sale; the greenery, steamy in the morning heat, was now replaced with tables laden with beer, pastis, wine, and soft drinks. "It's funny," he said, "we have a beautiful apartment with a lovely terrace, but sometimes it's just nice to—"

"Be in a busy square, surrounded by other people?"

"Exactly. To hear laughter, and chatting—"

"And a drunk street musician playing the guitar," Marine said, looking over her shoulder. "That guy has been around for years." She had lived in Aix all her life, save for her university years, which were spent in Paris.

The waiter returned with Verlaque's pastis, and he lifted his glass to meet Marine's. "To busy street life everywhere."

They talked of their day but were frequently interrupted by friends and colleagues who knew Marine, Verlaque, or both. Quick news was exchanged, along with a handshake or *bises* for good friends, and Verlaque was glad that the neighboring tables were already taken. Aix's examining magistrate, he'd had a long day and cherished this time alone with his new wife.

"Another one?" Verlaque asked Marine when they were finally alone.

"Why not? Although I'd forgotten that sitting across from the town hall on a warm summer night means we're going to be interrupted. All that talk of the importance of busy street life!"

"You're just too popular."

"Maybe we should go home—"

"Too late," Verlaque said. "Here comes another couple I think we know. They're slowing down and smiling at us." He recognized them, when they got closer, as neighbors who lived on their street. They shook hands and Verlaque sat back, impressed, as Marine recalled their names and the fact that they had just been on holiday in Lisbon.

"We lived like royalty in Portugal," the husband said. "Everything cost half what it would in Aix."

Verlaque flinched; he didn't like the idea of someone from an affluent country taking advantage of another country's weak economy. But as he listened he warmed to the couple; they had genuine enthusiasm for a city he had yet to visit and was now eager to see. Both he and Marine lit up at the couple's stories of Lisbon's fabulous museums, great food and wine, and antiquated trolleys speeding up and down its narrow, hilly streets. But the image of his worn copy of Tobias Smollett's *Travels Through France and Italy* popped into his head, and he couldn't figure out why. Then it clicked. The English author had made the same complaint about expensive Aix three centuries earlier, in 1765.

"Oh, you're reading the new Petitjean!" the woman said, seeing Marine's book.

"We loved it," her husband said. "It's almost as good as the early Barbier books."

"We were just saying the same thing," Verlaque said, realizing he should participate in the conversation, even if he hadn't yet read the book. But when Marine got out her ever-present notepad and began jotting down the names of Lisbon restaurants that the couple excitedly recommended, Verlaque drifted off, once again thinking of Smollett, who found the Aixois well bred, gay, and sociable. This couple certainly fit that description: the woman, probably in her early sixties, was perfectly coiffed and tanned, slim and immaculately dressed in long linen pants and a silk blouse; her husband, quite possibly a few years younger, was as fit and wore a pink Lacoste polo with perfectly pressed chinos. They were friendly but not nosy, obviously well traveled and intelligent, but also modest and sincere. *Bien élévés*. They said good-bye and walked off, arm in arm.

"You're dreaming about Lisbon," Verlaque said to Marine, who was staring off into the distance. "Accompanied by a rather rough version of 'Norwegian Wood.'"

"Is *that* what he's playing?" Marine asked, turning around to watch the guitarist. "But you're right. I haven't been to Portugal in years." She picked a black olive from a bowl and put it in her mouth.

"Correction," Verlaque said. "You're not only dreaming about Lisbon but also of those colorful ceramic tiles the Portuguese put everywhere."

"Azulejos," she said. "Given a choice, yes, I would put them everywhere."

Chapter Four

Aix-en-Provence,
Monday, July 5, 2010

Bruno Paulik loved summer. Provence became even slower than usual; there was still work to be done, but conversations lingered longer as colleagues exchanged vacation plans and news about which beaches had the best sand, parking, or *moules-frites*. Léa didn't have school, only choir and music notation lessons at the conservatory, and Hélène's grapes, fat but still green, hung heavily on the vines. Once a week Hélène's alarm went off at four, and she got dressed, went out to the barn, and climbed on the tractor. She worked until six or so, spraying the vineyards with sulfur to protect them from powdery mildew. It was a task for the early morning, when there was no wind. Bruno felt guilty that Hélène was up practically in the middle of the night and always waited until after she had left the bedroom to put in his earplugs. The tractor made a heck of a noise.

That morning Bruno had dropped Léa off at the conservatory, parked his car at the Palais de Justice, and began walking toward the cours Mirabeau, to have a coffee at the Mazarin. He knew who would be at the café: his boss, the examining magistrate, Antoine Verlaque; Verlaque's wife, Marine Bonnet, who had recently given up a university professorship to write full time; Jean-Marc Sauvat, a childhood friend of Marine's and a lawyer; and various other neighbors, café regulars, and early-rising tourists—usually German or Dutch. Bruno didn't usually go to the Mazarin—it wasn't really his crowd. As a farm boy who grew up in the Luberon, he felt cafés were places where one played foosball with buddies, not where one argued politics with friends who'd studied law in France's best schools. But he enjoyed Antoine's company—Antoine was a part owner of Hélène's winery and always wanted to know what state the grapes were in—and Bruno liked being with Marine and Jean-Marc, too. Besides, today he had big news.

It was almost nine when Bruno Paulik walked quickly across the café's crowded terrace, among the wicker chairs and round tables protected from the sun by a red awning. He knew his friends would be inside, and he didn't have time to say hello or give the *bise* to acquaintances who might recognize him as Aix's police commissioner. He almost ran into a black-tied waiter coming out of the café, carrying a tray full of coffee and fresh-squeezed orange juice. *"Bonjour*, Frédéric," Paulik said, standing aside and holding the door.

"Bonjour, monsieur le Commissaire," the waiter answered, winking. "You're lucky—your friend the judge hasn't yet eaten all the brioches."

"Save me two, Frédéric." Bruno walked in, making his way to the far corner, across the black-and-white floor covered with a light layer of sawdust. The café's golden-lit interior had remained unchanged for decades.

"Salut, Bruno!" Antoine Verlaque bellowed from their usual table. He held up a small basket and shook it. "Sorry, the brioches are all gone." The Mazarin only served pastries from Michaud's, across the street and arguably Aix's best patisserie.

"Liar," Bruno answered, setting his briefcase down on an empty chair. He gave the *bise* to Marine and shook hands with Verlaque and Jean-Marc.

"It's nice to see you here, Bruno," Marine said. "A new Monday morning ritual?"

"Perhaps." Bruno sat down, ordered an espresso from another waiter, and put his large hands on the table. "I'll get straight to the punch," he said. "You'll never guess who our new neighbor is."

"At La Bastide Blanche?" Jean-Marc asked.

"Yes," Bruno said, looking over his shoulder for the waiter.

Verlaque said, "Ah, so the unnamed buyer has revealed himself?"

"Or herself," Marine quickly added.

Bruno thanked Frédéric, who had just arrived with two brioches on a white porcelain plate.

"I only had one," Verlaque said, pointing to the brioches.

"You really are such a bad liar," Marine said, laughing. "Continue, Bruno."

"So guess who it is," Bruno said, pausing to take a bite of brioche.

"Let's play twenty questions," Marine suggested. "Obviously, they are famous. A family?"

"No."

"A man?" Jean-Marc asked.

"Yes."

"An actor?" Verlaque asked. "Aix is being overrun. I wish they'd all move back to Saint-Tropez or the Luberon. One of the secretaries at the Palais de Justice saw Brad Pitt on the Cours the other day."

"No."

"Not an actor, then. A soccer star?" Marine asked.

"No, but good guess."

"You're only supposed to say yes or no, Bruno," Verlaque said. "A politician?"

"No."

"A writer?" Jean-Marc asked.

"Yes."

Marine clapped. "This is exciting. Does he write fiction?"

"Yes."

Marine continued, "Do I like his books?"

Bruno set down his half-eaten brioche and looked up to the ceiling. "Yes. No."

She looked at him with a furrowed brow. "You don't know?"

Bruno shrugged.

"He can only answer yes or no," Verlaque said, laughing.

"Marine may like some of his books but not others?" Jean-Marc suggested.

"Yes!"

"Because after winning all kinds of awards and having his books made into films he switched genres!" Marine said.

Verlaque snorted.

"Yes," replied Bruno.

"Holy cow," Jean-Marc said. He was a shy and thoughtful man, and "holy cow" was as profane as he ever got. "It's Valère Barbier."

Bruno nodded. He couldn't speak; he was finishing the brioche.

"That's quite a scoop," Marine said. "What is the Great Man like?"

"A little awkward at first," Bruno replied after swallowing. "We met him down by the mailbox, and he was having a hard time looking us in the eye. But he took a shine to Léa and out of the blue invited us for tea the next day."

"You got inside the house?" Verlaque asked.

"Did you see Agathe Barbier's pots?" Marine asked.

"Or Valère Barbier's awards?" Jean-Marc asked, leaning forward.

"Photos with Mitterrand? Or Jacques Brel?" Verlaque asked. "Barbier apparently had many all-nighters with Brel and Georges Brassens. I think I took up cigars because of Barbier."

Bruno motioned with his hands. "One question at a time, please."

"When I was a law student, I used part of my monthly bursary to buy an Agathe Barbier bowl," Marine said. "A very small one."

"That I once used for cereal," Verlaque added.

"Yeah, well, let's just say you're lucky I forgave and married you," Marine said.

"You have an Agathe Barbier piece?" Jean-Marc asked. "You couldn't buy one now."

"Do you guys remember where you were when you first read *The Receptionist*?" Verlaque asked. "Barbier's books were so important for our generation."

"In the barn," Bruno said.

The group laughed, and he continued, "No kidding. I would sneak off from chores and read it. I hid it under a pile of burlap sacks."

"I don't remember how old I was when I read the book, but I sure do remember seeing Alain

Denis in the film," Jean-Marc said. "It was love at first sight."

Marine smiled. "Me too."

"In answer to your questions," Bruno continued, "the house is still very much in a move-in state. Boxes everywhere, some vintage designer furniture, but no big terra-cotta pots, no awards, no celebrity photographs. The house is imposing from the outside and has always freaked us out a bit by its sheer size. But the inside is very different—just as big but so worn down and . . . faded . . . that it's charming. The walls are peeling, revealing layers of paint—blue to green to pink then pale yellow—and many of the old floor tiles are broken. They clank as you walk over them. You can imagine a *Vogue* photographer shooting there with five or six skinny models wearing flowing white dresses, one of them with a parrot perched on her forearm."

Verlaque raised an eyebrow.

"Hélène buys *Vogue* from time to time. Anyway, the house has lots of potential," Bruno said as he bit into the second brioche.

"What did you talk about?" Marine asked.

"We hardly had time to talk," Bruno said. "Barbier went out to the kitchen, and by the time he came back we had to leave."

"Why?" the trio asked in unison.

"Léa had gone up the stairs to look at a fresco, and she came back acting like she had just seen

48

a ghost. She was breathless and burning up."

"That hardly sounds like Léa," Verlaque said. He was a big fan of Léa Paulik, a singer in the junior opera. She was polite, smart, and thoughtful. "She's such a solid little girl."

"I know," Bruno said. "That's why we made our excuses and left. Léa is stubborn and sometimes a bit of a know-it-all, but she isn't theatrical. We were a bit freaked out. But the weird thing is, Léa didn't even seem scared. She was . . . concerned, and . . . perplexed. But not frightened."

"How did Barbier handle it?" Marine asked.

Bruno Paulik thought for a moment before answering. "He looked terrified."

Chapter Five

New York City,
September 22, 2010

Justin excused himself and went to the rest-room. At the beginning of dinner he had placed his new iPhone on the table, with the microphone on. He had recorded forty-five minutes of Valère Barbier's story and now sent himself an e-mail with the file attached so he could delete it and begin recording anew. He had no idea how much memory the phone had and didn't want to take any chances.

"Lobster nage?" Valère asked as Justin returned to the table. He had put on his reading glasses and was looking at the evening's menu, printed on a sheet of white paper.

"Their signature dish," Justin replied. "Or so I've read. A lobster soup with squash and zucchini. The white burgundy will be perfect." He set his phone back on the table, and Valère smirked.

"You're expecting a call?" he asked.

"My boss wanted updates," Justin said. "So I just sent her a text message."

"You're honest."

Justin forced a smile. He continued to lie: "She's also a big fan of this restaurant, and I promised I'd send her our menu, dish by dish."

The soup arrived, followed by the sommelier. She walked around the table and showed Valère the bottle, a 2006 Puligny-Montrachet. "*Merci*," he said. "I think my young friend would like to test it."

The sommelier poured a little wine in Justin's glass. He noted its fine golden yellow, then swirled it a few times, keeping the base of the glass on the table, and slowly brought it to his nose. He breathed in, long and slow. "It's perfect."

Both the sommelier and Valère smiled. After filling Valère's glass and pouring more wine into Justin's, the sommelier said, "Enjoy, gentlemen," as she set the bottle into an ice bucket and carefully draped a white linen napkin over it.

"*Énorme*," Valère said, leaning toward Justin. "You could tell simply from the aroma whether it was corked."

Justin shrugged. "I watch a lot of wine shows," he said.

"While we eat this *nage*, should I continue my story?" Valère asked.

"By all means," Justin said, and he took a sip of wine.

• • •

I had, I think you can guess, another restless night. One of the good things about being retired is that you know you can have an afternoon nap. I tossed and turned for a while, trying to get comfortable in the heat and not think about the indentation I had seen on my bed. Around two or three a wind came in through the windows, and I had to pull up the blanket that was folded at the bottom of the bed. I lay on my right side, facing the door, and tucked the blanket up under my chin, finally feeling comfortable. Suddenly, the blanket pulled away. I froze. I very slowly and gently pulled it back over my body. I thought I heard a sound, like a low groaning. *It must be the wind,* I thought.

I tried thinking of errands that had to be done, and began making a list for Mlle Matton. I was at item five—buy a new hose for watering the garden, one that doesn't leak or kink up every foot—when the blanket was again torn off me from the left side. This time I sat up and fumbled for my cell phone, turning on its flashlight. I again heard noises, but there seemed to be nothing in the room. Something banged, and my heart leapt. I looked at one of the windows and saw that a shutter was wildly swinging back and forth, hitting the stone wall. I got up and ran to the window, fastening the shutters against the wall and closing the window. I'd roast with no fresh air coming in, but maybe I'd sleep.

I awoke to the sound of a car spinning on the gravel drive. It almost sounded like it had sped around in a tight circle before coming to a stop. You call that a donut, Justin? Well, doing a donut in your car is probably better for your health than eating one. I got out of bed and opened one of the windows that face south, over the front gardens. I knew right away it was Mlle Matton. The car was a real . . . how do you say it? Shit box. A little two-door Citroën AX that must have been thirty years old. She jumped out of the driver's seat before I had a chance to duck my head back inside the window. "*Oh là là!*" she hollered up to me. She laughed, pointing to her watch, a bright-pink plastic thing that was so big I could almost read it from my bedroom. "Someone sure sleeps in!"

I rubbed my eyes and looked at the bedside clock; it was almost ten. She was right. I quickly got dressed and as I did could hear her getting things out of the car and slamming doors. "I'll be right down!" I yelled. I wasn't sure she heard me, as the *cigales* were busy sawing away. It was the second time in two days that I had been awoken in my new home by a guest. I wasn't getting off to a good start. I once again stopped in the front hall to check in the mirror and run my fingers through my hair. I noticed that I looked even worse than I had for the Paulik family. I unlocked the door, and there she was in all her splendor.

You see, Justin, my working life had been spent in the literary salons of Paris and, later, New York. I had never really come face-to-face with such a woman before. She had her hands on her hips and was tapping the stone step with the toe of her enormous platform sandal. She thrust her hand in mine and said, "Sandrine Matton, at your service," and walked into the entryway, straight past me. She was tiny, even in heels, possibly just a little over five feet tall. Her bleached blonde hair was curly and gathered up, with a gold-colored elastic, at the top of her head. She was giving my house the once-over, straining to see the painting in the stairway and running her fingers along the surfaces as if checking for dust. And, yes, there was dust, as I hadn't done a single thing since she cleaned the house, before my arrival. She tapped one of her heels on the ancient—very ancient—black-and-white tile floor. "Cracked tiles," she said. "You'll be wanting to change these, no doubt. I'd put in shiny new ones. Marble is classy. Orange. Nice and bright."

I was so stunned that I could not reply.

"Still sleepy?" she said, laughing. "That's all right, as everything's up here—isn't it?" she said, pointing to the side of her head. "You must be up in the clouds, inventing those stories of yours."

I looked at her, not knowing if I should scold her or laugh. Had she read my books? And which ones? The books that made my name, like *The Receptionist*, or the books that made me rich?

"I brought my office with me!" she exclaimed, holding up a bucket of cleaning supplies and still laughing. "I'll get the coffee on, and then we can talk shop," she said, walking right through the living room toward the kitchen. "Looks like you could use some."

I followed like a punished child. I almost told her about the nightly visitor, or visitors, in my house, but she was already displeased with my apparent laziness, and I didn't want any more shame. But I knew at some point, if the visitations continued, that I could talk to her about it. And that she would be able to help me. That's how *cagoles* are. It's pronounced "cagaule" and it's slang in Marseille. The *cagole* is the girlfriend of the little Marseille *kéké*, the dude who has bad taste, isn't well educated, and is mostly interested in fast cars and drinking pastis and watching soccer. And she's even more vulgar than her male counterpart. She's loud. She swears. She's provocatively dressed in colors that I must admit look good in sun- and sea-soaked Marseille: neon yellow, hot pink, apple green. None of your Parisian black or gray. Are you getting the picture? Lots of makeup and jewelry, you ask? Right on, Justin. I think you have it.

But here's the thing, and it's especially true in the case of Sandrine Matton: *cagoles* can be the sweetest women on earth. They're affectionate and caring; they'll rest a hand on your shoulder as they talk and ask about how you are feeling. And they'll really listen to your answer. They're hard workers, often far more than their *kéké* boyfriends and brothers. They're fearless and make no apologies for their appearance or foul language. A sort of "take me as I am" attitude. That's it—I've just thought of it. They're honest. You can trust your life with them.

So I sat down at the wooden kitchen table that had been in the *bastide* for decades and watched Sandrine strike a match, light the burner, and get to work. Most girls from Marseille are dark, revealing their Italian or North African roots, but Sandrine had soft pale skin, big blue eyes, full lips covered in shiny gloss, a wide smile, and a little upturned nose. She was wearing an impossibly short skirt, its fabric covered in the stars and stripes of the good ole USA, and I almost wondered aloud how she was going to do housework in that getup. She wore a halter top, shiny green, which revealed a midriff that was taut and muscular, as were her thighs and calves. She whistled while she made the coffee, and I sat there twiddling my thumbs. I was exhausted and still thinking of the blanket being torn off me in the middle of the night.

"What a wind last night, eh?" she asked, as if she was reading my mind.

"Was it windy?"

She laughed again and shook her finger at me. "What, you didn't notice? It wasn't only wind but a mistral!"

Was it the mistral that had tugged at the bed-clothes? I'm a grown man and do know the difference between the wind and someone tugging at blankets, like Agathe used to do. Sandrine poured coffee into two café-au-lait bowls and added hot milk. She looked at me as she poured, seeing my fatigue and possibly other things too.

I took a sip of the coffee—she made it better than I did—and actually smiled. I felt better. "So, Mlle Matton, have you read my books?"

She sat down and crossed her legs, a sandal hanging loose off her right foot as she rocked it back and forth. "Have I!" She sighed and pretended to fan herself, and I knew then which books she had read. "I think my favorite is *Everything We Said*," she told me. "Such a sad ending, but somehow you don't feel bad. And I loved *Postcard Romance*. Such a good idea, to write a love story between travel writers who send postcards to each other! My sister Josy's favorite is *April in Paris*. We read it when we were teens dreaming of going to Paris." She shrugged and drank some coffee. "Maybe someday."

I stared at her. "You've never been to Paris?"

"Imagine that," she answered. "I'm thirty-six years old and have never been to our capital."

"But your uncle—"

"Oh, Uncle Guillaume comes here! He loves the South."

I went on, "It's only a three-hour train ride from Aix—"

"Only?" she asked. "And what do I do when I get there? My uncle is busy with work. Who would show me around?"

I wanted to say, *You just buy a map or a guidebook and wander to your heart's delight. Or sit in a café and people watch. Or visit the Louvre.* Justin, herein lies the difference between people who read my early books—the Pauliks, for example, I would imagine—and those who read my later ones, which as you know are filed in airport and train station bookstores on the romance shelves. The former are active and get things done. The latter can only dream about it.

I'm not being fair, you say? We'll see. I finished my coffee and realized that if Sandrine Matton really wanted to go to Paris, she would have. Right? But all she could do was dream about it. The safer choice.

Chapter Six

New York City, September 22, 2010

I've heard there are people in Jersey City who've never been to Manhattan," Justin said. "But that may be an urban myth." He looked at their empty glasses and, picking up the bottle, poured a little wine into each. He knew that was the sommelier's job, but she was nowhere to be seen.

Valère tapped the edge of his glass, and Justin continued pouring. "Do you want us to die of thirst?" Valère took a big sip and continued, "Sandrine is a really fascinating person. She's full of contradictions. She travels with her own tool kit and talks like a rough-and-tough city kid, and yet she's afraid to go to Paris."

Justin sipped his wine. It was just about the best thing he had ever tasted. "What's she so afraid of?"

Valère played with his wineglass, twirling it around by the stem. "Sandrine has her own ghosts to deal with as it turns out. She . . . no, that should come later. I'll get back to the morning when I first met her."

• • •

We finished our breakfast—stale croissants that Sandrine warmed in the vintage gas oven—and we did a tour of the *bastide* together, trying to figure out what to unpack first and where things should go. It was too big of a house for me, and she saw the worry and disappointment on my face. "M Barbier," she said, taking my shoulders in her hands, "we will unpack all these boxes and crates, and this house will fill up in no time. Plus, not only can I clean and organize, but I'm also a little bit of an interior design whiz!" I looked at how she was dressed and forced a smile. "What's in these crates, anyway?" she asked, pointing to one of the larger ones that sat in the middle of the dining room.

"My late wife's artwork," I answered.

"Sculpture?"

"Pots."

Sandrine looked at me with one eyebrow raised. "Huh?"

"Ceramic pots," I went on. "Agathe was a potter."

"Oh, I see," Sandrine replied slowly. She looked around the room, her index finger resting on her chin. "Do they have pedestals?"

"The smaller ones, yes, and the bigger ones stand alone."

"This is going to be fun!" she exclaimed. My

heart leapt a bit, for the first time in months. "I'll go get my drill to open these crates."

"Your drill?" I asked. I couldn't believe this woman. Like I said, Justin, I couldn't make this stuff up.

"I brought my tool chest," she went on. "And don't worry, the drill runs by battery, and I charged it this morning. I know you don't have electricity yet." She slapped her forehead. "But before I get the drill, I'll call the EDF and get them out here ASAP!" She pulled her cell phone from a huge bright-blue purse covered in sequins, dialed a number, and began, very politely, asking for the hookup service. She stayed calm while getting switched from person to person, and soon she had the third one laughing. I sat down on the bottom step and listened. She rang off, and came out into the front hall where I was sitting. "Tomorrow morning," she said. "They promise. One more night of campfires—eh, M Barbier?" She laughed and went out to get the drill.

We spent the rest of the morning getting Agathe's pots out of their crates. "These are good crates," Sandrine said. "We'll take them down to the basement later."

I mumbled in agreement but couldn't see myself ever needing them again. Sandrine was right: the place soon filled up with Agathe's pots, which we tried to place artfully around the downstairs rooms. I had missed them, with their rough surfaces and dark terra-cotta hues.

After a quick lunch of very decent egg salad sandwiches made by Sandrine (she had thought to bring ice, and beer, for my cooler), we began unpacking smaller boxes. Sandrine would remove an item—say, a crystal ashtray—hold it up in the air, and ask, "Have you used this recently? In the past year?" If I answered yes, as I did with the crystal ashtray, a gift from Jacques Mitterrand, she put it aside, in this case on an antique end table. If I answered no, back in the box it went, labeled "Emmaüs." The charity would come and collect everything after Sandrine arranged a date.

By the end of the day we'd furnished three rooms: the big salon, which Sandrine had taken to calling *la salle des fêtes*; the smaller salon, which she called *la salle de télé*, something I abhor; and the dining room. I was elated. She made it clear that she didn't appreciate my taste, a mixture of 1970s Italian and French antiques, but I was happy that she liked Agathe's pottery.

"What do you think, M Barbier?" Sandrine asked, hands on hips, as we stood in the middle of the dining room.

"It's wonderful," I said. "The furniture and Agathe's pots look so beautiful next to the faded blue walls."

Sandrine hummed to herself.

"I'm keeping the wall color," I added, knowing that her humming meant she didn't agree. "Faded elegance." The ceiling was about four meters high, and the walls had been painted decades, perhaps even a century, ago. Two-toned blue: dark midnight up to about hip height, and a lighter robin's-egg blue above. Over the doors, as is tradition in Provence, were little painted scenes, oval in form. They depicted the seasons, and I pointed out fall above the door that led from the dining room back into the foyer. "They're harvesting up there," I said.

"There would have been hundreds of harvests here," Sandrine said. "If only the paintings could talk—eh, M Barbier?"

"I'd like to taste some of the wine they were making back then."

"I'll bet it was plonk," Sandrine said. "My grandparents would add water to their wine, and that wasn't so long ago."

"You're probably right." I was about to say something about the oldest wine I have tasted—a 1929 Châteauneuf-du-Pape, Justin—when I stopped. A fast whispering interrupted me—so fast I couldn't understand it. "Pardon, Sandrine?"

She looked at me, frowning. "I didn't say any-thing," she said. "Should we stop for the day?" She was looking at me as if I were a dotty old man.

"Sounds like a good idea," I said, trying to act nonchalant. "Would you like a beer?"

"That's why I brought 'em!" she answered.

"I'm going down to the cellar to find a spot for the crates; then we'll really be done for the day."

"Let's do it tomorrow," I said.

She waved her hand my way. "No, I don't think so." That was obviously her way of saying she disagreed with me and was going to override my request. "I'll use the flashlight on my cell phone. Then it will be done." She almost skipped toward the cellar door, located behind the stairs, and opened it with the key that was hanging below the knob. In a few seconds she called up from down below. "There's lots of room down here!" I could hear her chatting with herself— *oh là là* this and that—and I grinned and went to the kitchen to get the beers. I was walking out of the kitchen, a bottle in each hand, when Sandrine came running up from the cellar, her face red, her eyes enormous. She rushed straight past me, toward the front door, and ran outside. I followed her, quickly setting the beers on the foyer console. She had stopped at a pine tree, and was leaning against it, panting.

"What on earth?" I asked.

She rubbed her neck, and tears formed in her eyes. "I couldn't breathe—"

"Was it too stuffy?"

She shook her head wildly back and forth. "No." She took a deep breath and felt up to her neck once again. "It was cold, not hot. But I couldn't breathe." I was going to ask her to stop being repetitive when she went on, "Someone was choking me."

I took a step back and almost tripped over the pine roots. I could see that she wasn't joking, nor was she being theatrical. "In that case," I said, "we have to call the police!"

"But there isn't anyone down there," she said. "How can there be? We've been here all day, working right beside the front door."

"I'll go down there, then." Don't laugh, Justin. I know I was being an idiot, trying to be the hero, but I couldn't let her see that the author of *Everything We Said* was a chicken.

"I'll go with you," she said, taking my arm. So she *could* see that I was a chicken.

"It might have been the wind," I mumbled as we stood at the top of the cellar stairs. I wanted to tell her about my sleepless nights, but it didn't seem like a good time.

"I'm staying here," she said, peering down into the depths of the cellar from the top step. "I'll shine my flashlight down the stairs."

"All right," I said, starting down the stairs, making a lot of noise.

Sandrine began singing an old Claude Nougaro song called *"Tu verras,"* which I thought was a really clever choice: "Ah, you'll see, you'll see. Everything will start again, you'll see."

Like she said, it was cold down there, and it

was vast. The walls were rough stone, and the floor was a dull gray concrete. "It's too musty down here for the crates," I called up, trying to be chatty. "We'll put them in one of the out-buildings."

I shone my light around, walking from room to room. Empty wine bottles, a broken chair, and stacks and stacks of old newspapers. If there had ever been more in the cellar, it had been cleaned out before I bought the *bastide*. An ancient-looking heating system took up one of the rooms. I vaguely remembered Sandrine's uncle, my friend Matton, telling me that it would need changing. The cellar was certainly eerie, but we were definitely the only people there.

I walked back up the stairs, relieved to see Sandrine's Stars and Stripes miniskirt. "Did you come down here when you cleaned the place for me?" I asked.

Sandrine shook her head. "It was locked, and the key wasn't there."

"You're right," I said. "I'm sorry. I just put the key there yesterday."

"I'm sorry, M Barbier," she said as I closed the door firmly, locking it. I showed her the key and put it in my shirt pocket. She added, trying to smile, "Maybe I imagined it."

"Let's drink those beers now. Outside." I wanted to tell her to call me Valère, but I also knew from experience that these sorts of working relationships should remain formal. No, Justin, you may not call me Valère. Very funny.

"I need something stronger," she then said. Her mouth trembled a bit when she spoke, and she bit her upper lip to stop it. "Like whiskey." She surprised me. Most French women don't drink hard spirits.

"That I can do," I said. "And I'll join you."

We sat outside, each of us on a chaise longue, staring at the vineyard. I smoked a big Montecristo double corona, and Sandrine took out a pack of those long, thin menthol cigarettes. As she lit one, she told me that she didn't smoke every day, only a few if she was drinking. "So that's not too bad for my health," she said, throwing her *"Marseille je t'aime"* lighter back in her purse. "Not like smoking those," she went on, pointing at my stogie.

I gave her a quick lesson in cigars, explaining that there are no chemicals added to the tobacco and, most important, that one doesn't inhale cigar smoke, so lung cancer isn't a risk. But with you, Justin, I'm preaching to the converted. I'll tell you right now, too, that I brought some Cubans over with me from France, to share with you tonight.

Sandrine asked, "But a big cigar like that must be so strong, no?"

A common misconception, I told her, and let her have a drag. It may seem like an intimate act, but sharing a cigar has never bothered me, especially if I can get a convert out of a cigarette smoker.

Her face lit up. *"Ça alors!"* she exclaimed, slowly blowing out cigar smoke like an old pro. "It tastes good! Very good!"

An hour and another whiskey later, Sandrine went into the house to get us some snacks. She came out with a bowl of peanuts and some salami that she had cut into big chunks. I tried not to wince: food thinly sliced always tastes better. Agathe taught me that. Sandrine chatted about Provence, the weather, her sister, Josy. I was as relaxed as I had been in months. At around eight or nine o'clock she stretched and reached into her purse for her car keys. She had been drinking a lot of water for the past hour, so I knew she'd be all right to drive. I stood up to walk her to her car, shook her hand, and told her what an enormous help she had been. "Can you come back tomorrow?" I asked.

"Of course!" she answered as she got behind the wheel. "We have the kitchen to do, and we can make some plans to redesign it." She put the key in the ignition, and the car made a sputtering noise. She sighed and laughed, patting the dashboard. *"Clochette! Allez, Clochette!"* Yes, she called that beat-up Citroën *Tinker Bell*. The car was making funny sounds and wouldn't start. You can see where this is going.

"Is it the battery?" I asked. As a Parisian, I know nothing about cars.

"It's a new battery," she answered. "You can hear the battery trying to turn over the engine." She looked up and smiled at me, thinking it funny I hadn't figured that out. "No, it's the fuel pump," she continued. "I had the fuel filter replaced when I had this problem before, but now I'm afraid I have to get the pump replaced. *Ô purée!*" That's a cute way, in the South, to say *putain*.

She got out her cell phone and dialed someone. I could hear a man's voice on the other end, and I stepped aside to give her some privacy. She was speaking a mile a minute, more yelling into the phone than actually talking. Her Provençal accent seemed to be dialed up. "*Connard!*" she finally yelled, and then hung up.

I walked over to the car. "I take it he can't help you out?"

"*Connard d'ex!*"

"Your ex-boyfriend?" I asked. Or maybe it was her ex-husband. Or ex-brother-in-law. I had no idea. At any rate, she called him an asshole.

"Yes! One of my ex-boyfriends. André!" she exclaimed. "He's at home watching the World Cup!"

"Soccer, right? Is that on now?"

Sandrine whistled. "Wow. It's the last game tonight. What planet are you from?"

"And Josy?" I asked, ignoring her jab.

Sandrine paused before answering. "She's gone on holiday."

"Don't worry," I reassured her. "It's probably better that you don't drive after those whiskies."

She sighed and got out of the car. She patted the hood and said, "It's not your fault, Clochette."

She began searching through the contacts on her phone, but I could see she didn't look convinced that anyone would come. Her hand trembled slightly.

"You bought enough sheets to set up a small luxury hotel," I said. "You can take your pick of any of the bedrooms, and we'll get a pizza delivered from the village for dinner. I'd drive you into Aix, but I've had more whiskey than you. Tomorrow we'll get a mechanic out here. I noticed that there's a garage in the village."

"I'm so sorry, M Barbier," she said. She looked up at the house, and I wasn't sure if she was sorry that she was inconveniencing me or she was afraid to sleep in La Bastide Blanche. She shrugged and said, "At least I'll be here if EDF shows up early tomorrow morning."

We walked back to our chaises longues, and I went into the house to get my cell phone and a bottle of wine. During one of my walks into Puyloubier, I had put the pizza place's phone number in my phone. The village was only a kilometer or so away, but I didn't feel like walking, and it would soon be dark. Sandrine went into the house and brought out two wine-glasses and a corkscrew; she was definitely a take-charge kind of woman. I asked her what kind of pizza she wanted, and we agreed on chorizo with mushrooms and red peppers. The call made, we sat back again, and I poured some wine. "M Barbier," she asked, "what made you decide to start writing your wonderful romance books?"

This is a question I have been asked over and over again, but I guess Sandrine hadn't read my standard answers. "I was heartbroken after Agathe's death," I said. "I wrote the first romance—"

"*Another Day!*"

"Right," I replied, "as an homage to Agathe. I wasn't thinking *I'm going to switch genres.* I was just writing what was in my heart, and what I thought I needed to say."

"Your older books you didn't write with your heart?" she asked. She put her hand to her chest for extra effect.

"No," I answered slowly. "They were more up here," I said, pointing to my forehead. "Émile Zola once told his friend Paul Cézanne that he, Cézanne, was more talented because he painted with his heart while Zola wrote with his head."

Sandrine listened, furrowed her brow, and then smiled, understanding what Zola meant. "And you kept writing romances."

I wished she would stop calling them romances. In the trade they're referred to as "contemporary women's fiction." "I did. Especially after the success of *Another Day*. I found writing those books an emotional release. Cheaper than therapy."

"They made you feel good."

"Exactly." I didn't add, "and rich."

"That's why I love cleaning," she said. I tried not to look surprised. She went on, "I'm helping other people, and it makes me feel good. I can organize their stuff, so they feel better about themselves too."

I lifted my glass to hers and gently tapped it. "You have already, Sandrine. Thank you."

"How did Mme Barbier die?" This question, people usually don't ask. They either know, because it was all over the press, or they don't want to ask.

"We're not sure."

Now it was her turn to look at me, surprised.

I continued, "The case was never solved; in fact, it's still open. Agathe fell into the sea. At least that's how I remember that night. We were on my publisher's sailboat—Alphonse Pelloquin was his name. He died of cancer a few years ago. We had all had a lot to drink, and it was late. The waves were choppy, though they hadn't been earlier. I was down below, having a nap . . ."

Sandrine stared into her wineglass, silent. A whining noise and the sound of crunching gravel came from off in the distance. Soon a tiny light approached the house, getting closer and closer. It was our pizza.

The little moped, with one of those bright-red wooden boxes attached to its rear, stopped about ten feet from us, at the end of my driveway. The delivery guy got off, and took our pizza from the box. I had the money ready, and we met halfway. He slowly took off his helmet, and I could see he was a kid, maybe twenty. He stared at me, and gulped before speaking. "M Barbier," he began, "it is . . . an honor."

"To bring me my pizza?" I asked, trying to laugh. I think the whiskey and wine were getting to me.

The kid laughed and handed me the pizza. "No, it's an honor to sort of meet you," he said. He reached out with his skinny hand, and I shook it. I was going to ask him if his name was Dylan, and then chastise him for writing on the living room walls, but he introduced himself as Thomas.

"How do you do, Thomas," I said. I realized that in all the commotion I had used my real name when ordering the pizza. Usually I'm M Dupin. George Sand was born Aurore Dupin.

"I just want to say," Thomas said, his voice

cracking, "that *Red Earth* is my favorite book of all time."

I turned around, hoping that Sandrine wouldn't burst in and want to talk about *Postcard Romance*, but she was busy lighting candles on the terrace table.

"I'm thrilled," I replied earnestly.

"We had to read it in high school," he said. "But I want you to know that I've kept reading it, over and over, since then." He gestured toward the scooter and said, "I'm doing this for a summer job."

I nodded. "Good man. Having a summer job is important. What are you doing in the fall?"

"Going into my second year of *prépa*."

"Clothilde did *prépa*!" Justin cut in. "Pure hell, she called it."

"That's exactly what it is, a hellish two years of study—*préparation*, in order to try to pass the entrance exams into *une grande école*."

"Yeah, but if you get in, those elite schools are free, aren't they?" Justin asked.

Valère chuckled. "If you gain entry into one of them, they're not only free; you're paid a salary. For being a student! I asked Thomas which school he wanted to go to."

"Sciences Po," Thomas answered. "I want to be a journalist."

Sciences Po is—yes, you're right, Justin—a political science school, with lots of courses in the humanities. "I wish you all the very best," I said to Thomas, shaking his hand again. "And please be careful on that contraption." I pointed to the scooter.

"I will, M Barbier!" he shouted, as he put his helmet back on. I wanted to offer him some kind of job around the house, gardening or something, to get him off that thing. Maybe I would. I was a new man, one who wasn't getting any sleep, but one who was very different from his former depressive Parisian self.

"*Oh là là*," Sandrine called over. "Are we eating a cold pizza or what?"

Chapter Seven

Aix-en-Provence,
Monday, July 5, 2010

Instead of taking the tiny passage Agard, normally the quickest way back to the Palais de Justice, Bruno Paulik walked along the rue Thiers, one of his favorite streets in Aix. He liked the elegant but faded hotels that lined the curved street, and the fact that here there were still mom-and-pop stores that had been around for decades. He walked into one of them now, a shoe store called Cendrillon, which he remembered being dragged to by his mother and older sisters on Saturday shopping trips into Aix. "*Bonjour, mesdames*," he said politely to the other shoppers—all female, all looking at him curiously—as he carefully closed the door behind him.

"*Ah, bonjour, monsieur le Commissaire*," said a well-preserved woman in her late sixties who was helping another woman choose a pair of dress shoes.

"I'm here for my daughter," he explained.

"I'll be with you in a minute," the saleswoman answered.

"You go ahead," her client said, "while I try walking around the store in these shoes a bit."

"*Merci, madame,*" Bruno said. He looked around the shop and swore it hadn't changed in decades, except for the prices, which were higher and no longer in francs. But the summer sales were on, and Léa needed new sandals.

"*Et votre maman?*" the saleswoman asked, and Bruno realized that she must be Anne-Marie, the shop's owner. "*Vos soeurs?*"

"They are all well, thank you," he replied. Anne-Marie had somehow recognized him and knew that he was a policeman, but he hadn't recognized her. "Maman and Papa are still very active," he went on. "I'll tell her you said hello."

"Likewise," she said. "And if you could tell your mother that we're closing in two months, and we've appreciated her business over the years."

"You're closing permanently?"

"I'm afraid so," she replied. "Early retirement. We just can't compete with . . ."

Bruno nodded. "The chain stores. I'm so sorry."

She shrugged. "You're looking for shoes for your daughter?"

"Yes, sandals, in size 36. She wants the ones made in Saint-Tropez," he answered. "I have specific orders. She wants them in light-brown leather."

Anne-Marie smirked. "I'm not sure if I have any left in brown in 36, but I'll check."

She went in the back room, and Bruno smiled as the other client walked around the room, testing her new heels. "A summer wedding," she said. "My niece." She walked over to Bruno and whispered, "It's costing a fortune. They're renting the Château Grimaldi in Puyricard."

"I'd better start saving," Bruno said. "My daughter is almost twelve."

The client laughed and walked over to a mirror to look at her shoes. Bruno realized that one of the most pleasant weddings he had been to recently was Antoine and Marine's, a year ago, in a tiny Ligurian village. Anne-Marie came back with a shoe box in her hands. "Great," Bruno said.

"Not exactly," she replied. "They're not brown, and I know how selective little girls can be. They're the Tropeziennes brand, but in silver. It's a very chic color right now." She pointed to the small metal emblem on one of the straps, to prove the shoe's authenticity.

He looked at the sandals, flat with five delicate straps that surrounded the foot. They had been favorites since Brigitte Bardot made them famous in the late 1950s. His sisters had always worn them, and he noticed that girls and women in Aix still did. "I'll take them," he said.

Marine left the café, kissing Verlaque good-bye and wishing both him and Jean-Marc a good day, and made her way up the rue Clemenceau in the direction of their apartment near the cathedral. For the first year of their married life they had each kept their apartments, but she recently sold hers, located in the chic quartier Mazarin, and they had just begun to look for a house in the countryside. The prices made her stomach flip, as did the fact that her husband didn't flinch seeing renovated farmhouses near Aix selling for multiple millions of euros. He claimed it was because he was used to Parisian prices, but she knew that it was really because of the wealth he had grown up with. Antoine's grandfather, Charles Verlaque, had earned the family fortune in flour mills, Antoine's father, Gabriel, halfheartedly took over in the late 1970s. The mills were sold to a multinational in the late 1990s.

Marine cherished mornings in Aix, especially in summer, before the tour groups arrived. When she was a girl, she dreamed of living in a big city, Paris or Rome, and wished that her hometown wasn't so sleepy. Now she found herself wishing there were fewer people in Aix. In a few minutes she arrived at the place de l'Archevêché, now called the place des Martyrs de la Résistance, but the former name would always be engraved in her mind. It was the one she had grown up with. Instead of turning right, toward their apartment, she decided to walk on and visit the cathedral. She had a long day ahead, researching the war years of Simone de Beauvoir and Jean-Paul Sartre, and needed a few moments of inspiration. When her book proposal, a biography on the couple's working, and loving, relationship, had been accepted by a prestigious Parisian publishing house, she resigned from her position as a law professor at the Université d'Aix-Marseille. Quitting her job hadn't been a rash decision—she had been thinking seriously about it for over a year—and with Antoine's blessing her book deal helped her deliver her letter of resignation to the dean. Almost a year on, ex-colleagues told her that the university still hadn't hired a replacement, and she felt relieved to be away from the slow-turning wheels of French academia.

Saint Mitre's carved face greeted her as she stood outside Saint-Sauveur. The saint was beheaded in the fifth century, and he held his own head in his hands. It was so much more elegant, mused Marine, than having it lie on the ground at his feet. Or perch on a platter, as Judith often does with the head of Holofernes. She stopped to give a beggar beside the front doors a euro. The beggar said *merci*, and Marine saw that he was blind. She went inside, leaving the bright sunshine for the darkened church. It was mercifully cool, as the morning was already hot. As much as she loved living downtown, she relished the idea of their future country house, whose thick walls she imagined would keep them cool. She frowned, realizing that her guilt about the probable cost of the new house was quickly diminishing.

The chapel of saint Mitre was on the left-hand side of the nave, and Marine walked through the church with purpose. Her aim wasn't to visit the saint's sarcophagus, which was in the chapel (*Who knows whose body is under all that stone,* she thought). She wanted to do something she had been doing since she was a child and had always brought her luck—or at any rate helped her to think straight. On the column to the right of the tomb, about three feet off the ground, was a hole about the size of a large coin lying on its side. Legend said that the hole released a miraculous liquid that could cure eye diseases. She bent down and slowly put her finger in the hole, thinking of the beggar outside, and closed her eyes. Blocking out the noises in the church, she tried to concentrate on her book. But visions of a stone country house kept interfering with her attempts to organize the next chapter. Opening her eyes, she slowly felt along the smooth cold surface of the hole's interior. She sighed. She couldn't feel any liquid, but, then, she never had.

To sell the book idea, Marine had organized the chapters as simply as she could. The book would cover two long lives, in one of history's most tumultuous centuries, so she ordered the chapters chronologically. Once the contract had been signed, she thought she could be a little more daring with the narrative and perhaps go back and forth in time, but in the end it proved logical to keep the chapters as they were. All day she worked on organizing chapter 3, 1937–39, and toward the end of the day typed in a chapter title, "The Oncoming War," before closing her laptop. Verlaque had transformed the mezzanine, which gave onto his living room, into an office for Marine. "What about your office?" she asked. "I have an office already," he said. "At work, at the Palais de Justice. The only work I do at home is bill paying, and that I can do at the dining room table."

Conscious of the fact that she was about to go out into the scorching heat, Marine drank a tall glass of water. She then grabbed her car keys and purse, and headed out of the apartment to pick up her goddaughter, Charlotte. Charlotte and her mother, Sylvie, Marine's best friend, lived around the corner. Twelve years ago, Sylvie had had an affair with a married man and kept the resulting pregnancy a secret from him, against the advice of almost all her friends, including Marine. That evening, Marine and Charlotte were invited to dinner at Hélène and Bruno Paulik's, as Léa and Charlotte were good friends. Verlaque was going out that evening, with cigar friends, visiting downtown apartments in the hopes of finding one suitable to rent as a clubhouse.

Charlotte was waiting in the street, beside her front door, when Marine arrived. It shocked Marine to see Charlotte standing there alone, and she forgot how grown up she was at eleven years old. "Where's Sylvie?" Marine asked after exchanging the *bise* with her goddaughter.

"She had to leave," Charlotte answered. "She was late for an appointment."

Marine nodded and said nothing, thinking that "an appointment" probably meant a date, and Charlotte didn't want to talk about it. Charlotte had never met her father, but Marine knew that he was a well-known photographer from Berlin, with children of his own.

"*Maman* spent hours in the bathroom getting ready," Charlotte said.

Marine looked at her goddaughter and smiled. "Oh yeah?"

"I had to brush my teeth at the kitchen sink."

"Poor you!" Marine said, trying to have fun with it. She was unsure where the conversation was going, and if Charlotte's feelings were hurt.

"She finally came out of the bathroom and then ran right back in again and wiped off most of the makeup she was wearing," Charlotte said, "and then changed her clothes for the third time."

Marine whistled. "Sylvie looks good no matter what she wears. She needn't worry so much."

Charlotte smiled. "Yeah, *Maman* is really pretty." She reached over and held Marine's hand, and they walked toward the underground lot where both Marine and Antoine kept their cars, their arms swinging in motion as Charlotte told Marine about school. Next year Charlotte would be in junior high, and she was determined to take the exams to enter into the bilingual French/English class at Collége Mignet. Antoine Verlaque was her English tutor. Léa Paulik would surely be admitted into the intensive music program, also at Mignet, and the girls were thrilled at the possibility of studying at the same downtown school.

In less than twenty minutes, they were driving up the dusty gravel road leading to the Pauliks' house. Verlaque had convinced Marine to buy a new car, showing her photographs of small, sleek Italian and German race cars. She instead bought a small four-door Renault Clio. "Made in France," Marine said, "plus my parents always buy Renaults."

"I know," Verlaque said, his expression exaggerating the sadness in his voice.

Marine laughed. "My family has been a customer at the Aix Renault garage for years, and I know they won't rip me off when it comes to repairs."

Today the temperature read 34°C, and she was thankful that the Clio had air-conditioning. "There's the mountain!" Charlotte called out, leaning forward to get a better look at mont Sainte-Victoire.

"It looks like it's leaning over us, it's so close," Marine said. She swerved the car to avoid a pothole. "As if it's protecting the vineyards."

"It's so white!" Charlotte exclaimed. She shielded her eyes and Marine laughed.

"Here we are, and there's Léa waiting for you!" Marine said as she parked the car under an oak tree, hoping it would provide a little shade. Léa came running and embraced Charlotte as soon as she stepped out of the car. Marine smiled as the girls chatted. Charlotte was almost a head taller than the short, plump Léa.

"*Âllo*, Marine!" Léa called, and she ran to Marine to give her the *bise*.

Marine embraced her and said, "You sure do a lot of running, Léa."

"I'm not allowed in Mom's wine lab," Léa said, wiping some perspiration from her brow. "She's afraid I'll break something!"

"That's probably a good idea!" Marine said, laughing. "Hélène's wine is very expensive these days."

Léa shrugged, having no idea of, or interest in, the prices of her mother's wines. "Let's go to my room," Léa said to Charlotte. "I have some new *Alices*." The girls ran off to look at the adventures of the French Nancy Drew.

Hélène and Bruno Paulik walked out of the house and called over to Marine. "It's cooler inside, believe it or not," Hélène said.

"I believe it," Marine said.

They exchanged the *bise*, and Hélène ushered Marine into their vast kitchen. "I'll pour you a big glass of water," Hélène said, "and then we have a surprise. We're invited to our neighbor's for an aperitif."

"Chez Valère Barbier?" Marine asked.

"Yes," Bruno answered. "Apparently, he has a gift for Léa."

"It's a bit like meeting a rock star," Marine said after taking a sip of water.

"You'll see," Bruno answered. "He's just a regular bloke."

Hélène said, "He's even a bit . . . melancholy."

"He's probably never gotten over the death of his wife," Marine offered.

Hélène smiled, knowing that her newly married friend was a romantic.

Marine finished the water and went on: "And the fact that Agathe Barbier died mysteriously—"

Bruno waved his hand. "No amateur sleuthing, please." He adored Marine but worried for her safety when she stuck her head into police business. "She drowned."

"The case is still open," Marine quickly said. "I looked it up."

"You're supposed to be writing your book," Hélène said, shaking a finger and laughing.

"You're so right," Marine said. "I thought when I retired from the university I'd have all kinds of time to write. But the days seem to fly by."

"You guys, it's time to go," Léa said, calling from the front hall.

Bruno rolled his eyes. "Our alarm clock."

"I heard that, Papa," Léa answered.

"Do you know who this is?" Valère asked Léa. They were sitting on the cool tiled floor of the bigger salon, gathered around an opened cardboard box, looking at a black-and-white photograph. Charlotte sat beside them, and Hélène, Bruno, and Marine were seated on armchairs formed in a circle around the box. Sandrine was in and out of the room, bringing in chilled rosé for the adults and Orangina for the girls. Sandrine was thankful the electricity was on—but the EDF guys warned her that one day the ancient wiring would need to be entirely redone.

Léa smiled and stared at the photograph. "Of course I do," she said.

Bruno winced; his daughter was getting more and more haughty as she got older. But Valère Barbier adored her assurance and egged her on. "So then, do tell me," he said.

"Why, it's Maria Callas," she answered. Léa brought the photo closer and said, "She was so beautiful."

"Yes, she was," Valère said.

"Did you take the photograph?" Charlotte asked, as she twirled a colorful silk scarf that had also been in the box around her shoulders.

Valère laughed. "No, that's me in the photo, beside Maria."

"The sailor?" Charlotte asked, leaning in to get a better look.

The adults laughed, including Valère. "It was a sort of fashion back then, in the early seventies, on the Côte. I paid a lot for that white linen jacket and blue cap. Pierre Cardin!"

"What was she like?" Léa asked, not interested in designer clothes.

"Always hungry," Valère answered. "Poor Maria loved food but had to watch her weight. We'd go out to eat, and she'd bug the chef about the dishes we had all eaten—but not her. Then she'd write down the recipes on little pieces of paper and stuff them into her purse. She loved cakes and desserts but could never eat them."

"But you have to eat to sing," Léa said.

"I agree!" Valère answered. "Maria ate lots of salad and raw beef."

"*Beurk*!" the girls cried in unison.

"We listen to her at the conservatory," Léa said. "My teacher says that her middle ranges were perfect, but she was too shrill in the higher registers."

"She was more than perfect in the middle ranges," Bruno said. "She was hauntingly beautiful."

Valère turned to face Bruno. "You're an opera fan?"

"Since I was so high," Bruno answered, placing his hand, palm down, about three feet off the floor.

"And are you also in the wine business?"

Bruno laughed. "No, I'm a police officer."

Valère dropped the photograph and tried to laugh. "A cop, eh?"

"*Police officer*," Léa said. "Daddy is the commissioner."

"Léa," Bruno said, "please don't correct adults."

Valère waved his hand. "It's quite all right. 'Police officer' is the correct term. I for one hate to be called a romance writer."

"Did you know Maria Callas very long?" Marine asked.

"Only very briefly," Valère said. "She was . . . difficult."

"'I am alone, always alone,'" Bruno said. "That's what she said at the end, right?"

"Exactly," Valère said. "It's odd, how often writers and actors and singers say that. Here we are, surrounded by people—our characters, our fans, our public—and yet often we feel alone."

"Snacks!" Sandrine called out as she walked into the room carrying a tray of small bowls.

"And here I am, living in the country for the first time in my life," Valère continued.

"My husband and I are thinking of buying a house in the country," Marine said. "But I've lived downtown all my life. He—Antoine—works downtown, so there will be days when I'll be alone at the house. I love being surrounded by my fellow Aixois."

"Night is worse," Valère began.

"Who would like something to eat?" Sandrine cut in. "We have pistachios, expensive English potato chips, cherry tomatoes, and olives from the market."

Léa didn't answer. She was still staring at the photograph. Valère looked at her and said, "I'd like you to have the photo, Léa."

She looked up at him wide-eyed. "Are you sure?"

"Yes, M Barbier, are you sure?" Hélène asked.

"Absolutely," he answered. "Sandrine is forcing me to throw out things I haven't used or looked at in the past few years. I had even forgotten about that photograph."

"Let's get it framed, M Barbier," Sandrine said. "We're already going into town to get your late wife's drawings framed. That way you can sign it for Léa."

"Excellent idea," Valère answered. He looked at Charlotte, who was still playing with the silk scarf, twirling it this way and that. "And you, Charlotte, may keep the scarf."

"*Merci beaucoup!*" Charlotte said, beaming. "I love it!"

"A woman's scarf I'm certainly not going to use," Valère added, laughing.

"The scarf didn't belong to Maria Callas, I hope?" Bruno asked.

"Oh no," Valère replied, staring at the scarf, "I don't think it did."

The front door knocker sounded, but before anyone could move, a voice bellowed from the front hall. "You have no idea how expensive a taxicab is from the TGV station to Puyloubier!" Hélène, Bruno, and Marine swung their heads toward the voice, and Valère and the girls instinctively jumped up. Sandrine set down the tray and put her hands on her hips.

The visitor walked into the salon, a woman somewhere between sixty and seventy-five years of age, tall, and heavyset. She had short jet-black hair and wore bright-red glasses. Her lipstick matched the glasses. She said, "Valère, thank you for the welcoming committee. Did you not get my text messages? I was lucky and got a taxi driver who lives here, in the village, but when I gave him the address he quickly made a sign of the cross. What's going on

91

here?" She laughed and looked around at the group. "And, Valère," she went on, "what on earth is that child doing wearing my Hermès scarf?"

Chapter Eight

New York City,
September 22, 2010

"Of course I had seen Michèle's text message. I thought if I ignored it she wouldn't come," Valère said. "But that was very stupid of me. She never listens to a word anyone says."

"So who is this Michèle?" Justin asked.

"Michèle Baudouin, my archrival. She sells more books than I do. In fact, I think she may be one of the best-selling authors in the world."

Justin shrugged. "I imagine I would know the name if she's that well known. What's her pen name?"

"Rosalie di Santi." Valère waited and watched Justin. "Ah! I see from your amazed expression that even a millennial like you knows the name of Rosalie di Santi."

"Hey, millennials are cultured!" Justin almost added "more than you lucky-to-be-born-in-the-fifties baby boomers," but he kept silent.

"I'm not making a judgment against every kid born in your decade, so stop complaining or I won't let you choose the next wine."

Justin smiled and picked up the wine list, turning many pages until he got to the reds. He looked up and said, "Go on. I'm all ears. And I already don't trust her."

I've always hated her pen name; di Santi sounds like a cross between an Italian countess and a flamenco dancer, and Rosalie sounds like a made-up Disney name. But she's stuck with it. Michèle and I go back, way back. We grew up together, on the same street in Paris. We were rivals all through school and then at university— just like Simone de Beauvoir and Jean-Paul Sartre were—albeit Michèle and I had much lower intellectual ambitions, and, unlike the philosophers I mentioned, neither of us has a political bone in our body.

The French press love writing about us, given that we've known each other since we were kids and we both ended up being famous writers. They even tried to link us romantically, which was terrible for me and especially for Agathe. Now, I'm not saying I was never physically attracted to Michèle; that would be a lie. She is a handsome woman, though her beauty has faded as the years have passed. When she was young, she was tall like Agathe, but rounder, not as skinny and frail looking. Michèle had olive skin and big eyes and big lips and big . . . Cut it out, Justin. I was going to say big hair. It was thick and jet black, with a white streak that ran down the front. She drank and smoked like my buddies from the newspaper; in fact, she's a cigar smoker, and a mutual friend just told me that she recently married a Cuban man thirty years her junior, all in order to be able to buy a house in Havana.

When you're writing, a little devil sits on your shoulder, always nagging you about how really shitty your first draft is. The devil may be one of your parents or your favorite writer or an old teacher. But mine is Michèle. Despite all our drunken arguments—once we were both thrown out of the Café de Flore for yelling too much—she's my conscience. She's the little critic in my head who urges me to be a good writer. And when Agathe died, Michèle was there almost immediately. In fact, I always wondered how she got to the sea so quickly. But she's a superwoman. Her books have been translated into over forty languages—okay, so have mine—but Michèle has been on the *New York Times* best-seller list for over twenty years, without a break! She writes two books a year, on average, and takes a one-day break between each. One day! Sometimes I don't write for months. And besides her romances, she's now a best-selling cookbook writer and appears on all those horrible competitive chef shows on television. Poor Agathe couldn't even fry an egg.

And so there was Michèle, like a ghost,

standing in my newly organized living room. I jumped up and introduced her by her real name, not as Rosalie. Sandrine was on the ball and brought Michèle a glass of chilled rosé, then ran upstairs with her suitcase. Michèle was in a good mood, and Charlotte recognized her from television. Michèle brushed it off with a wave of the hand and told everyone that she wrote cookbooks; no one asked any questions. They *must* have recognized her as Rosalie di Santi, but perhaps not. My new neighbors—my new friends—don't seem to be interested in fame or fortune, or who knows whom, like so many chic Left Bank Parisians are. We got back to talking about Maria Callas, and then Aix in general, with Michèle asking lots of questions—totally out of character, by the way—and then she had everyone in hysterics with a story about a recent trip to Scotland she made for a cooking show, where she threw up on camera after eating haggis. (She insisted it had nothing to do with the haggis; she said she had a stomach virus.)

Time flew by and eventually Sandrine nudged me and lifted her right eyebrow, signaling that perhaps our guests might want to go home for dinner. But before I could speak, Bruno and Hélène, who had been off to one side whispering, turned and invited us all back to their place for dinner. "Bruno was going to barbecue tonight, and he always makes way too much food," Hélène said.

"You have room for all of us?" Michèle asked. "I was going to have Valère take me out to Aix's finest restaurant tonight."

"Nonsense," Bruno said. "It's too hot to eat in a restaurant, and we have more than enough food."

The little girls cheered, which was quite adorable, and we told the Pauliks we'd be at their place in thirty minutes so they could get things ready and Michèle could have a quick swim after her train journey. Sandrine got to work clearing away the aperitif dishes, and something seemed to be bothering her, so when we were alone I said, "You're invited too, Sandrine." I was worried that perhaps she felt a little out of place, as she was—thank you, Justin, yes, the hired help. But having spent the past few days with her, I felt like she, too, was a friend.

"Oh, I know I'm welcome there," she answered.

"Then why are you pouting?" I asked.

She nodded her head in the direction of the swimming pool, where Michèle was splashing and yelling, "*J'adore Provence!*"

"Michèle?" I asked. "She's nice once you get to know her." But, then, Michèle had been perfectly amiable that evening, despite her abrupt entry.

"Well, I just got a text message from the garage that my car is ready. So I'll be on my way. I've made up her room, and I'll come back to help you once she's gone."

"Oh, for heaven's sake, Sandrine," I pleaded. "I need you here during the day. Michèle will be no help whatsoever. She'll be down at the pool all day, talking into her Dictaphone. She still gets her books typed up by a secretary. So will you come back tomorrow? We still have so much to do."

Sandrine snorted. "I don't trust her."

I laughed and she gave me another raised eyebrow.

"And what are you basing that on?" I asked. "You know nothing about her."

"She wants something—that's all. Besides, I know who she is. She writes romances too. I recognize her from her book jackets. But Josy and I prefer your books. They're . . . smarter."

Our conversation was stopped by the appearance on the doorstep of a dripping wet, raucous swimmer. "I'll get you a towel," Sandrine said, looking Michèle up and down. "I mopped the floors this afternoon."

"Oh dear," Michèle answered with an audible amount of sarcasm in her voice. "Then I'd better stay outside. I say, Valère, bring me a shot of whiskey. I'm getting cold."

Sandrine went upstairs and seemed to be taking forever to find a towel, and by the time I had handed Michèle a tumbler of whiskey Sandrine still wasn't down. "She doesn't like me," Michèle whispered. I then knew she'd overheard our conversation.

"Just what are you doing here, Michèle?" I asked.

She threw her head back and laughed. "Why, I'm here to see you, darling Valère!"

What in the world is a succotash, Justin? Oh, just a bed of sweet corn? More corn? Then why don't they say that? But these deep-fried frogs' legs, they're fantastic. What are they battered in? Yes, you're right—it's shredded filo.

The Pauliks didn't have food as adventurous or glamorous as this, just a barbecue of lamb chops and sausages, as they had promised. But Hélène had made a fantastic potato salad, and for dessert we had oodles of fresh strawberries, nothing else. The conversation was very interesting, just as interesting as any conversation in Paris. Marine, their friend, asked about my books. She said, "Valère, if I may call you that—"

"You may," I answered.

"Thank you," she replied, very courteously. She had a very proper way of speaking, and before she began a sentence, you could see her brow begin to furrow, as if she were carefully choosing the best words. "I recently read an interview in *Le Monde*, with an American author whose name escapes me, who said that writers never talk about their stories—I mean the plot, or the characters—when they're together. It's more about the form—the narrative, for example—or the language. Is that true?"

"Absolutely," I said, impressed by her question, and equally *sous le charme* of her beauty. "The things we had drilled into us in a high school or university—plot, theme, symbolism—don't come up in conversations with fellow writers. But if we're experimenting with the narrative—the form—we talk about that. Once you decide on the narrative form, the book can almost write itself."

"I disagree," Michèle cut in. And we finally had a glimpse of the real Michèle Baudouin, in all her bossy glory. "The story is everything. The characters rule."

I could see Bruno, Hélène, and Marine looking at each other with confused faces. So Sandrine had recognized Rosalie di Santi, but not my neighbors. That gave me huge satisfaction, being the competitive and jealous asshole that I am. "Ladies and gentlemen," I announced, waving my arm in Michèle's face, "may I introduce my old school friend, known to the general public as Rosalie di Santi."

They all gasped, even the big guy, Bruno. The little girls giggled, aware that there was something exciting going on but not knowing what.

"You can wipe that smirk off your face, Valère,"

Michèle said as she downed her glass of red wine. "I'm not at all upset that these fine people didn't recognize me as the romance writer, because, Valère, do you know how many of my books are in print right now, as we speak?"

"A few million?"

She roared with laughter. "Four hundred million."

"Is that a lot?" Léa asked.

"*Oui, ma chérie*," Bruno answered. He looked like someone had just punched him in the lower stomach.

Hélène poured Michèle more of her delicious Syrah from 2004, as if egging her to go on, which she did: "Romances are story driven, and it's a hell of a job writing them. The writer must have a keen ear for dialogue and be able to craft deft sentences, create page-turning tension, and give the reader compelling characters. They are written by women for women, and I'll defend them to the ends of the earth, even if none of you here have read them. If a man writes them," she said, looking at me, "they are called women's fiction, or not even given a label. If a woman writes them, they are called romances, and they are never reviewed by the major newspapers, nor are they ever made into films."

"But I've read about you in *Le Monde*," Hélène said. "Or perhaps it was *Le Figaro*."

"Yes, you read *about* me," Michèle said,

"but you didn't read a review of my books."

Hélène nodded. "I think you must be right."

"I've never thought about it like that," Marine added. "My husband, Antoine, is a bit of a snob—" Here Hélène and Bruno laughed, and I was getting curious about this Antoine guy. Marine continued, "A few weeks ago we were in Paris, on the Métro, and most people were looking at their cell phones, not reading. That got Antoine cursing under his breath. When we finally did see someone reading, it was—"

"A woman of a certain age," Michèle said.

"Exactly," Marine replied. "And she was reading one of your books. Antoine made some disparaging comment, but I defended your books, saying that I much preferred to see someone reading than not at all."

"Odd logic," I said. "It's like giving students Abba lyrics to read in a poetry class."

"Shut up, Valère, you little twerp," Michèle said.

"If I may," Marine said. "I think the problem many people, including myself, have with romance fiction is the obligatory happy ending. It gives women unrealistic expectations."

"But my books aren't bodice rippers, where the ultrawealthy man meets the governess or secretary and they hate each other but are in each other's arms by the end of the book," Michèle explained. "Jane Austen invented that, by the way. In my books, my heroines are strong, they have unusual occupations, and they may not even want to get married in the end. Besides, women are smart; I think they know the difference between reality and fiction."

"There's also an assumption that if a book has a happy ending, it's light reading, and if it has a tragic ending, it's more important," I said.

"Finally, you've stopped talking gibberish," Michèle said.

"My lighter books were huge sellers but panned by the critics, and my earlier, dark ones won every literary prize in the book."

"Except the Nobel," Michèle said.

"I'm saving that one for my next opus," I replied, grinning.

"You haven't written in years," she said. "You've lost—"

"Dessert time!" Hélène said, standing up. "Léa and I bought strawberries at the market this morning." She looked over at her daughter, who was bored with our bickering and playing a game with Charlotte. I'll do it for you now, Justin. Reach over and grab the tip of my chin, and now I'll grab yours. I'll sing the rhyme; the first person who starts laughing loses. You'll have to excuse my singing voice. *Je te tiens, tu me tiens, par la barbichette*; *le premier de nous deux qui rira aura une tapette*! *Je te tiens, tu me tiens, par la barbichette*; *le premier de nous deux qui rira aura une tapette*! That was bad, Justin. You only lasted two verses. Plus you spewed out wine all over the table. Léa lost after about ten rounds, as Charlotte was an expert at keeping her face still. When the girls finished, Michèle turned to me and said, "We used to play that when we were kids, didn't we, Valère? I've got you, you've got me, by the little beard." She reached over and grabbed my chin and added, "I've got you, don't I?"

I haven't yet told you why Michèle was there, what she had on me, but you'll know soon enough, perhaps by the time our dessert comes. I hope there's no corn in the dessert. We left the Pauliks' just before midnight, and Michèle and I walked up the lane to the *bastide* with the help of a flashlight. We heard noises—an owl, and then a branch snapping—and she grabbed my arm and said, "I'm sorry, Valère, but your new house gives me the creeps."

"It's scary at night," I replied, "but that's only because the blasted *cigales* have stopped their racket, and the sounds seem louder, exaggerated."

"No," she argued, "it's more than that. Like the taxi driver making the sign of the cross as he turned up your lane."

I laughed. "Some kind of Provençal village superstition." And I really meant it. "Who knows what—"

Another breaking branch caused Michèle to jump and pull me in closer. She turned around and grabbed my arm, pulling me along. "Faster," she said. "There's someone behind us."

"Don't be daft," I said. And again I really meant it. She was getting on my nerves. "You're a novelist. It's normal to imagine things and be under the spell of a centuries-old house."

"I'm no stranger to centuries-old houses," she replied, almost running. "I own one in the Loire, built during the reign of Louis XV, and it has good karma!"

We got to the front door, and she almost grabbed the keys out of my hand. "Hurry up, Valère! You were always so slow!"

When we stepped into the front hall, we were both breathless. I showed her how well I was locking the door, giving each lock—there were three—an exaggerated thump as I turned them. "Okay?" I asked.

"I need a nightcap," she said, leaning against the banister.

"Help yourself," I said. "Sandrine set up the drinks cart in the big salon."

"Won't you join me?"

"No, I'm exhausted. Help yourself to anything, and I'll see you in the morning."

I practically had to pull myself up the stairs by the banister. I scowled at the lady in the pink dress, who seemed to be having such a good time watching me and the cast of characters who came and went in and out of my house. I brushed my teeth and got dressed for bed, too tired even to read. But for the first time in a few days, I wasn't frightened to go to sleep. Sandrine's hysterics in the cellar and now Michèle's marathon up the lane made me see how ridiculous we were all being. It was an old house in the country, just like the Pauliks' house, and I would bet my fortune that all three of them were already sound asleep, with no imaginary goings-on. I turned off the light and could vaguely hear Michèle downstairs, chatting to herself and moving about. I fell asleep to voices and conversations in my head— most writers will tell you this. It's often dialogue you're working on—your characters never give you a break—but since I wasn't working on a book, the voices that accompanied me as I tossed and turned, trying to get comfortable, were the Pauliks', the children's, Marine Bonnet's, and mine and Michèle's. And, of course, Sandrine's *"I don't trust her."* Again, just like the taxi driver's, a Provençal hunch; a superstition.

I don't remember falling asleep—who does?— but I do remember waking up. I always will. I woke up with the very vivid impression that wet lips had been whispering in my right ear. They had spoken quickly, and with much forced importance, for some time. I couldn't even tell what the language was. French? English? I

106

couldn't move. The voice stopped, as did the humid sensation in my ear. "Michèle?" I whispered. I held the sheet up around my chin, and my heart pounded against my pajama top. I closed my eyes and must have fallen back asleep, as I later awoke with the distinct impression that someone had laid a hand on my right shoulder. This time, I shot out of bed and ran out of the room.

I stood at the top of the stairs, panting. Turning on the lights, I ran down the hall to Michèle's room and swung open the door. Her bed was empty and still made up. "Michèle!" I called out. "I know that was you!" I flew down the stairs, turning right at the bottom, to go into the big salon. Michèle was sprawled across the sofa with a half-empty bottle of sixteen-year-old Lagavulin sitting on the floor beside her. Was she faking it, Justin? If so, she was pretty good at fake snoring. The noise she was making would have woken up any ghost wandering around the house! I pulled a small mohair blanket over her and poured myself a glass of whiskey and took it to my office, where I spent the rest of the night reading, on the Mies daybed, rubbing my right ear, trying to rid it of that most unpleasant feeling.

Chapter Nine

Aix-en-Provence,
Tuesday, July 6, 2010

I can't believe you invited Valère Barbier to my cigar club!" Verlaque hollered to Marine from the bedroom. He fluffed up two pillows, wanting to read a little poetry before turning off the light. He had a headache. Fabrice and Julien had argued all night about the potential clubhouse, each detesting the other's choices and prerequisites. And yet they were best friends. Four of them—Fabrice, Julien, Jean-Marc, and Verlaque—had visited three apartments with a young, very patient realtor who had carefully chosen what he thought would suit the club's demands: a large kitchen and dining space for at least sixteen members, a fitted bathroom, a terrace, and a salon. Fabrice insisted the salon be big enough for each member, or almost each one, to have his or her own leather club chair. Julien and Verlaque thought that impossible, and ridiculous. Jean-Marc, ever the diplomat, tried to argue both sides.

"I know!" Marine called from the bathroom. "Wasn't that a good idea?!"

"No!" Verlaque called back. "It's tomorrow night, as you know, and I have to check with the club about whether I can bring a guest. It has to be *approved*."

"Who wouldn't approve Valère Barbier?" Marine finished brushing her teeth and made a gurgling sound, then spit into the sink.

"That's not the point," Verlaque yelled. "It could be Queen Elizabeth—or, let's say, Winston Churchill back from the dead—and I still couldn't invite them without approval."

Marine laughed through the bathroom door. "That's ridiculous," she said. "You'd think you guys were some kind of elite top secret club, like the CIA or MI6 or something."

"I couldn't hear you," Verlaque called. "What did you say?"

"Nothing." Marine began to change for bed.

"You don't need to wear a nightgown," Verlaque called. "It's hotter than Hades in here. A fourth-floor downtown apartment in July . . ." If the poetry didn't cure his headache, perhaps a little . . .

Marine appeared, wearing a long cotton night-gown with big blue letters across the chest: BONNE NUIT.

"Good night?" Verlaque asked. "Not my favorite nightgown. I guess you're too tired to make love?"

"I don't feel that great," Marine said.

"I'm sorry to hear it," Verlaque said as Marine got into bed. He kissed her forehead and held her hand. "I hope you had fun this evening?"

"Yes, it turned out to be full of surprises, with all of us, including Rosalie di Santi, eating at the Pauliks'."

Verlaque sat up. "Rosalie di Santi? For real?"

Marine laughed. "In all her glory."

"What's she like?"

"Very droll," Marine answered. "We had a very interesting discussion about form versus story when writing—"

"That sounds more interesting than Julien and Fabrice arguing about whether our clubhouse needs two ovens or one, or a gas or induction burner—"

"You guys are so spoiled. So many people in the world don't even have clean water."

"That's beside the point."

"I know," Marine said. "I like your cigar club, which is why I thought Valère would like it too."

"I'll call Fabrice tomorrow," Verlaque said. "He's the president."

Marine had her eyes closed, and Antoine wasn't sure if she was listening. She opened them and said, "When I think about it, Rosalie—Michèle is her real name—was very extroverted, but it was almost forced, like she wanted to entertain us for some reason. Make us all like her. As if there was a hidden agenda—"

Verlaque smiled and rubbed his hands together. "Nobody fools Marine Bonnet."

Marine pulled the sheet up to cover her shoulders and turned toward her husband. "There is an ocean of history between Valère and Michèle . . . I sense that not all of it is clean." She yawned and said, "Michèle was just the tiniest bit aggressive with him."

"Poor Valère," Verlaque said.

"Picking sides?" Marine asked, smiling.

"I'd defend anyone who wrote *Red Earth*."

"Me too. But perhaps we're being biased, given our literary tastes. Maybe Valère deserves her antagonism. Who knows what went on between them? Besides, Valère has an eye for the ladies."

"Really?" Verlaque asked. "Did he make a pass at you? I'm sure you can defend yourself."

"No, not a pass as such," Marine slowly answered. "But he's the kind of man who looks at a woman with a certain intent, an intent that is very clear to the person being gazed upon."

"Have a good day with the philosophers," Verlaque called to Marine before shutting the door. Out on the rue Adanson, he felt so happy he could almost sense his heart swelling and constricting with each beat. He had spent years as a grumpy bachelor, and now here he was, married to someone who made him happy every single minute. He was realistic enough to know that their marriage would not always be this easy—his own parents' had been a disaster—but for now he would allow himself to bask in the glow of newlywed bliss. "Bliss," he said aloud, using the English word, slowly emphasizing the double *s*. "Bliss."

By the time he got to the Palais de Justice he was hungry, even though Marine had forced him to eat granola for breakfast (he refused to eat it with yogurt—that seemed entirely too healthy—and he poured milk in instead). He walked through the giant central courtyard, where a statue of Mirabeau himself—Honoré-Gabriel Riqueti, orator, politician, spendthrift, and skirt chaser—pointed in the direction of a law chamber, although the inside joke was that he was indicating the toilets. Verlaque nodded in Mirabeau's direction and headed up the stairs to his office, where he knew his too-posh secretary, Mme Girard, would be waiting for him to approve and sign a stack of papers.

"*Bonjour*, Mme Girard," he said as he saw the well-coiffed sixty-year-old walking toward his office with, yes, a stack of papers. She was tanned and had just returned from a two-week vacation somewhere in the Caribbean but he couldn't remember where. No tropical island held any interest for him, except Cuba.

"*Bonjour, Juge,*" she answered, trying not to look down at the judge's belly, which, in her opinion, seemed to get bigger every day. "The *commissaire* is on his way." She handed him the papers and almost did a little curtsy before turning around to walk back to her desk.

"Thank you," he answered, taking the papers with a bigger than necessary smile. He walked into his office, leaving the door open for Bruno Paulik. Turning on the espresso machine that sat on a glass-top console—he had brought in his own furniture, just one of the many reasons, he knew, other Palais de Justice employees thought him a snob—he sat down, getting out his grandfather's fountain pen and a jar of ink.

"Knock, knock," said Paulik as he walked into the office.

"Good morning," Verlaque said, looking up. He saw that the commissioner held a small white paper bag. "Michaud's? Brioches?"

"One for each of us," Paulik answered, setting the bag on the desk. "I'll make the coffee."

"The machine should be ready," Verlaque said. "What's on the books for today? Besides paperwork and the incredibly fascinating case of the mayor's extortion ring. Bus pamphlets, right?"

"There were signs too."

"Huh?"

"The communications company was paid for signs too," Paulik said, while bent down, hands on knees, watching the thin stream of espresso pour into a porcelain demitasse. "You know, those big signs they put in bus shelters."

"Have a seat and let's go through it together," Verlaque said, opening the bag from Aix's best patisserie and taking a glazed brioche. It was so fresh that he almost crushed the soft dough between his fingers.

Paulik carried the espressos over and sat down. "Well, Yvette Tamain—"

"Remind me how long she's been mayor."

"Twenty-three years." Paulik bit into his brioche. "Her term finishes next year. She and her party recently paid a company called AixCom to design and produce pamphlets and signs explaining the new municipal bus routes. The company charged 250,000 euros for the work, but apparently it only cost 40,000. An intern at the municipal tax office caught the discrepancy."

"Incredible," Verlaque answered. "Bravo for the intern, but not to the missing 210,000 euros of public funds. They will have to be brought before me and officially put under investigation. Does this intern have enough proof?"

Paulik nodded. "Yes, she does. And she claims she can follow the money to Tamain's next election campaign and a long weekend she and her cronies spent at a five-star hotel in Saint-Tropez."

"Who's in on it?"

"Tamain and her campaign manager, Damien

Pacaud, and the CEO of this AixCom, Gilles Gavotto. After the bus campaign, AixCom was hired to publicize the opera festival and a recycling campaign."

"Payment for their cooperation," Verlaque said. "I'm not looking forward to this. Tamain and I have never liked each other." He leaned back and sighed. "Why does my colleague in Nice get all the interesting investigations?"

Paulik laughed. "I read about that this morning in *Le Monde*. The kidnapping of the heiress?"

Verlaque nodded. "Did you see the cast of characters who made up the kidnappers?"

"You could make a Hollywood movie about it," Paulik said. "A retired Michelin-starred chef, a hotel manager, a loser paparazzo, and an ex-boxer from the Ukraine."

"Well, let's get the intern in here with her paperwork," Verlaque said. "I'd like her to show me everything before we call Tamain."

Paulik got up and left the office, pulling his cell phone out of his jacket. Mme Girard was on her way in, and she paused in the doorway. She saw the empty Michaud's bag and tried not to scowl. "There's a retired magistrate on the phone for you, Judge. His name is Daniel de Rudder. I was about to take a message when I saw the *commissaire* leave."

"Oh! Rudder was one of my professors in Bordeaux," Verlaque answered. "I'll take it.

"*Âllo?*" Verlaque said into the phone. "*Juge Rudder?*"

"The one and only," the judge answered and then fell into a coughing fit. Verlaque held the phone's receiver away from his ear and tried to estimate how old Daniel de Rudder was. Possibly eighty. "Sorry about the cough," Rudder went on. "But when you're eighty-eight, these things are bound to happen."

Verlaque raised his eyebrows at his poor guess. "It's great to hear from you! Where are you living these days? Still in Arcachon?"

"Yes, I'm sitting here with a woolen throw across my knees like an old man, staring at the flat gray ocean. My daughter-in-law, a retired nurse, keeps bringing me tea. All day long. I hate tea. Do you remember Nurse Ratched from *One Flew Over the Cuckoo's Nest*?"

Verlaque laughed. "So you're living at your son's? I'm glad about that."

"Yes, having children was the best thing I ever did," Rudder answered. "Especially now, when they can take care of me." He laughed and exploded into another coughing fit. "I heard you too have finally settled down, and may I say congratulations? Marine Bonnet is a fine woman."

"You've met?"

"No, I've read her articles in the law journals," Rudder answered. "At least I did. But now articles exhaust me. Tintin is about my speed these days."

Verlaque laughed, not able to believe that Daniel de Rudder—champion sailor, beloved professor, then terrifying magistrate—was now staring at the ocean and reading comic books. "You're probably wondering why I'm calling you out of the blue," Rudder said.

"It had crossed my mind."

"I hear that Valère Barbier is living in Aix."

"Yes, coincidentally Marine had dinner with him last night, at a friend's house."

If Rudder was impressed, he didn't say. "Nurse Ratched is helping me clean up my affairs and go through old documents. Last night I stayed up way too late and reread my diary from the time of Agathe Barbier's drowning."

Verlaque slowly nodded. "You were the magistrate investigating that case . . ."

"Yes, it was my wife's insane idea to move to Cannes to see some blue sky once in a while. We hated it. We were only on the Côte for two years, but I was there when Agathe Barbier had her accident. A few things are still bothering me . . ."

Three hours later Verlaque closed his office door and headed out for lunch. He had remained on the phone with Daniel de Rudder for another twenty minutes, chatting about friends and the weather, and Rudder agreed that he would arrange to send documents concerning Agathe Barbier. Verlaque imagined Rudder sitting in his wicker chair, tying up the packet of documents with a string, his age-spotted hands trembling, the tea-crazed daughter-in-law hovering in the door-way.

As Verlaque headed out into the noon heat, uncertain where to go, he winked at Mirabeau's statue—how could a man with a deformed foot, too many missing teeth, and an oversized head have been a lady-killer? He took out his cell phone and called Marine, to see if she was at home, but got her voice mail. She was probably at the library or eating with friends. Marine seemed to know half of Aix.

And so he did what he usually did when he had no lunch plans. He wandered. Wandering in Aix wasn't as fun for him as wandering in Paris; when he was a teenager his father had jokingly told a friend that Antoine was going to get his PhD in *flânerie*. In those days he could leave the family home in the 1st arrondissement in the morning, walk up to the top of the *butte* of Montmartre, then walk back downhill and cross the river to eat lunch in a Left Bank café. Nowadays he couldn't imagine walking *up* to Montmartre, but he could possibly walk downhill, if a good dinner met him at the end of his stroll. But Aix, despite its small size, was still a town that surprised him. It held lots of secrets, little gems hidden in its gold stone. Myths, stories, hopes, and wishes that the Aixois had held on to for centuries.

The impending investigation of the mayor depressed Verlaque and at the same time bored him. He walked up the rue Mignet, hands in his pockets, humming a Van Morrison song. "Caravan," he thought it was called. His paternal grandparents, Emmeline and Charles, would play the record after they had worked a long day in the garden and had poured themselves each a celebratory aperitif: Pimm's for Emmeline, who was born in London and held fast to certain English traditions, and an inexpensive whiskey, diluted with water, for Charles. Emmeline would sing along, and Verlaque's grandfather would tease her. She was a much better watercolorist than singer.

He stopped before number 9 and watched as a couple walked out the door, excitedly talking. "*Ça alors! C'était magnifique!*" the woman said, squeezing her partner's arm. "*Mais oui! Plutôt insolite,*" her partner replied, turning his head around to look back down the narrow passageway before closing the door. Verlaque loved the word *insolite* and asked the couple what lay beyond, as there was no sign or lettering on the front door. "*Une boutique surprenante!*" they replied almost in unison, and he thanked them, opened the door, and stepped inside.

It was immediately cool in the damp passage-way, and as his eyes adjusted from leaving the bright sun he saw dozens of metal objects hanging from the stone walls on either side. Soft music played, and he could see the green of a garden at the end of the passage. He walked on, and the green got closer—it was bamboo, and it cut off the courtyard from the private garden beyond. On small wooden tables and chairs were set out more objects fashioned out of wrought iron, and a middle-aged man with a goatee walked out of a makeshift cabin, rubbing his hands on a blacksmith's thick gray apron. "*Bonjour*," he said.

"*Bonjour*," Verlaque replied, looking around in awe. "I've lived in Aix for years, but never knew—"

"Yes," the artisan answered. "Many people don't know. I don't advertise." He had a trace of a Spanish accent.

"You're a blacksmith?"

"Yes. I've made these objects, and I take commissions for bigger objects too. Furniture, gates—things like that."

Verlaque saw candelabras, trivets, fireplace utensils. None of those things interested him, but the idea of a gate for their future country house did. "I'll come back with my wife," he said.

"I'd be delighted," the blacksmith said.

Verlaque turned to go and then saw, in a corner

of the covered terrace, a rickety green wooden bookshelf. "Used books?" he asked.

"Yes, I have too many books," the blacksmith answered. "So every now and then I sell them."

Verlaque could see that some of the bindings were old, and he bent down, his head tilted to one side, to read their titles. *Insolite* certainly suited this shop and its owner: "out of the ordinary." A blacksmith and a bibliophile. Down a narrow hallway in Aix. An unmarked door. And then Verlaque saw it: *Red Earth*. He had no idea where his own copy was. Not at his apartment. Possibly in a box in Paris. He saw that the clothbound book was old and gently pulled it out, opening it to the copyright page: 1975. It was a first edition, and was signed, in a flourish of black ink, under the publishing house's name, by Valère Barbier. "How much?" Verlaque asked, holding up the book. He hoped his voice sounded casual.

The blacksmith smiled. "It's a signed first edition."

"So it is," Verlaque said, laughing.

"But I need the money. I'll sell it to you for fifty euros."

"Sold," Verlaque said, pulling his wallet out of his back pocket, thankful that he had gone to a bank machine that morning. It would be a great gift for Marine, and he could show it that evening to M Barbier, who had left a message via Bruno Paulik saying that, yes, many thanks, he would attend the cigar meeting. Verlaque turned to the last page, eager to remind himself of those words he had so adored when he was a teenager, the *flâneur* wandering around Paris, blissfully unaware of the kind of life that lay ahead for him.

Chapter Ten

New York City,
September 22, 2010

I'd like you to go back a bit," Justin said, leaning away so the waiter could set the lamb medallions in front of him.

"Where to?" Valère asked, already cutting his lamb.

"The part about Michèle's taxi driver making the sign of the cross before heading up the drive." Justin carefully cut a small piece of lamb and dabbed it in the dark-red *jus*. He couldn't believe he was here, eating in this restaurant, hearing these stories from Valère Barbier's own mouth. Except for the comings and goings of the waitstaff and the discreet sommelier, Justin felt like he was alone, in a bubble, with Barbier; he had no idea if the restaurant was full or empty, or even what time it was. He was wearing a watch but didn't want to look at it and risk appearing rude or bored.

"Are you superstitious too?"

"I'm Chinese American," Justin said. "Of course I am."

Valère laughed and picked up his wine, taking what Justin thought was too big a sip. More of a gulp. "Good choice, this Châteauneuf-du-Pape."

"Thanks."

Valère wiped his mouth and continued.

Bon. The next morning Sandrine showed up, as I suspected she might. Despite her threats, she's too hard a worker not to—and, well, I sort of threatened to fire her if she didn't. Don't look at me like that, Justin. I had no choice: I needed Sandrine. There was too much to do, and, yes, I didn't want to stay alone in the house with Michèle. I yawned continuously as Sandrine made coffee, and when she handed me my bowl of café au lait, I said, "Thank you, Sandrine," looking her in the eye. "Thank you for everything." That's exactly what I said.

She smiled, recognizing my apology. "I won't leave you, M Barbier." That's exactly what she said. Did she sense what was going on? Did she know about the nighttime visitations? I could hear Michèle snoring in the big salon, and I thought it might be a good time to fill Sandrine in. She must have wondered why I was always so exhausted in the morning. "Sandrine, this place, at night . . ."

She stopped buttering a baguette, set the knife down, and looked at me. "*Oui?*" she asked.

I rubbed my face, hoping what I was about to

say wouldn't sound completely insane. I may write fiction, but I do know that ghosts do not exist. "There's someone else here, in the house," I began. "They pull at my bedcovers, they walk around at night, and last night the . . . person, or whatever it is, whispered in my ear as I slept."

Sandrine raised an eyebrow and began to spread apricot jam on the bread. She handed me a piece and said, "I'm not surprised."

"What? You don't think I'm crazy?"

She shrugged. "Don't you remember what happened to me in the cellar, M Barbier? And, well, they talk about this place in the village—"

"They do?"

"Well, sure. Gérald couldn't believe I took a job here."

"Who in the world is Gérald?"

"The mechanic who fixed Clochette!"

Justin, Sandrine has this annoying habit of saying something out of the blue and expecting you to understand it, which of course you don't, and when you ask her to explain, she treats you like an imbecile. "What did this Gérald say?"

She leaned forward and whispered, "Gérald says that the Bastide Blanche is haunted, and it always has been."

"When I said that someone's been tugging at my sheets, I meant a real person," I said. I got up to get us some more coffee.

"I did ask Gérald for more details," Sandrine

said, ignoring my comment, "but he didn't know when or why the stories about the Bastide Blanche began."

A noise in the hallway made us both jump. Michèle appeared in the doorway. "I have the worst headache in the world," she muttered.

Sandrine didn't hide her smile as she walked over to one of the kitchen cabinets and took out a box labeled FIRST AID. Isn't she incredible? Even my dear, *très froid* retired secretary, Ursule Genoux, wasn't that organized. Sandrine thrust a box of aspirin into Michèle's hands. I added, for comic effect, "Take two and call us in the morning!"

"Very funny," Michèle muttered, and walked away.

I could see the look of loathing on Sandrine's face as her eyes followed her out of the room. "Michèle's not that bad," I whispered, wanting to keep peace in my house.

"Oh yeah?" Sandrine replied. "I overheard you two talking last night."

"What?" I asked, concerned that Sandrine was listening, intentionally or not.

"*Mais oui,*" she continued. "I don't think she's being fair, M Barbier. To threaten you like that."

"Sandrine, it doesn't concern you."

She made a dismissive grunt and sat down. "You're my boss, M Barbier," she began. "You asked me, and I told you why I don't like her. Josy always says to be careful with women like that—"

"Can we change the subject?"

Sandrine tapped the table with her fingernails, each painted in red, white, and blue. "As you wish." She took a big bite of her *tartine*. "So," she said, wiping her mouth with a paper napkin. "What did the voice say last night?"

"I don't know," I answered. "I was in one of those moments when you've been tossing and turning but don't know if you're awake or asleep. The voice spoke quickly, almost hissing. And the funny thing is, it didn't sound like French."

"English?"

"No, closer to French than to English."

Sandrine clapped her hands, then grabbed my arm. "Occitan!"

"You may be right," I said. "I've only ever heard Provençal a few times, but it could have been."

"It's an old ghost then," Sandrine went on.

"Sandrine," I objected, "I don't believe in ghosts. That's all superstition. I'm a well-respected writer—"

"Who was scared out of his wits last night, right? I can see you didn't sleep."

"Point taken."

"Well, from what I know of ghosts in old houses, and we have one here who might have lived over one hundred years ago, they're not mean, just confused."

I burst out laughing, which I shouldn't have. Sandrine started sulking and crossed her arms. She asked, "Do you want my advice or not?"

"Yes, please." Can you believe it, Justin? I felt like a schoolboy being scolded.

"The ghosts still think the house is theirs. We need to explain to them that it's yours."

I tried not to roll my eyes, but we didn't have much to go on. They visited me every evening and had frightened Sandrine, and even little Léa had felt their presence. "What do we do?" I asked. "Walk through the house with a candle, chanting, and ask them to leave?"

Sandrine didn't pick up on my sarcasm, or if she did, she ignored it. "No, we don't ask them; we *tell* them," she said. "We need to be *firm*."

"How do we go about it?" I asked.

She sat down and got out her cell phone. "I'll just look it up," she said. "Why hadn't you thought of that?"

"I still forget, perhaps intentionally, that nowadays one can find almost anything on the Internet. Books are no longer—"

"Yeah, whatever," Sandrine said as she stared at her screen. "M Barbier, you need to get with the twenty-first century! There. I've only just begun to search, and already there's all kinds of advice."

"Let me guess," I said. "You've found a Web site called Sisters in Sorcery or Ten Easy Ways to Rid Your Home of Unwanted Ghosts?"

Sandrine looked up at me. "How did you know?"

I laughed and she narrowed her eyes.

"You're teasing me. That's not nice, M Barbier."

"I'm sorry, Sandrine," I replied. "Please tell me what we can do."

Sandrine began reading. "The first thing this guy stresses is to be polite about it."

I snorted. "They're the ones keeping me up."

"You don't want to anger them," Sandrine continued, giving me a raised eyebrow. "If you've *politely* asked them to leave, and they don't, it may be because they're trying to communicate something to you. But do not try to communicate with them. 'Do not' is in bold letters, M Barbier."

"Noted."

"If you need to communicate with them, find someone that is—"

"*Who* is."

Sandrine sighed. "Experienced."

"*That* should be easy. Anyway, I have no wish to chat with them."

Sandrine smiled. "I think it could be very interesting. But I'll read on. The next bit is called 'Cleansing the Home.' As your housekeeper that should be my job. Ah, it says to use holy water."

"Can you just buy that stuff?" I asked.

Sandrine shrugged. "I'll look into it. I haven't been to Mass since . . ." She got out a little notebook and made a note to herself. "Sprinkle holy water everywhere in the home, including closets, doorways, attics, and basements. And don't forget outside too. Many people have succeeded by saying the Lord's Prayer while sprinkling."

"I can't remember it."

"Surely you can," Sandrine said. "Or you can say any prayer. I'll bet you can even make one up."

"Because that's basically what a prayer is. Made-up hocus—"

Sandrine cut me off: "Here's the bit for you. 'Nonbelievers can burn a sage stick.' "

I broke out in laughter. "Does this person live in New Mexico by any chance?"

"I don't know where that is," Sandrine answered curtly. "But we have plenty of sage around here. I think can make you a sage stick."

"You can probably look up directions on the Internet," I suggested.

She didn't get the sarcasm and answered, "You're right! You're catching on, M Barbier!"

We heard a vehicle pull up on the pebbled drive and honk its horn. "The electrical guys are back," I said. They stayed for the rest of the morning, Sandrine following them around the house, asking questions and taking notes. The whole house would have to be rewired. They were surprised I was even living in it, given the state it was in.

Chapter Eleven

Aix-en-Provence,
Wednesday, July 7, 2010

It was a long time—perhaps over two years—since Verlaque had been to his friend Jacob's house, north of Aix. The last time was also for a cigar event, and it was also a warm summer evening. He remembered that Marine had been with him, and how much she liked Jacob's old stone house. This time he had Jean-Marc with him. Jean-Marc, as a choice, not from necessity, didn't own a car.

"The only time I'm tempted to buy a car is when I'm in yours," Jean-Marc said, running his hand along the 1963 Porsche's padded dashboard.

"Seriously?" Verlaque asked as he veered the car to the right at a fork in the road. The top was down, and they could hear *cigales* in the trees. "I thought you hated cars."

Jean-Marc shook his head. "Actually, I really like cars—well, at least beautifully made ones like this. But I'm a practical man, Antoine, and I live downtown. When I do the math and calculate how much per month a car would cost, with the garage rental, and gas and insurance, I realize I'm far better off renting one on those rare weekends when I need a car."

"I get it," Verlaque replied.

"And thank goodness for Monoprix grocery delivery," Jean-Marc said, laughing. He leaned his head out into the warm evening air and looked at the valley as it rose and fell below the road, bright green vineyards dotted with silvery olive trees. "This is a beautiful part of Provence."

"That's exactly what Marine said when we went to Jacob's a few years ago. And it's only twenty minutes north of Aix." Even though Jean-Marc was Marine's childhood friend, Verlaque felt like he too had known the mellow lawyer for years. Jean-Marc impressed Verlaque with his calmness and his easy acceptance of others', and his own, situation in life. He had once had a live-in lover, Pierre, but they were no longer together. And yet Jean-Marc never complained, remaining ever the discreet and dependable friend. If Verlaque had become a better person since he met Marine— and he knew he had—it was partly due to Jean-Marc's kindness and steadfastness.

"Marine sent me a text message this morning about meeting Valère Barbier," Jean-Marc said. "She seemed rather impressed with him. Is it true he's coming this evening?"

"Yes, if he can find his way. I gave Marine

directions to forward to him since it was her insane idea to invite him."

"Insane idea? You're not okay with it?"

Verlaque sighed. "The cigar club is sacred to me," he began, trying to find the words to explain himself. He glanced over and saw his friend nod in agreement, so he continued, "With you guys, I'm no longer a magistrate—"

"You're one of the guys. And Virginie?"

Verlaque laughed. "Including our glorious, cigar-loving pharmacist, Virginie. I can let my hair down at the club, as the Americans say. I'm not a Parisian, or a judge, or the son of a wealthy industrialist. I'm just Antoine, another crazy person who closes his eyes when he starts to smoke a Cuban cigar and all his worries seem to disappear."

"I think we all share that feeling," Jean-Marc said. "You wanted to keep the club to yourself, so to speak. And Valère Barbier isn't one of us."

"He very well could be," Verlaque said. "But right now he's living next to my commissioner, and I've sort of linked Barbier to work, as silly as that seems." He slowed the car and turned into a pebbled drive lined with plane and umbrella pine trees. At the end of the drive the large but unpretentious old house appeared, and Verlaque parked the Porsche beside a black Mercedes he didn't recognize.

"Paris license plate," Jean-Marc said as he

got out of the car and looked at the back of the Mercedes. "It must be the Great Man's."

Verlaque laughed. "He'd better get rid of those Parisian plates if he wants his car to stay in one piece around here." They walked to the back of the house, along a stone path lined in lavender that was blooming and at its peak. Fat, ecstatic bees flew in and out of the flowers. When the men got to the end of the path, they stopped and looked at the stone terrace, where a group was gathered, drinking champagne and smoking cigars.

"*Oh, mon dieu*," Jean-Marc whispered, having immediately recognized Barbier. "Fabrice and Julien have Valère Barbier cornered." Jean-Marc looked at Verlaque with worry. "What do you think they're saying?"

"When I told you my misgivings about inviting Barbier here this evening," Verlaque replied, "I wasn't being entirely honest."

Jean-Marc grinned. "You were worried about what some of our members might say to Barbier—"

"Yep. Kind of."

"Well, let's go get some champagne and find out."

They walked across the terrace, exchanging *bises* with fellow club members and choosing cigars from a wooden Partagás box that Virginie held open for them. "One of my clients was just in Cuba," she said. "The cigars are half the price there."

"For now," Verlaque said, "until the embargo is lifted. Then they'll be expensive even in Cuba. Thank you so much for bringing these."

"Antoine, come here!" Fabrice hollered.

Verlaque excused himself and walked with Jean-Marc to where Fabrice and Julien—best friends and both in their early sixties—had more or less cornered the writer with their imposing stomachs. Fabrice, the club's president, took Verlaque by the arm and asked, "Antoine, what's the better book? *Red Earth* or *The Receptionist*?"

Julien said, "I think—"

"Shut up, Julien," Fabrice said.

"Pleased to meet you," Verlaque said, reaching a hand toward Barbier. "I'm Antoine Verlaque, Marine's husband."

"Delighted to meet you too," Valère said, shaking the judge's hand.

"Antoine?" Fabrice asked. "Which one?"

"Well, that all depends," Verlaque said. "I always think one's favorite book or film coincides with how old one was when one read or watched it, especially the first time. A few years down the road, you can change your mind, and another book might become your favorite."

Fabrice waved his hands. "Please give a yes or no answer and none of this diplomatic wishy-washy stuff."

"We have money riding on this," Julien added.

"Oh, for heaven's sake," Verlaque said. He looked at Jean-Marc, who was smiling. "*Red Earth*," he said.

Fabrice raised his hands in the air and yelled.

"Thanks," Julien said. "I just lost fifty euros." The two friends—who were both financially well off, Fabrice thanks to dozens of plumbing stores across the South of France, and Julien courtesy of a string of luxury used-car lots—seemed to always be betting. Verlaque had the feeling they never actually paid each other, or if they did, that it all came out in the wash. Each seemed to win as often as he'd lose.

Verlaque continued, "But *The Receptionist* is a very close second, and one of my favorite films."

Fabrice leaned toward Valère, drawing him in close to him with his arm. Verlaque cringed. Fabrice went on, "As you well know, Alain Denis was in that film. Antoine here, our examining magistrate, was on the Île Sordou a few summers ago, trying to have a nice quiet holiday, when Denis—"

"That's enough, Fabrice," Verlaque said, smiling, trying to be light. He thought of his conversation with Jean-Marc in the car. As he'd feared, he was no longer simply Antoine: Fabrice was casting him as the examining magistrate.

Jean-Marc joined in. "As a lawyer, Fabrice, I advise you to stop talking."

137

"Judge? Lawyer?" Valère said. "Is everyone in this club involved in the law?"

Verlaque looked at the famous writer, detecting the tiniest bit of . . . apprehension? Nervousness? Even a slight distaste? But it wasn't the first time this had happened during a social occasion. He was used to it.

Verlaque walked away to drop some of his cigar ash into an ashtray. Jean-Marc joined him and whispered, "We needn't have worried. Both Fabrice and Julien seem to have read Barbier's better books."

Verlaque smiled. "Never judge a book by its cover."

"That's another thing I love about this club," Jean-Marc said. "We come from all walks of life; some of us have multiple diplomas, some of us none, but it doesn't matter when we are together."

The wind picked up, and the group was forced to move inside for dinner. Jacob had ordered lamb couscous from a small Moroccan restaurant in Aix, and, as usual, each member of the club had a role to play in helping to prepare for dinner, whether it was cutting the bread, setting the table, opening wine bottles, or—Julien's specialty— folding the linen napkins into funny shapes.

The conversation moved from food and wine to local politics, with Valère Barbier sometimes taking part in the conversation but more often just sitting back and listening intently. Verlaque thought this polite behavior for a first-time guest and was impressed. Barbier's star quality diminished after a few glasses of wine, and by the end of the meal and their second, much larger cigar Barbier was not a famous writer but just another cigar lover and epicurean.

"When did you start smoking cigars?" Virginie asked Valère after dinner, in Jacob's living room. Verlaque remembered this room from his previous visit: long, with thick stone walls, honey-colored oak beams, and original highly polished terra-cotta floors.

Valère took a long, slow puff of the Hoyo de Monterrey double corona and leaned his head back. "I was in Cuba, in 1982. I had just won a prize, in France—"

"Mr. Modest," Jacob said, smiling. "It was the Prix Goncourt."

"Yes, it was," Valère replied, nodding. "And I was invited to Havana because my Spanish translations were selling well there. My publicist and publisher were thrilled to come along—they were cigar smokers. Well, we spent a lot of time waiting for Fidel—we were supposed to meet him—and it became a joke. Instead of waiting for Godot, we were waiting for Fidel."

"Huh?" Fabrice asked Julien, louder than he meant to.

"I think it's a book," Julien whispered back.

"It's a play, you dolts," said Gaspard, a law student and the club's youngest member.

Verlaque looked over at Jean-Marc, who was looking at his knees, his shoulders heaving and his face red from suppressed laughter.

Valère crossed a leg and continued: "To pass the time, the other guys smoked, and I loved the smell. After the second day, I looked around me, and said to myself, Valère, either you can try one or you can be an idiot and just sit here twiddling your thumbs and miss out on experiencing all this fabulous island has to offer. To break me in, they wisely chose a smooth Romeo y Julieta double corona—it's still one of my favorite cigars. Whenever I smoke one, it takes me back to those humid afternoons, sitting on the rocking chairs that lined the hotel's roof terrace, with that big, crazy, pastel, multicolored city laid out before us. One of my regrets in life is not having bought a house in Havana."

"That's difficult, isn't it?" José, a writer for *La Provence*, asked. "You have to be married to a Cuban."

"Alas, yes," Valère replied.

"And so, what happened?" Virginie asked.

"Oh, I got hooked," Valère replied. "I started reading about the history of cigars, and we visited some of the factories, and I've smoked Cubans ever since."

Virginie laughed. "No, I meant with meeting Fidel."

"Ah. He was a no-show," Valère said. "After five days it became clear to us that he wasn't coming, and we were only going to be there for a week. So we explored the city as much as we could. On our last day a minor government official took us to a fabulous restaurant in a kind of no-man's-land surrounded by what looked like abandoned apartment buildings. But the back of the restaurant faced the sea. You'd sit there on the narrow terrace and watch fishermen—"

"Rio Mar!" Julien and Fabrice said in unison.

Valère snapped his fingers. "That's it. Best lobster I've ever had."

Julien and Fabrice had an ongoing bet to see who could visit Cuba the most. Since they usually went together, it was another redundant challenge.

Verlaque's cell phone vibrated inside his pocket, and he quickly snuck a look at it. Cell phones—and he was one of the biggest enforcers of the rule—were frowned upon during their get-togethers. It was a text message from Officer Goulin: There's been an accident at La Bastide Blanche. The commissioner thinks M Barbier may be with you. Can you please bring M Barbier to Puyloubier? Tell him to brace himself. Sophie Goulin

Chapter Twelve

New York City,
September 22, 2010

A n accident?" Justin asked. "What happened?"
"So," Valère leaned back and continued,
"I was in the car with the judge, and I wasn't
nervous as we drove back to the Bastide Blanche.
We chatted about this and that—current French
politics, Parisian restaurants—as Verlaque's
friend Jean-Marc followed, driving my Mercedes.
It made me nervous at first, as it's a very nice
car . . ."

"Do I need to know that?" Justin asked, anxious
to hear what had gone on at the *bastide*.

"Whoa! Yes, otherwise you'd be scratching
your head later tonight, trying to figure out what
we did with my Merc." A waiter walked in,
pushing a trolley laden with cheese. Valère sat
upright and looked over the selection of more
than twenty French cheeses, all perfectly ripened.

"*Les fromages*!" Justin said, relieved thanks to
the waiter's perfect sense of timing. He realized
he'd spoken out of turn but was annoyed all the
same by the interruption.

Valère held up his knife and bounced it a few times in Justin's direction. "Cheese. The perfect dessert. Look at this delectable, runny Saint-Marcellin."

"Was someone hurt?" Justin asked, not looking at the cheeses.

"Okay, I see I'd better continue or you'll never be able to choose."

Verlaque didn't know any more than I did, or why the officer had thought it necessary that Verlaque drive me home, like I was an old man. But I'm famous—or at least I was once—and perhaps the commissioner thought I was accustomed to star treatment. I wasn't worried. In fact, I was fairly certain that the house had been broken into. Sandrine would have left for the evening, and Michèle was probably passed out again, deaf to the sound of burglars walking around, opening drawers, and emptying cupboards. But what did I even have to steal? An acquaintance in Paris once had his massive apartment in the avenue Foch burgled, and they took nothing! After all, what did he have? Books, records, a silver tea service that was priceless and sitting out on an equally expensive rare Scandinavian buffet. The thieves were looking for money, which he never kept in the house, and electronic equipment—iPhones and computers—and jewelry. His cell phone was on him, and he only owned one computer, which was in his office in the 1st arrondissement. He was a bachelor, so no diamond necklaces. La Bastide Blanche was very much the same as that guy's apartment: there was little in it that an eighteen-year-old thief would want. Would he care about Agathe's pots? Never.

As we entered the village, my palms began to sweat, and I could sense that Verlaque was tensing up too, his hands tightening their grip around the steering wheel. I then realized that I might have been targeted by professional art thieves who knew the value of Agathe's work. For all the police knew, this may have happened to me before, which is why they asked the examining magistrate to drive me home. They didn't want me driving through the streets of Aix like a lunatic, endangering myself and others, in desperation to get back to my house. I assumed that was why I had been warned to brace myself: I had been robbed, and somehow not only did the thief or thieves know the value of Agathe's work, but they had been organized enough to get the pots out of the house and into a truck kitted out with protective cases for them. If these guys were skilled enough to steal van Goghs from famous museums, my old house would be kids' play. Could they have done all this with Michèle there, even if she was asleep? Yes. Michèle could sleep through anything. Anyway, it would have been easy work to tie her up and shove a napkin in her mouth. At this point, as we neared the house, I started quietly laughing. Verlaque gave me a quick, nonjudgmental look. He thought it was nervousness, but in fact I was laughing at the back talk I imagined Michèle would have given the young thugs, and I pictured them running around the house looking for something to shut her up with. The linen napkins would have been easy to find; Sandrine had been ironing them when I left for Aix.

I took a handkerchief out of my pocket and blew my nose. Verlaque brought his little car to an abrupt stop, jerking me forward in my seat. I looked up and saw a police car, Thomas's red pizza-delivery motorbike, and an ambulance with its lights flashing.

Verlaque was quicker to get out of the car than I was, so by the time I reached the ambulance, the attendants were closing the back doors and getting ready to go. Paulik didn't seem to be around. I heard one of the guys say to Verlaque, just before jumping into the driver's seat, "The commissioner is with her." Who? My mind raced, and just as I had imagined the theft scenario while driving home, I now had a dozen scenes flashing through my head. *She* must mean Michèle. Or had Sandrine stayed on late? Sandrine openly disliked Michèle and may have made some excuse to stick around, in order to keep an eye on her. Had there been a household accident, and Sandrine was hurt? Did Michèle have a stroke? She was no spring chicken: my age down to the month. I arrived at the back of the ambulance and looked at the closed doors. And then, starting in the pit of my stomach, I began burning up. The heat rose up through my lungs, my neck, and then my face burned with heat. I began sweating. Beads of perspiration dripped down my back. I felt nauseous. I looked up at the ambulance as it drove away. *Paulik must be in the back,* I thought, *with Léa.*

Jean-Marc quickly made himself useful, preparing coffee for everyone. I stood in the kitchen doorway in a daze, watching him set out cups and milk and sugar. I could hear Sandrine wailing in another room, arguing with the police officer who was speaking to her. "M Barbier!" she called out to me. "Tell this officer that I never would have done such a thing! Tell her!"

Verlaque came to me and gently put his hand on my arm. "They are taking statements in the living room," he said. "Come with me."

I followed like a lost puppy. "But how is *she?*" I asked.

Verlaque turned around. "The ambulance attendant said that I should phone the hospital in an hour or so."

I nodded and followed him into the big salon.

Sandrine saw us and jumped up and ran toward me. It was as if we had known each other for years and not just days. I guess that's what tragedy does. She wrapped her arms around me and then quickly pulled back, apologizing. Her eyes were puffy and red from crying. "She said that I did it!" Sandrine cried out before falling back onto the sofa, exhausted.

"Who says?" I asked, sitting down on a foot-stool near her. "The policewoman?"

The policewoman—officer, I should say—looked at me and slowly closed her eyes, then opened them again. "Sandrine is my employee," I offered. "She wouldn't hurt a flea."

"The victim said she was pushed," the police officer quietly said, "just before she lost consciousness."

"She fell down the stairs," Verlaque added. I had no idea how he knew this, but he must have been very quickly debriefed while I was watching Jean-Marc prepare coffee.

"Poor little thing," I whispered, burying my head in my hands. I could not bear the thought of Léa hurt.

"Poor little thing?" Sandrine whimpered, her nose running and her voice catching. "She's an old cow! But still, I didn't push her!"

I looked up, bewildered. Then Bruno Paulik came into the room, followed by Thomas, the pizza boy.

"Bruno!" I called out, jumping up. "Where's Léa?"

"At home, asleep," Paulik answered, looking around.

"Then who . . ." I began to ask, then stopped. I realized that the ambulance attendant must have meant that Paulik was in the house, with Sandrine. "Was it Michèle who fell down the stairs?"

"Yes," Paulik answered. "Thomas was delivering pizza, and when no one answered the doorbell, he walked into the foyer, as the front door was wide open. That's when he found Mme Baudouin, lying at the bottom of the stairs."

"I feel queasy again," Thomas whispered. He sat down, and Jean-Marc came in with the tray, setting it quietly down on the coffee table. Sandrine sat there, staring at the coffee, so the policewoman began pouring it out.

"Why didn't you answer the doorbell?" Verlaque asked Sandrine.

"I was going to," she answered. She was beginning to sound angry. "But I was upstairs, with my hands full of folded laundry. I yelled down for him to come in, but he didn't hear me."

"I've taken Thomas's statement," Paulik said. "And Officer Goulin has taken Mlle Matton's. But, Thomas, I'd like you to repeat to Judge Verlaque what Mme Baudouin said to you when you found her."

Thomas nodded and began: "She was bleeding, and her face was an awful color." He stopped to swallow, and then continued. "But she managed to open her eyes and whisper, 'She pushed me.' Then . . . um . . . she passed out. Blood started coming out . . ." He closed his eyes, taking a breath. "I started yelling."

"That's when I heard you," Paulik said. He turned to Verlaque and explained. "I was outside checking a leak in our garden's automatic drip system. Hélène kept bugging me about it, and it was only in the evening that I remembered to check it. I ran to the *bastide*, and by the time I got here Mlle Matton was on the phone to the emergency services. Thomas told me what Mme Baudouin had told him, and I called the police station."

"This is a serious accusation," Verlaque said to Sandrine.

At that point a young male police officer walked into the house. "I've finished checking the grounds," he said.

"Anything, Officer Schoelcher?" asked Paulik.

"No, nothing. No sign of a disturbance outside or upstairs."

Sandrine began weeping and repeating over and over that she hadn't pushed Michèle, and I believed her. But it looked bad, and as my new cigar friend suggested, Michèle was accusing Sandrine of attempted murder. Very serious indeed. At that point a loud thump sounded and each of us turned around. It was Thomas, who had fainted and fallen off his chair and onto the floor.

In less than an hour everyone was gone. One of the police officers parked Thomas's moped in one of the outbuildings, called his boss explaining Thomas's absence, and drove Thomas home. Sandrine was to stay with me at La Bastide Blanche. She was in no shape to drive, and that way I could keep an eye on her. In fact, I thought we could keep an eye on each other, as I suddenly felt very lonely. I offered to call her sister, Josy, but Sandrine refuted that idea with a wave of her hand. Verlaque nodded, approving the idea. I believe I saved him from launching into one of those "you must not leave the country" speeches they make in the cop shows. Neither Sandrine nor I offered any information about the night visitors: Sandrine's scare in the cellar and my nightly tug-of-war with the person in my bed. We were too tired, I think, and I suppose we had both quietly decided that things were looking bad enough for Sandrine without mentioning ghosts. Or whatever they might be. Verlaque and Jean-Marc left together, the former promising to visit me the next day and keep me updated on Michèle's condition. I gave Sandrine a sleeping pill and closed her bedroom door. I lit the hall light and was halfway down the hall when I heard her snoring, almost as loudly as Michèle had. I was almost at my room when the light went off, and I ran the remaining three or so feet to my room, charging in like a bull, fumbling for the light switch, panting. It wasn't the first time that had happened, but with everything else in the house, it had hardly seemed worth getting upset about. But that night it did.

I dressed for bed, dropping my cigar-scented clothes in a heap on the floor. I thought about Michèle saying, "She pushed me." If the person was *behind* Michèle, she might not have seen them. She would have assumed it was Sandrine, the only other person, to her knowledge, in the house. It could have been a woman or a man. I went back to my original thief idea: they had been in the house, getting ready to steal, and saw Michèle at the top of the stairs. It may have been an accident; the thief, in a hurry to leave, rushed past her, causing her to fall. But Thomas would have seen them leaving, and he had said nothing.

I looked around the room and somehow had a premonition that it would never be changed. The ocher-colored walls were decorated with plaster carvings painted dark gold. At first I had found this *gypserie* hideous but after a short time I had come to like it. My wrought-iron bed was now in the middle of the room—Sandrine's solution, to help with my sleep— but I wasn't convinced about the bed's new position, as the room was so big. I felt like I was on a raft drifting in the middle of the sea. I watched the shadows cast by the pine trees dance around the walls. Then something on the floor, beside the fireplace, caught my eye. I sighed, too tired to go pick it up, not caring if I would be chastised by Sandrine for laziness or slovenliness. I tried ignoring it but felt myself drawn in. Each time I closed my eyes they would open within seconds, fixed on what I now believed to be a piece of fabric. I finally got up and walked over to it, my heart pounding. Bending down, I lifted it by a corner, as if it were hot or poisonous. Holding it up, I saw that it was indeed fabric: a linen handkerchief, embroidered with the initials AF. I recognized it immediately and held it to my chest. It was Agathe's favorite.

The wind suddenly stopped, and the night became still. Not a sound outside, not a frog, nor cricket, nor passing car. I went back to bed and put the handkerchief under my pillow, too tired to ask why or how it had shown up in my bedroom. It had probably fallen out of a box or suitcase when I unpacked, although I didn't remember packing it in Paris.

My eyelids burned with fatigue. I closed them and must have immediately fallen asleep, because when I next opened them the bright sun was shining through the windows, and the *cigales* were just beginning to make the noise that would go on for the next twelve hours. It was nine o'clock, and I had slept through the night for the first time in months, perhaps years. I stretched, then remembered Agathe's handkerchief. I reached under the pillow and took it out, holding it to my cheek.

Chapter Thirteen

Aix-en-Provence,
Thursday, July 7, 2010

Antoine Verlaque spent the morning going over the Yvette Tamain case with two associates, breaking at eleven thirty. They agreed they would meet again the day after Bastille Day—the fifteenth of July—to finalize their line of questioning before they called in the mayor, her campaign manager, and the CEO of AixCom. As soon as his colleagues left, he picked up the phone and called the hospital; Michèle Baudouin was still in a coma. After lunch he would go to Puyloubier and pay a visit to Valère Barbier and his housekeeper. He had some questions concerning Mme Baudouin's accident: blanks in the evening's events that had been bothering him all morning.

No sooner had he finished his call to the hospital than his phone rang again; it was Mme Girard, in the next room, telling him he had a call from Judge Sennat in Cannes. He thanked his secretary and took a deep breath before accepting the call. It had been years since they had spoken.

"Verlaque here," he said, realizing he sounded colder than he had intended.

"Hello, Antoine," the magistrate said. "How are you?"

He sat back and tried to calm himself. "I'm fine, Chantal. How are you?"

"Busier than the devil," she answered.

"Any news on Mme Blechman's kidnapping?" He had recently seen Chantal Sennat on M6, being interviewed by journalists. She hadn't aged, not like he had. Her long, jet-black hair was as thick and wavy as it had ever been; it was the kind of hair that shampoo companies hired models for. Verlaque watched her as a journalist asked a repetitive question, holding his microphone too close to her face; her dark blue eyes focused on the unfortunate young man, at once intimidating and seducing him.

"Nothing, nada, zilch," she answered, not disguising her frustration. "It's been three days now. . . . I'm getting pressure on all sides, including Paris."

He nodded, knowing that Paris meant the *Élysée*. He realized there might be a positive side to only having to deal with a crooked mayor and not having to explain to the president of France why you haven't yet caught kidnappers. He asked, "I assume you're calling about the information concerning Agathe Barbier that Daniel de Rudder requested be sent to me."

"Yes, although Rudder has pissed me off royally. If he has concerns or worries, he should ask me to go through that stuff."

"But with the kidnapping . . ."

She sighed. "Yes, I'm passing the affair on to you, but *only* because I'm too busy. A car driven by two of our slower officers left here two hours ago with the Agathe Barbier report. They should be there any minute, unless they stop in Saint-Tropez for lunch, in which case their next assignment will be at a school crossing."

He laughed, remembering her humor and her impatience.

She went on: "You'll have to send the papers back here in a police car. Or you could bring them yourself."

"I'm too busy."

"As you wish," she replied. "I have no idea why Rudder is all of a sudden interested in reopening that case. He must be senile. Agathe Barbier died in 1988. That's when we were . . ."

Verlaque cleared his throat. "Yes, it was a long time ago. You must be married with teenage kids by now."

"Divorced, no children. And you?"

"Married, no children." He didn't think it any of her business to know that he was only recently married.

"My sister says that having children is the only important job one can do while on earth."

"Well, then, we both seem to be failures," he said, playing with his pen. Chantal could have easily asked an underling to call him about the delivery, but here she was, making the call herself. She probably had the *président de la République* on hold on the other line. Chantal Sennat hadn't changed a bit. She did as she pleased, not caring who she offended or kept waiting. It was one of the things that had attracted him to her when they were studying in Bordeaux together. That, and . . .

"So it seems," she said, sounding amused. "My sister may have six children, but she's an unhappy wretch. Plus, when she and her good-for-nothing husband decided to have kids, they forgot that three would be in university at the same time. Guess who's working her ass off to pay for their studies, as none of them got into a *grande école*?"

"I'm sure they'll remember that when you're old," Verlaque said, laughing.

"Yeah, right. Well, you sound good, Antoine. I've got to go. Rudder is wasting your time, but, still, you'll contact me if you discover any overlooked evidence when you go through the boxes?"

"Certainly," he answered.

"You're such a liar." He could hear her breathing, and she waited a few seconds before adding, "Listen, think again about coming to Cannes . . ."

"I don't think so, Chantal."

"That's what I thought you'd say," she answered. "But when it comes to women, you always change your mind—don't you?" She hung up.

"*Merde*!" Verlaque hissed as he hung up his phone. He got up and paced the room. He walked over to his bookshelf and opened his small mahogany humidor, pulled out a short but thick Partagás D4, snipped off the end, and, fumbling with his lighter, lit it. He opened the windows of his office and sat on the ledge, smoking. Memories appeared before him like color postcards: weekends with Chantal in Prague or Rome. Wine-filled evenings with friends, in garret apartments that overlooked the gray city, before Bordeaux had been cleaned up and gentrified. Verlaque had money, even as a student, and she had energy and drive in spades. In that way they were a good match and the envy of their fellow students: he was a posh Parisian who excelled at debate and rugby; Chantal was a fiery beauty who was raised in the remote region of Corrèze by a mechanic and a beautician, and had worked her way up from a mediocre village school to one of France's most elite law schools.

His stomach growled, and he decided to go for lunch in Puyloubier. And he knew exactly who to invite. He stubbed out his cigar and left it in his hiding spot, safely wedged between the outside wall and a metal bracket on the shutter. Grabbing his jacket and phone, he walked out just as Mme Girard was gathering her things. She looked at him and curled up her nose.

"I'm going to lunch and then to Puyloubier, if anyone asks," he said, trying to ignore the cloud of cigar smoke that seemed to have followed him. "Any minute now there will be a delivery of important evidence from Cannes, escorted by two policemen. Could you call down and tell the guys at the front door to keep it with them under lock and key until I get back?"

"Certainly," she answered, picking up the phone. "Have a nice lunch."

"Thank you. You too," he answered. Mme Girard, in his opinion, was far too thin, and he didn't like to imagine her meager lunch of a bit of cold tomato and tuna from a can. He was in a sour enough mood that he almost said his thoughts aloud. A younger Antoine Verlaque would have. But he stayed quiet and walked downstairs and out of the building as quickly as he could. As he walked up the rue Mignet, to get his car out of the garage, he scrolled through the list of contacts on his phone. He wasn't sure if he still had Auvieux's phone number, but it was there, third from the top. He dialed, and after three rings Auvieux answered.

"Jean-Claude, it's Judge Verlaque. How have you been?"

"*Monsieur le Juge*! Well, my oh my. I can't believe it's you," Auvieux answered, with obvious delight in his voice. Verlaque smiled; it was the kind of response he had hoped for. The one he needed.

"I have business in Puyloubier this afternoon," Verlaque said. "Are you free for lunch? I know it's last minute."

"You mean, that nice restaurant . . ."

"Yes, on the *rue qui monte*."

"Well, I say, this *is* a nice surprise! I'll just put my *daube* back in the fridge."

Verlaque smiled. Only an old peasant—one who worked outside every day—would be eating beef stew on a hot July day.

Jean-Claude Auvieux read the menu, holding it tightly with his large, rough hands. Verlaque watched the farmer, his brow furrowed and his mouth partly open. Auvieux wasn't that much older than Verlaque, but his childlike naivety made him seem almost elderly. His name didn't help either: Auvieux meant "of old." His face was red and weathered—the face of someone who worked outside, in the sun and wind—and he had lost most of his hair, save for the short white whiskers that covered his face.

Auvieux flinched when the young waitress brought over a small blackboard and propped it up on the edge of their table. "The chef's daily specials," she announced, beaming, her shoulders thrust back and her back straight, as if the dishes were brilliant offspring.

"Oh my!" Auvieux cried, setting the menu down. "I'll have to start all over!"

"I'll have one of the specials," Verlaque said, trying to make the choice easier for Auvieux. "The cod with fennel and orange."

"Excellent choice, monsieur!" she cried.

"Osso bucco?" Auvieux asked, looking at the blackboard and then at Verlaque.

"Veal," Verlaque replied.

"But the chef has made an unusual osso bucco today," the waitress explained. "With white wine, fennel, and artichoke hearts." She lifted up her right hand, gathered the tips of her fingers, and pressed them to her mouth, making a loud kissing noise. Verlaque looked down at the table to try to control his laughter, and Auvieux beamed.

"That's that, then!" Auvieux exclaimed, lifting his hands into the air. "I'll have the osso . . . whatever it is."

"We'll have a white burgundy," Verlaque said, putting on his reading glasses to look at the short but well-put-together wine menu. "From Rully, the—"

"If I may be so bold," the waitress cut in, "as to suggest a white côtes du Rhône. Its floral bouquet will be excellent with both the cod and monsieur's osso bucco."

"Thank you. That sounds fine," Verlaque said, handing her the menu. "And might you have a first-course recommendation?" He loved this girl and couldn't wait to tell Marine that she still worked here.

She leaned in and whispered, as if revealing state secrets. "For you, monsieur, the foie gras *poêlé*, since you have chosen *un plat legér*. The chef has prepared an exquisite apricot chutney to go with the foie gras. The best local apricots he could find, *bien sûr*."

"It was a bumper crop for apricots this year," Auvieux added, smiling. "I had hundreds."

"Perfect," Verlaque said. He didn't care what kind of chutney the sautéed foie gras came with; simply the liver and browned butter were enough.

"And for your friend," she continued, "to balance the veal, and the acidity of the white wine and artichokes, might I suggest the roasted chèvre?"

Auvieux rubbed his stomach.

"I think you can take that as a yes," Verlaque said.

Auvieux nodded and took a large gulp of water, as if preparing his palate.

"Very well," she said. "I'll be right back with the wine."

Verlaque smiled and leaned back, glad that Auvieux had been available at such short notice and feeling slightly guilty that it had taken him so long to call and invite him out. He thought back to the Bremont case, trying to remember exactly when it was that he had first met Auvieux, caretaker of the Bremont estate, while investigating the case involving the brothers Étienne and François.

The wine was opened and the first course came. They talked about the weather, the food, and Aix's rugby team's losing streak. After the waitress had taken their plates away, Verlaque poured them each another glass of wine and rested his forearms on the wooden table. "Jean-Claude," he began, "what do you know about the Bastide Blanche? It's just down the road, on the way out of the village."

Auvieux bit his lower lip. "I've never been there. It's a big place, very old."

Verlaque nodded, but Auvieux stayed silent. "Yes, it's hundreds of years old," Verlaque continued. "Tell me, what's its history? A friend of mine has just bought it, and he said that some of the villagers make the sign of the cross before going there."

"Oh yes, oh yes. That they do, that they do."

Verlaque tried to remain patient with Auvieux's repetitive nonanswers. "Some old tale?" he asked.

"They say it's cursed and haunted."

"By whom?"

Auvieux looked up at the ceiling. "Why,

someone who once lived there, I suppose," he replied. "I've never really known. We were simply told it was haunted and not to go near it. Bad things happened there many years ago."

Verlaque sat back. That would explain the villagers' apprehensions but not how Mme Baudouin fell down the stairs—that is, if she wasn't pushed by the housekeeper. "The new owner is a famous writer," Verlaque said.

Auvieux nodded. "I know. Everyone knows."

"Do the villagers like him?"

Auvieux shrugged. "We hardly know him," he said. "He's just arrived and stays at the house. But he does have the housekeeper buy his food at the market and in the village shops, so he's well liked for that. He doesn't send her to the *hypermarchés* in Trets or Aix."

"Anyone else new in the village?"

Auvieux rolled his eyes. "It's summer! The village almost doubles in size! Let's see, a Dutch family is renting old lady Coydon's house for a month while she visits her grandson in Lyon," he said. "There's a German couple, two men, who have just bought *une maison du village* and are restoring it. Oh, and there's a Parisian, very well dressed she is, very proper. Someone said she's a retired librarian. She hardly goes out, only to buy food. But you can hear her coming down the sidewalk."

"Why is that?" Verlaque asked.

"Her cane," Auvieux said.

"She's elderly?"

Auvieux shook his head, ready for the judge's questions to end. "Blind," he said.

"Are there any ruffians in the village?"

"*Quoi?*" Auvieux asked. His gaze was fixed on the waitress, who was coming toward them, carrying two steaming dishes on a tea towel that stretched between the two plates.

"You know," Verlaque said, realizing he was running out of time with the farmer. "Bad boys. Ne'er-do-wells."

Auvieux smirked. "The Pioger cousins. Hervé and Didier. They've both been in jail, one for theft and the other for roughing up his ex-wife. They live together in an apartment above the old hardware store."

"Cozy."

"I wouldn't say that," Auvieux replied, not understanding, or not acknowledging, Verlaque's sarcasm. "One of my friends saw it once and said it looked like a sirocco had blown through it." Verlaque smiled, imagining that hot desert wind that in its wake left red sand on every surface.

The waitress set down the plates, warning that they were hot. Auvieux rubbed his hands together as the aroma from his osso bucco wafted into his face. "*Bonne continuation, cher Monsieur le Juge!*"

• • •

For dessert the two men shared a cheese plate, and then finished the meal with espresso followed by a hard-to-find Roger Groult calvados (the chef was from Normandy). Verlaque quickly paid the bill before Auvieux could argue. He hadn't got much useful information from Auvieux, except for the names of the Pioger cousins, but he'd had a thoroughly good time. He remembered his grandfather Charles, although vastly wealthy, making a point of dining every week with his managers and mill superintendents. "You don't learn anything from sticking to what you know," Charles had told his grandson. "You have to get out of your comfort zone. Besides, I like my men." Emmeline, Charles's English wife, had done the same: she was equally at ease with her bohemian art-school friends, their wealthy Parisian neighbors, and the no-nonsense farm wives who lived near the Normandy manor house the family used on weekends and holidays. Verlaque and his brother, Sébastien, had not been raised to mingle with others who did not live as they did—in a grand house in central Paris—and Verlaque, the few times that he saw his real-estate-mogul brother, knew Sébastien would never be able to mix with anyone who did not have the same kind of hefty bank account. Verlaque had always been very aware of his family's wealth and at university had made an effort to make friends with all different kinds of people. Rugby, he knew, had helped enormously. As had Chantal. He realized that he did have something in common with all of them—the rugby men, his old friends from law school, the cigar club, the farmer: they all loved good, real food. *I guess I'm still a snob in some ways,* Verlaque thought as he parked his car beside La Bastide Blanche, having taken Auvieux home. No, as much as he respected his secretary, Mme Girard, he could never be friends with her. What would they eat?

He walked across the lawn to the ancient front door, which was wide open. Given that the house was in the country, and it was a warm summer day, the open door did not entirely surprise him. But was it often left open like that? The Pioger cousins could have easily scoped out the grounds, knowing that the old worn-down house, now occupied by a rich and elderly man, was an invitation—gold-embossed—for breaking and entering. *Breaking isn't even needed,* thought Verlaque as he called out "Âllo!" *Anyone can just walk right in, as I'm doing now.*

He stepped into the elegant entryway and curled up his nose. Something was burning. "*Âllo!*" he called out again.

"Shhh!" Sandrine whispered as she walked down the long hallway, holding her index finger to her mouth.

"What's that awful smell?" Verlaque asked in a soft voice.

"I'm asking you very kindly to leave my home," Valère Barbier said as he came out of the living room, holding up a clump of burning branches. He saw Verlaque and winked. "This is my home now, and you must all leave." He walked across the hall and into another room, waving the burning branches above his head. "I appreciate that you may have lived here once, but, well, time goes on . . . *Que sera, sera . . .*"

Sandrine winced. "He's not even trying!" she whispered.

"What *is* that branch?" Verlaque asked.

"Sage," Sandrine said, leaning in toward Verlaque. "I made it."

Valère came back into the hallway and walked out the front door, still talking to the spirits. Verlaque and Sandrine followed him and watched as he made a halfhearted attempt to sway the burning sticks around the perimeter of the house. "Holy water up next," Sandrine said. "I bought it at the cathedral in Aix."

"Indeed?" Verlaque asked. "Is the house haunted, then?"

Sandrine nodded.

"Don't you think that's just village gossip, Mlle Matton?"

Sandrine waved her index finger back and

forth. "Is it village gossip that keeps M Barbier awake all night?"

"Perhaps M Barbier has worries that keep him up." Verlaque watched as Barbier disappeared around a corner.

"What worries could he have?" Sandrine asked. "He's a world-famous writer. Look at this house." She gestured toward the *bastide*, which Verlaque had to admit looked majestic on a sunny summer day.

"Wealthy people have problems too." He thought of his parents, stuck in their mansion a few streets from the Louvre, and never communicating. His mother had died, as she had lived: unhappy. "Perhaps even more," he added.

Sandrine blew a bubble with her bubblegum. "Nothing's as hard as cleaning. And loving and losing someone."

Verlaque turned to her. "I'm sorry," he began.

"I'm out of sage!" Valère called as he came toward them from the southeast corner of the house. "I almost burned my fingertips!"

Sandrine put her hands on her hips. "What am I going to do with you? I made four of them—don't worry."

"Care for a break?" Verlaque asked Valère.

"Go ahead," Sandrine replied. Verlaque looked at Barbier to see if he cared one way or another that his cleaning woman bossed him around. He seemed not to.

Sandrine looked at the men and said, "I'll leave you two and go clean up our lunch dishes."

Verlaque nodded, and Valère led him to the edge of the terrace, where a wrought-iron table and four chairs were set out. "Please, take a seat," Valère said.

"Thank you," Verlaque said, sitting down and looking out over the view of purple lavender, silver olive trees, deep green vines.

"May I tell you how charming I think your wife is?" Valère asked.

Verlaque nodded. "It's the best decision I ever made. Thank you." He reached into his jacket and pulled out a small leather cigar carrier, big enough for two coronas. He slipped off the lid and held it out to Valère. "Please," Verlaque said. "Friends of mine buy these in Havana. They're hand rolled by a guy named Gustavo."

"Gustavo! In that little room up above Villa Conde's courtyard!" Valère said. "I haven't had one of these in a while." He reached in and gently pulled one out. They cut and lit their cigars. Valère crossed his legs and sat back. "Marine, your wife, reminds me of Agathe."

"Really?"

"She's beautiful but she doesn't know it. Or doesn't flaunt it. They're both tall women too—unusual in our country. Is Marine Breton?"

"One grandmother was," Verlaque answered.

"That's where she gets her height and auburn hair and green eyes."

"Marine is beautiful, and Agathe was beautiful in a strange way; she was taller than the Parisian girls, and she had a long straight nose and high forehead that made her look quite regal. She didn't have the pouty lips and upturned nose that so many Parisian girls have."

Verlaque laughed.

Valère, encourage by his attentive listener, went on. "To her I was a renegade, a kid from the 13th arrondissement whose mother worked as a nurse and whose father died in World War II, the guy always writing bits of verse on the backs of envelopes and little bits of paper he found. That was her nickname for me—*Lambeau*. Scrappy."

Verlaque smiled. It was a good nickname. "The beginnings of a writer . . ."

"Agathe worked harder than I did; she had more originality," Valère quickly said. "I knew early on what the critics would like, what kind of book would make more famous writers pat me on the back and refill my whiskey glass."

Verlaque couldn't figure out why Valère's mood had suddenly soured. "But you won the Prix Goncourt."

"Popularity contest. I also received the Légion d'honneur and was on the short list for a Nobel in 1987—but lost to Wole Soyinka, for obvious political reasons."

Verlaque laughed. "I'm sorry," he said. "That must have been tough."

"My ego was bruised—that's all. I laughed it off, and Agathe said, 'A little group of sixteen or eighteen Swedish nationalists might be able to pick the year's best Swedish author, but how can they ever really know what's best in the entire world's literature, with all its styles and different traditions?'"

"Nineteen eighty-seven." Verlaque knocked some white ash into the ashtray. He looked at Valère and waited.

"Yes. A year later Agathe was dead."

Sandrine came out, carrying a bottle of cold mineral water and two glasses. "Perfect, thank you," Valère said. "You're missing the—"

"Whiskey," Sandrine said. "I couldn't carry it. I didn't forget. I'll be right back."

Verlaque said, "I hear that Mme Baudouin is still in a coma."

"Yes," Valère replied, nodding. "I called this morning."

"How well do you know Mlle Matton?" Verlaque asked after Sandrine had gone through the front door.

Valère looked surprised. "She's the niece of my friend and lawyer, Guillaume Matton. I've known him for years."

"But not her."

"No, that's true," Valère answered. "But Matton

would hardly have recommended her if she were . . . troublesome . . . or unreliable."

"She seems to think that your house is haunted."

Valère shrugged. "I'm at a loss to explain what's been going on around here, and Sandrine's ideas—however New Age they may seem—are worth a try at this point. I can't handle another sleepless night."

Verlaque crossed his legs and looked up at the house before asking, "Is it possible that Mlle Matton is trying to frighten you?"

Valère shook his head. "It started before she got here. Almost as soon as I moved in."

Verlaque noted that Sandrine Matton may have known—thanks to her uncle—the exact day that Valère took possession of the house. "Can you think of anyone else who might want you out of the house?"

Sandrine came back out with a bottle of Laphroaig, curtsied, and left.

"*Merci*, Sandrine!" Valère called after her. "Few people even know I've left Paris," he continued.

"What exactly has been happening here?" Verlaque asked. "Can you explain it to me?"

Valère sat back and began describing to the judge the odd goings-on at night. He was relieved that Verlaque nodded and listened carefully, not passing judgment.

"You realize there may be logical explanations

for these incidents," Verlaque said once Valère had finished.

"I know, I know. The wiring is older than the hills; it needs to be completely redone. That could explain the lights going on and off. And I know that old houses make noises. But what about the voices? The impression of another body on my bed?"

"Who gains from trying to frighten you? Is there anyone who hates you?"

Valère laughed.

"Someone angry at you?"

"Yes," Valère slowly answered. "But she's dead."

Chapter Fourteen

Aix-en-Provence,
Thursday, July 8, 2010

Marine was a great believer in following a recipe, down to the minute details. Like many daughters of well-educated women who grew up in France in the 1970s, she wasn't taught how to cook. Her mother, Florence Bonnet, a noted theologian and professor at Aix's university, believed the right to work and attend university had been earned by French women after the Second World War. Her daughter would be free from the shackles of the country-house kitchen, as she herself had been.

Marine laid a bottle of olive oil on the *Elle* recipe page, to keep it flat and stop it from turning. She had borrowed the magazine from Sylvie, who was a subscriber and liked to chide Marine for not buying what she considered essential *bonne lecture* for every French woman. Marine understood what her best friend meant: *Elle* was full of well-written reviews of currently released books and films, articles on relationships, politics, and of course dazzling fashion pages—but the clothes were not too expensive, as in *Vogue*. But it was the recipes in the last pages that attracted Marine: simple meals made from easy-to-find ingredients that reflected the seasons, and for the most part written for women her age who, like her, hadn't been taught how to cook.

Both she and Antoine loved to eat well, and she was competitive enough to want to strive to be a better cook than her husband. His kitchen—their kitchen now—was a joy to cook in, with its smooth marble countertops, gas range with five burners, and very sharp German knives. How had she managed for so long with dull knives, in her simple kitchen on the other side of Aix?

The door to their fourth-floor apartment opened, and Antoine walked in, shouting, "*Coucou*!" as he usually did. Marine replied with her standard, "*Buonasera*!" While pouring dark-green olive oil into two glass baking dishes, she continued, "I'm afraid I'm losing my Italian."

"It doesn't look like it," Verlaque replied, pointing to the olive oil.

Marine laughed. "I don't mean cooking. The language."

"Let's buy an apartment in Venice, then."

"You're joking!"

"Not at all," he said. "Apartments in Venice are now half the price of the same in Paris."

Marine set down the olive oil and stared at him. "Are you serious?"

"I can show you," he said, taking his cell phone out of his pocket.

"No no," she said. "I believe you. I want to get this in the oven."

"Is it all right if I spread some papers on the dining room table?"

"Sure. I thought we'd eat outside on the terrace."

"Great." Verlaque held up a faded green folder about two inches thick and said, "The report on Agathe Barbier's drowning, from 1988."

"Should you have that here?"

Verlaque shrugged, thinking of Chantal's demand that the dossier be sent back to her accompanied by police officers. "Probably not. But I wanted your opinion."

"Okay, I'll look at it after you've gone through it."

"I'll save you the good bits." He took a few steps toward the dining room and then turned back. "There's only one problem with an apartment in Venice," he said.

"The city is sinking?"

"No."

"*Acqua alta*?"

"No."

"Too many tourists?"

"Not in Castello."

"I give up."

Verlaque frowned. "There isn't a direct flight from Marseille."

"Ah, that would complicate quick weekend getaways. By the way, it's an all-vegetable dinner tonight."

Verlaque mimed stabbing himself as he walked back into the dining room.

Verlaque leaned back in his chair, wiping the corners of his mouth with a large linen napkin. "Excellent," he proclaimed.

Marine squirmed. She thought her husband was being overcongratulatory. "Thank you," she answered. "Too bad the rosemary was burnt."

"You're too hard on yourself." Verlaque poured the rest of the wine into their glasses, and his stomach made a rumbling sound.

"Was that your stomach?" Marine asked. "You can't be hungry?"

"Maybe I'll just grab a few slices of salami from the fridge. Do you mind?"

"Go right ahead," she answered, laughing. "Was the Agathe Barbier dossier revealing in any way?"

"Fairly straightforward so far," he said, getting up from the table. "I managed to read all the interviews while you were cooking."

"Don't waste a trip," Marine said, handing him a few dirty dishes as he made his way to the kitchen.

She leaned back and looked over the rooftops. The cathedral's octagonal steeple was lit up, and she suddenly heard the chorus of the opera break into song, just a few meters from their apartment. Verlaque came back upstairs carrying a small plate with thinly sliced salami and said, "Cheapest opera seats, right here."

"And we can eat as we listen."

"And drink," he said, lifting his glass to hers.

"Who was on the boat when Agathe went overboard?" Marine asked, picking up a piece of the salami and putting it into her mouth.

"They were five," Verlaque answered. "Agathe and Valère Barbier; Valère's publisher Alphonse Pelloquin and his wife, Monica; and Valère's secretary, Ursule Genoux."

"His *secretary?* On vacation?"

"The commissioner in Cannes asked the same question when she interviewed Genoux," Verlaque replied. "They were finishing up a book, and apparently she was always present when Valère was working. It was still the 1980s."

"Right," Marine said. "No computers."

"Valère dictated to her while she typed."

"But on a boat?"

"They had been in Sardinia for three weeks," Verlaque said. "Monica Pelloquin is Italian and has a house there."

Marine winked. "Lucky them. I remember my parents talking about the accident. It all sounded so sordid. One imagines too many gin and tonics, too much sun, and then arguments and fights. You know, like those Hollywood stars in the thirties. What on earth was Agathe Barbier doing on deck during a storm anyway?"

"She was seasick," Verlaque replied. "No one knew she had gone up on deck, except for Alphonse Pelloquin, who warned her about the bad weather. The others were down below. Pelloquin claimed that when she insisted—she had been very sick all day, which the others confirmed—he told her to harness herself to the lifeline near the bow of the boat. He went back to the cockpit to steer, and just minutes after that she was gone. Over the storm's racket he hadn't heard a thing."

"Suicide?"

"They all said that was impossible, knowing her even temperament and good nature."

"Where are these people now?" Marine asked.

"In Paris," Verlaque replied. "Except for Alphonse Pelloquin, who died of cancer in 2001."

Marine finished her wine, and then frowned and shook her head.

"What's bothering you, my dear?" Verlaque asked.

"Why didn't Agathe tie herself to the lifeline, like she was supposed to?"

"Because she couldn't? Perhaps she fell off

180

before she had a chance to tether herself to the boat?"

"And Daniel de Rudder wants you to find something in the dossier, right?"

Verlaque nodded. "There are some photographs of the boat in the file. You used to sail, right?"

"Hardly," Marine answered. "A boy I dated in high school had a family boat in Marseille. I remember the nuts and bolts, I suppose. Rudder took you out, didn't he?"

"Many times," Verlaque replied. "Very good memories, those." He thought of Rudder, standing at the stern, with his tanned face and flyaway blond hair, yelling instructions to eager young law students, many of whom had never been on a boat in their lives. And there was Chantal . . .

The sound of hundreds of people leaving the opera festival filled the square just around the corner from their apartment. Marine made a comment about the opera being finished, but Verlaque didn't seem to hear. She stared at him and said, a little louder this time, "Let's go inside and look at the photographs. I feel like tea. Would you care for any?"

Verlaque looked up and said, "Tea? Yeah, sounds good."

Marine gathered the rest of the dishes and watched Verlaque, who had moved to the edge of the terrace and was looking out over the city.

She loved resting her eyes on her husband when he wasn't aware of it; she adored his thick black-and-gray hair, his crooked nose, his barrel chest and wide shoulders. He rested his elbows on the terrace's stone wall and watched the crowd, some of whom would take the rue Adanson as a shortcut, others because they were lost, and still others because they simply felt like meandering on a warm summer night, perhaps inspired by Mozart's opera. Verlaque stood motionless. Marine shrugged; she had at least expected a wisecrack about the tea.

"Such bad haircuts," Marine said, looking at the black-and-white photographs laid out before them.

Verlaque muttered in agreement. "Even the rich and famous weren't immune to the Vidal Sassoon shag, circa 1985."

"And the women's bangs that look like sausages," Marine said, pointing to a passport photo of Monica Pelloquin. She picked up a photograph of a snarling adolescent boy. "Who's this?"

"Erwan Le Flahec, Agathe's son," Verlaque answered, picking up one of the police reports and reading it. "It says here he was born in Vallauris in 1972, so he would have been sixteen when his mother died."

"But he wasn't on the boat that night, right?"

"No."

"Thank God."

Verlaque continued reading while Marine carefully looked at the photographs, frowning and biting her bottom lip. Verlaque laughed and said, "The Cannes police gave each subject an evaluation when filling out these reports, like in grade school. Everyone on the boat received a 'very disagreeable' in the category of 'cooperation while questioning.'"

"Needs improvement," Marine said.

"Three out of ten. See me after class," Verlaque added, laughing.

"Even the kid," he went on, "who was questioned in Paris, was, quote, 'extremely uncooperative.'"

"No wonder," Marine mumbled. "His mother died."

"The secretary claimed that she overheard Agathe and Alphonse Pelloquin arguing earlier that afternoon."

Marine looked up. "Five people on a small sailboat. I don't doubt it."

"Exactly. They could have been arguing about anything."

Marine said, "It must really bother Rudder that the case was never solved. He was an unbeatable judge, wasn't he?"

"Yes, but he was also human," Verlaque said. "Rudder's grandson, who must have been Erwan

Le Flahec's age at the time, was sick. Very sick, with leukemia. He died the next year. Rudder and I had drinks together one night a few years after that. Well, it went into the morning, and he confessed that the Barbier case still haunted him. He admitted that he should have taken a leave of absence, but he kept on the case, convinced he could do both—make visits to the hospital and resolve a suspicious death. He gave much of the work to a young colleague, who was in over his head. Rudder was already in his sixties then, and perhaps should have retired."

"It was a high-profile case," Marine said. "It was Valère Barbier, for heaven's sake. I still can't believe that Barbier lives here, and we've met him. You know, it's crazy . . . He's such a big deal. I think because we've now joked with him, and chatted about this and that, we're forgetting his importance to this country's culture."

"I'll have to be more nervous around him when I see him again," Verlaque said.

"And despite his joking and guy-next-door easiness," Marine said, her voice getting higher as it usually did when she was excited, "I do remember Valère making cracks about me being married to a judge and Paulik being a policeman. Like he was nervous . . ."

"He did that at the cigar club too," Verlaque said. "But let's not get carried away."

Marine picked up a stack of photos of the boat.

"When did the police arrive on the scene? I mean the boat, in this case."

Verlaque slipped his reading glasses back on and turned the pages of the report. "Almost immediately," he answered.

"How is that possible?"

"As it turns out, the boat was close to the coast," he said. "Alphonse Pelloquin sent out an emergency call, and it says here that the coast guard arrived in under an hour."

"But things on the boat could have been changed by then, moved around."

Verlaque shook his head. "True, but Valère wouldn't let anyone move until the coast guard came. I read that before we sat down to dinner. When he was interviewed, he told the police that he made the two women stay in the cockpit, tethered to their lifelines. He and Pelloquin tried shining lights on the sea and throwing buoys overboard, but it was no use."

"If they were close to the shore, why did Agathe's body never wash up?"

"Good question."

Marine snickered as she handed a photograph to Verlaque. "The kitchen," he said, looking at the photograph of the ship's small galley. "Judging by the number of used limes in the sink, you were right about the cocktails." She leaned in toward Verlaque and continued, "Katharine Hepburn. That's who I was thinking

of. Didn't she get in horrible drunken rows with
. . . with . . ."

"Spencer Tracy."

Marine snapped her fingers. "That's him. *Guess
Who's Coming to Dinner*! He was her husband in
that film and in real life too, right?"

"Lover," Verlaque corrected. "He was a
Catholic and wouldn't divorce his wife."

Marine raised an eyebrow. She fumbled
through the photographs until she found one of
Agathe Barbier, and passed it to Verlaque. "See
the baptismal medal around her neck?"

Verlaque nodded. "It doesn't mean she was
devout." He picked up a photograph of the boat's
foredeck and brought it closer, then handed it to
Marine and flipped through the report until he
got to the passage he was looking for. "Listen to
this," he said. "Monica Pelloquin, when interviewed, insisted that Alphonse was a maniacally
thorough skipper. One of the other guests—I
think it was the secretary—said the same thing."

"Obviously the storm wasn't his fault," Marine
said.

"But look at that foredeck," Verlaque said,
pointing to the photograph.

"*Oh là là.*" Marine brought the photograph
closer and narrowed her eyes, looking at it from
left to right. "*Quel bordel!* Why isn't the anchor
in its well?"

Verlaque smiled. "You do remember something

186

about sailing. I remember Daniel de Rudder was a fanatic about using the anchor well. And look at all those lines on the deck, the ones that belong in the cleats and bow fairleads or whatever they're called. They should be coiled and stowed away. Rudder always said that an untidy deck was an accident waiting to happen—anyone could trip and fall overboard."

"Do you think that's the detail that Rudder wanted you to see?" Marine asked.

"I'll call him first thing in the morning."

"It's not much to go on," Marine replied, setting the photograph down and frowning.

"But if Pelloquin was such a good sailor, he would have a tidy deck, no?"

"So you're saying he intentionally left out the anchor and lines? To trip Agathe?"

Verlaque got up from the table and began clearing away their teacups. "I know, I know," he replied. "It's a long shot."

Marine sat back and folded her arms against her chest. "To begin with," she said, "we're missing a motive."

Chapter Fifteen

New York City,
September 22, 2010

Justin felt relieved that Valère was enjoying the cheeses and thus taking a break from talking. He wasn't sure where the conversation was going, but he was certain the famous writer was wracked with guilt and had somehow chosen a young editor to pour out his heart to. Perhaps it helped that Justin wasn't French, or perhaps their age difference made it easier for Valère to be honest—that is, if he was telling the truth.

Before their meeting, Justin had spent a few hours reading newspaper articles about Agathe Barbier's accidental death. He was thankful he had picked up enough French at NYU to understand the details of the reports. But he wanted Valère's version and so far wasn't getting it. Certainly the episode would be an important part of Barbier's memoir. And was that why the author was so guilt-stricken?

"Your wife . . . Agathe . . . She was from Brittany, right?" Justin asked. "I had a French professor at NYU who said that the Bretons are the most distinctive people in France. She'd make us sing Breton songs."

Valère wiped his mouth with his napkin. He crossed his arms and smiled. "Agathe was born Agathe Le Flahec, in Crozon, just south of Brest. Beautiful wild clean beaches, with no one on them. She hated Mediterranean beaches, but I can't stand cold water, and, let's face it, in the sixties and seventies all the beautiful people were down on the Med, not in bloody freezing Brittany."

Justin laughed. "Were her parents artists as well?"

"Her father was a country doctor, and her mother stayed at home with the kids but was an accomplished watercolorist. Agathe went to the village elementary school, but it was decided that for *lycée* she would go to Les Loges in Saint-Germain-en-Laye, outside Paris. You've probably never heard of Les Loges. The school—and there's another one just like it in Saint-Denis—was set up for the daughters, granddaughters, and great-granddaughters of decorated soldiers. They were prestigious boarding schools that were free to those girls, and still are. Agathe's grandfather, Erwan Le Flahec, was a general in the First World War. So off she went to Les Loges in 1961, then the École des Beaux-Arts in 1964, from which she graduated with a master's in fine art in 1969."

"I used to walk by the Beaux-Arts all the time," Justin said. "The students were snooty and as soon as they heard our American accents would refuse to talk to us."

"Well, it seems like you had no problem in chatting up Clothilde," Valère said, laughing. "But I know what you're saying about the art students. They acted like that when I was your age. I was intimidated, but my wild friend Hugo, a reporter, wasn't. He used to claim that the male Beaux-Arts students were all insane, and the women all beautiful, so we'd have a good chance of scoring with the girls."

"And so you met Agathe." Justin pinched himself, realizing how lucky he was to be hearing all this. He wished his own parents were as open.

Valère smiled. "Agathe used to joke that the high point of her time in Paris was discovering clay at the Beaux-Arts. In second place was meeting me. I had just graduated from the Sorbonne and was working my first job, as an assistant editor at *Le Monde*. Hugo and I would finish up correcting the sheets and then head out to the cafés and bars to pick up girls. I think that's one of the many things we have in common, Justin."

Before Justin could reply, Valère's mood changed. His brow furrowed and he said, "Back to the Bastide Blanche."

"Right," Justin agreed, coughing. "Judge

Verlaque's visit must have thrown you for a loop."

I'll say. After he left, Sandrine was even more fidgety than she usually was. She kept checking her cell phone and insisted we get outside and take an early evening walk. As we started down the drive, we came across Léa, who was sitting under an oak tree, reading. "You're not reading in our attic today?" I asked. Léa had been visiting us more frequently as of late, often spending hours at a time in the attic. Sandrine thought it odd, and I thought it completely normal. I did the same at Léa's age, only not in an attic, as we lived in a Parisian apartment, but in the pantry.

"*Maman* said I had to get some fresh air," Léa replied.

We chatted for a bit, and Sandrine told Léa that we had taken the photograph, the one with me and Maria Callas, into Aix to get framed. In fact, the framer's shop was next to the hospital, and we explained that we had been in to see Michèle, whose condition had not changed. I asked Léa if she knew of any good walks in the area, and she jumped up and called to her mother, who was walking between the barn and the house, carrying what looked like beakers full of red wine. Hélène yelled hello and gave Léa permission to accompany us. In fact, it was the other way around. Léa hurried down the road and said to follow her. Instructed us, really. We must have made a curious trio: the old writer, whose apparitions I was now convinced stemmed from guilt; the short-skirted, fast-talking housekeeper, who may or may not have pushed my fellow writer down the stairs; and a little girl leading us along.

We walked in single formation when we got onto the main road, which isn't that busy, but, still, when those village boys drive, they drive quickly. A taxi approached, leaving the village toward Aix, and as it drove by we stopped walking and, naturally, watched it go by. An old woman wearing sunglasses and a large straw hat sat in the back seat. "The blind lady," Sandrine said.

"It would be terrible to be blind," Léa said, "but worse to be deaf."

"You think so?" I asked.

"Not to be able to see your parents?" Sandrine added. "Or see flowers or your mother's vineyards?"

"But it would be worse," Léa answered, "if I couldn't hear their voices." I now knew the Paulik family better, and was aware of Léa's musical gifts. Neither Sandrine nor I argued, and we let the conversation slide into other, less melancholic, subjects.

"Are we almost there?" I joked after about fifteen minutes.

Léa ignored me and turned up a dirt road that led southeast of the village. We obediently followed. I was going to make another joke, about the blind leading the blind, but it was corny, and, besides, Léa wasn't blind. She knew exactly where she was going.

The road twisted and turned around two or three old stone farmhouses and one garish, recently built yellow stucco bungalow. I almost pointed out the ugliness of the bungalow—its obvious cheap materials, its unimaginative blockiness, the windows that were too small (here, in the country, one could have big windows!)—but I decided to stay quiet. Sandrine probably grew up in such a house, on the other side of Aix, where her sister, Josy, might still live.

Then we saw, at the edge of an olive grove, where Léa was taking us. It was a quintessential snapshot of Provence: a small white chapel, its front door flanked by two light columns and topped by a semicircular window. There were two tiny arched windows on either side and a bell tower at the roof's peak. A very large, old cypress tree guarded the chapel. The only blemish was a bright yellow watering hose that had been left out on the front lawn, parched from the sun. Someone from the village must water the lawn, or make an attempt to, but judging from the golden grass, watering in this summer heat was a losing battle.

"*Venez!*" Léa called to us as she began running, not into the chapel, whose door I could see was open, but around to the back. When we got to the far side of the chapel we could see her sitting on a rocky outcrop in the middle of the lawn, taking off her sandals. She waved and yelled, "Saint Pancrace!" then she stood up and slowly began walking on the smooth rocks.

"Who in the world is Saint Pancrace?" I asked Sandrine.

"Don't ask me," she answered. "Josy and I would sneak novels into Mass. We never listened."

"Probably my books, you little heathens," I said.

"Look, you two!" Léa said when we finally reached her. She was putting her little feet into a set of worn-out footprints embedded in the rocks. "These are the footsteps of Saint Pancrace!" she said. There were four, and Léa skipped back and forth between them.

"Is that so?" I asked.

"Yes," Léa answered matter-of-factly. "Saint Pancrace walked here from . . . I can't remember, but it was far . . . and he sat here and rested his feet in this hollow in the stone, which was full of water, because it had rained. And when he rested his feet, a miracle happened. The stone turned all mushy and soft, and his footprints were left in the rock. Look!"

194

What, Justin? You believe in that kind of stuff? I figured you did. Let me continue.

"You have to do this," Léa said quite seriously. "It's good luck to put your feet in his footsteps. We did it in May. A bunch of us kids from the village, after a Mass in the chapel."

"How does it bring you good luck?" I asked.

Léa answered, "Because you're following in his footsteps, and . . . well . . . it will help you have a good life."

I didn't comment that it surprised me that the Pauliks went to Mass. They seemed too liberal. But that was my Parisian Left Bank intellectualism screaming out. They may have made an exception for that May Mass, like one goes to Mass at Easter or Christmas but never at any other time. Or perhaps they did go every Sunday. I didn't really know, nor was it my place to judge.

I asked Léa to show us the church, and she sat down and put her sandals back on, then jumped up and was off like a rocket. Sandrine grinned and we followed Léa back around to the front of the chapel. At the front door Sandrine put her hand on my forearm, signaling me to stop. A siren was singing, an angel. We crept into the chapel and stood with our backs to the wall. It was too small for pews; I wondered what they did for the May celebration. Léa was standing perfectly still, with her back to the stone altar, facing us. I'm not an expert in choral music; in fact, I know nothing about it. Perhaps I could pick out bits of Bach's *St. Matthew Passion*. But I love choral music when I hear it, and always regret that I don't pay better attention to it. I glanced over at Sandrine, who had her eyes closed, her face lifted up to the tiny chapel's rounded ceiling.

The song gave me goose bumps. The lyrics were so simple: about a little lamb. Childlike, and yet with the deep, low notes it became profound. It was utterly beautiful and transcendent. It was the last line that floored me. I knew the song. I had heard it sung in London, with Agathe. I think in the early 1980s.

Léa ended her song, and we held our breath. Outside there was no sound, as if the world had stopped. No ghosts, past or present. Sandrine began clapping, and I followed. Léa stood there, grinning, and curtsied.

"What was that song?" I asked. My heart was pounding.

"A piece by John Tavener," Léa answered. She frowned, frustrated, as the composer's name was difficult for her to pronounce. That was it. John Tavener's "The Lamb." Agathe and I had seen its world premiere. "Our teacher chose it for us. She said that it was difficult to sing, even if the lyrics looked simple."

"Do you often sing in the chapel?" I asked.
She nodded.

"It does feel very nice in here," Sandrine said.

"That's what I mean," Léa said. "It feels good. Like at my house. Most of the time I don't have a problem singing at the conservatory, except in one room, on the top floor. My teacher says I don't have to sing there anymore."

Sandrine looked at me and then at the girl. She asked, "What happens in that room?"

Léa rubbed her neck. "I can't breathe," she said. "And I get too hot."

"Like what happened at my house," I suggested, immediately regretting it.

"Until I started singing the lamb song in your house," Léa said, unbothered. "Since then, I feel fine, even in the attic." She then called out, "Papa! Papa!" and ran out of the church.

Sandrine and I looked at each other, and I shrugged my shoulders. "I've heard her singing up there, in the attic," Sandrine whispered. We followed Léa outside, which was all stillness and quiet. Not even a bee buzzed. But suddenly dust gathered on the dirt road, a low rumbling sounded, and Bruno Paulik's ancient Range Rover came into sight.

Chapter Sixteen

Paris, Friday,
July 9, 2010

"All is well with the world," Verlaque said, unfolding his starched linen napkin and putting it on his lap. He leaned back and closed his eyes.

"The world is going to hell in a handbasket," Marine answered. "But you are so happy when we're in Paris, and we're in one of your favorite restaurants." She looked around at the ancient tiled floor, carved wooden bar, and gilt mirrors on the walls, so diners who faced the wall could see the rest of the restaurant and, more important, the other diners.

The TGV had arrived in Paris just before noon, and a taxi had whisked them—along the river— to the restaurant. Marine had a vague idea where they were—not far from the Elysée Palace and the British embassy and Place de la Concorde. It was the kind of restaurant where Antoine felt at home: good old-fashioned food, expertly prepared. And one paid highly for that quality. She knew, from articles in *Le Monde* and in Sylvie's

*Elle*s, that younger, more international restaurants were the rage in Paris—their staff and clients both young, and usually tattooed, the interiors all blond wood and bare lightbulbs. This was not one of those places, and Marine felt relieved. A middle-aged woman wearing a white blouse as starched as the tablecloths and napkins took their drink orders and moments later came back with their aperitifs and a plate of thinly sliced peppery *saucisse*. Two men and a woman at the next table—for the tables were very close together, naturally—discussed the minister of education's current bill in a way that made it clear they not only knew him but worked for him. Marine took a sip of her ten-year-old port and asked, "Who is first on your list of interviews?"

Verlaque replied, "Ursule Genoux. Valère Barbier's private secretary. She's retired and lives not far from here. After that, I'm going to the 16th to visit the publisher's wife, now a widow. Are you off to the Bibliothèque Nationale?" Marine usually did research on Sartre and Beauvoir in France's national library, located in four gleaming towers in the east of Paris.

"No, not this time," Marine answered. "But I will go to Montparnasse and visit their graves; then I'm going to Sèvres."

"Sèvres? The leafy suburbs?"

"To the ceramics museum," Marine said. "I

called ahead, and they're letting me look at Agathe Barbier's archives."

"Did you tell me that already, and I've forgotten?" Verlaque asked. He leaned back so that the waitress could set a breast of duck in front of him.

"No," Marine said, laughing. "I forgot to tell you—that's all." She pointed to his plate. "You copied me, by the way, by ordering the duck."

"I did not! I had decided on it as soon as I walked into the restaurant."

"Even though you hadn't yet read the specials?"

"A good restaurant like this always serves duck breast," Verlaque argued. He cut into the meat. "Perfectly rare. Bon appétit."

No. 7 rue de Surène, Ursule Genoux's apartment building, was less than a five-minute walk from the restaurant, in this neighborhood that was much like the overpriced one where Verlaque grew up and his father still lived. It lacked in grocery and hardware stores; instead the streets were lined with designer shops, government offices, embassies, and mediocre overpriced sandwich shops that quickly fed those who worked in the shops, offices, and embassies. He was glad he had remembered the name and address of the restaurant where they had lunch, even if Marine gasped when she saw the bill.

Oddly enough, there was a *bar-tabac* beneath

Ursule Genoux's apartment, one of the few, Verlaque imagined, in this part of the 8th arrondissement. He rang the brass buzzer labeled GENOUX, and a female voice replied, instructing him to go up the stairs to the first floor. He had wondered how a secretary—even one who worked for a famous writer—could afford this neighborhood. A first-floor, street-side apartment partly explained things: noisy and dark. Or she may have bought it decades ago—that is, if she owned the apartment.

Mme Genoux was standing inside her open door when Antoine got to the top of the stairs, and she held out a long thin arm and shook his hand. "Please come in," she said, stepping aside. He quickly took in the small entryway that was surprisingly painted a bright, cheery yellow that made him think of van Gogh. Two old-fashioned umbrellas stood in a ceramic stand and a selection of straw hats hung on hooks. She ushered him into the living room, which, despite his prediction, was not dark but bright thanks to three very tall windows.

"Lovely room," he said. The walls were covered in small oil paintings and prints of lakes and mountains—that he could have expected of an elderly professional secretary—but the furniture was polished, and the antiques from periods he admired, like the Regency. The walls were painted the same yellow as the entryway.

"Thank you. Please, sit down," she said, gesturing to an armchair covered in blue silk.

"You must have been surprised to have received my phone call," Antoine began.

"But you didn't call," Mme Genoux answered. "Your secretary did."

Verlaque couldn't tell whether he was being chastised. Perhaps Mme Genoux was insulted that the magistrate hadn't called himself, or she may have simply been pointing out his good secretary's work. "Yes, of course," he answered. "What I meant was, you must have been surprised to receive a call about the death of Agathe Barbier after all these years." While he waited for an answer, he looked at the former secretary. She was tall, as tall as Marine, but with wider shoulders. The hair that fell to those shoulders was fine and straight, and streaked with gray. Her eyes looked light brown, but he couldn't quite tell.

"No, that didn't surprise me either," she answered.

He looked at her, slightly shocked by her reply. "Would you care to explain?"

"I've never believed that one can just fall off of a boat."

"The sea was rough—wasn't it?"

Mme Genoux answered, "Yes, but Agathe wasn't a dimwit. She would have been careful."

"But I understood that Mme Barbier was

202

very ill with seasickness. She would have been desperate for fresh air, and her illness may have thrown her off balance."

Mme Genoux pursed her lips. "So why are you here?"

"The magistrate at the time—"

"Daniel de Rudder."

"Precisely," Verlaque answered. "Rudder has requested that the case be reexamined." Verlaque did not explain why, nor would he have if Mme Genoux had asked, but she did not. "How long did you work for M Barbier, Mme Genoux?"

"Thirty years and three months," she answered. "I began in 1979, shortly after *The Receptionist* was published."

"Did you have an office?"

She made a sweep of the room with her hand. "Here. There's a small office between this room and the bedroom. M Barbier would walk across the pont des Invalides every morning from their apartment in the 7th, carrying a recorded tape of the chapters he'd dictated the day before. He called it his morning constitutional."

"And so you wouldn't have done much work for Mme Barbier?"

"Oh yes, I did," she replied. "M Barbier didn't write every day—especially as he was becoming more and more well known and in demand. Interviews and such. So we agreed that on the days when he didn't need me to transcribe his drafts, I would do errands for madame, if she needed me, that is."

Mme Genoux seemed to relax more, especially as she explained her duties for the Barbiers. Verlaque tried to continue with questions of a similar theme. "Did M Barbier ever learn to type his books into a computer?" he asked. "That must have been so much work for you."

"But it was my job," she answered. "And I loved it. No, he bought himself a laptop a few years ago, but he said it was enough work returning e-mails and looking up the weather, so he would keep using the Dictaphone for his books. And by then his books had changed—"

"Indeed," Verlaque said. "The romances."

"They were longer books, so they took more time to type, but they were . . . less . . . complicated."

Verlaque smiled. "And that week in Sardinia in 1988," he continued. "You went because M Barbier was writing a book?"

"Yes, I usually went along when the Barbiers took long vacations."

"How did everyone get along that week? And afterward, on the boat?"

"There were arguments," Mme Genoux answered, picking at her long linen skirt. "I told the Cannes police at the time, after Agathe . . ."

"Yes, you told them that the day Mme Barbier

died, you overheard a fight between her and M Pelloquin."

"Yes, but I couldn't hear what they were saying, as the wind had picked up. We were all there, except for M Barbier, who was napping down below. He was drinking a lot in those days."

Verlaque remembered the spent limes in the sink and noticed that Mme Genoux referred to her boss of thirty years by his surname but called his wife by her Christian name. "What was Alphonse Pelloquin like?"

Mme Genoux squinted and pursed her lips. "I didn't care for him. I thought him an opportunist."

"And his wife?"

"Oh, her! She was—is—a prima donna. A spoiled girl who never grew up."

"Would Agathe Barbier have reason to commit suicide?"

"Certainly not," Mme Genoux replied, her voice raised. "And I told the police the same thing. She was happy, had a brilliant career, and was very talented."

"Do you have any idea why M Barbier was drinking heavily? Were there marital problems?"

"I have no idea," she answered. Her voice had reverted to the crispness it had when he arrived.

"Did M Barbier keep an agenda?"

"From the year 1988, you mean?"

Verlaque smiled and nodded.

"Yes, he kept an agenda, and we went through

it together every morning. The agendas would now be in his possession, if he still has them."

"Thank you, Mme Genoux," Verlaque said as he got to his feet. "May I contact you in the near future if I need to?"

"Yes, use the cell phone number. But I warn you that it's new technology for me, and I'm just getting used to it."

"I could ring you on the land line."

She hesitated and then answered, "I may go and visit my niece and her family in Picardy. Best to use the cell phone." She got up and walked him to the door.

"Thank you once again," Verlaque said.

"Indeed," she said, opening the door.

As Verlaque walked to place de la Madeleine, he thought about how patient Ursule Genoux had been, all these years, if she really believed Agathe Barbier was murdered or that foul play was somehow involved. Why not speak up? But the elderly woman seemed like the sort of person who would never raise a fuss, who would shy away from conflict. Perhaps she had been silently waiting all these years to speak her mind. He shrugged, then hailed a taxi that was driving around the gray bulk of the Madeleine. He had never liked it and wished that some Italian artisan had gotten his hands on it and painted it a pastel yellow or pink like so many churches in

Liguria or Sicily, although those churches were baroque and not neoclassical. He gave the driver Monica Pelloquin's address in the 16th and sat back and enjoyed the view of his favorite city, at the same time trying to imagine white and gray Paris painted in Mediterranean colors. By the time they arrived at Mme Pelloquin's apartment near the Trocadéro, he'd decided that Paris had best remain gray, to match the Seine. There was no sparkling blue sea here.

At the door, he buzzed at Pelloquin, and an accented woman's voice told him to take the elevator to the fifth floor. Unlike first-floor apartments, fifth-floor apartments in classic Haussmannian buildings were Verlaque's favorite: high enough for a view and lots of light, and with a *balcon filant*, for Baron Haussmann had decided that only second and fifth floors would have balconies. From the street, their uniformity made them look like ribbons of iron running the width of the building.

When he stepped out of the elevator, Verlaque saw a young woman standing in the doorway to one of the apartments. "This way," she said. He thought her accent might be Portuguese.

"I'm Judge Verlaque from Aix-en-Provence," he said, stepping inside the vast entryway tiled in black-and-white marble.

"Yes, just a minute please." The maid—he assumed that's who she was, as she wore a traditional black apron—turned and left him, walking through a set of double doors. A few seconds later, she came out and said, "Please, you may go in." He hadn't had much time to glance around the foyer, but did see some gaudy Venetian masks—the kind tourists buy on the Piazza San Marco—hanging on the wall. He much preferred Mme Genoux's apartment, at least so far.

The living room was so big that Verlaque at first had trouble locating the apartment's owner. Mme Pelloquin said hello, and he turned and saw her standing beside a massive fireplace at the far end of the room. It was the kind of stone fireplace normally found in Burgundian châteaus—too big, and too rustic, for a Parisian apartment. *"Bonjour, madame,"* he said, and walked across the room to shake her hand. Mme Pelloquin did not meet him halfway but stayed standing beside the fireplace. Had she been a friend, he would have made a joke about the long walk. "Thank you for agreeing to meet with me on such short notice."

Mme Pelloquin shrugged her shoulders. Her rudeness did not faze or intimidate Verlaque, but it did irritate him. As it didn't seem like he was going to be offered a seat, he jumped into questioning, already anxious to leave. "I have been asked by the former magistrate of Cannes, who officiated over the accidental death of Agathe

Barbier in 1988, to make further inquiries," he said. Since Mme Pelloquin was being non-communicative, he decided to give her the barest of details. If she wanted to, she could look up Daniel de Rudder and see that he was now retired and living in Arcachon. He went on, "You were asleep when Mme Barbier fell off the boat that night."

Monica Pelloquin rubbed her eyes with her right hand. "It was so long ago," she slowly answered, as if it physically pained her to speak. Verlaque did not respond, wanting Mme Pelloquin to continue unprompted. He looked at her and saw what Mme Genoux was referring to when she called the publisher's widow a spoiled girl. Although Mme Pelloquin must have been in her late sixties, she was wearing an outfit that Verlaque thought Marine might consider too young even for herself: a flowered empire-waist cotton dress that ended well before the knees, with pink high-heel sandals. She had long black hair, tied up in a bun, and luminous pale skin made more striking by her red lipstick. She took her hand away from her eyes and looked at Verlaque. He said, "Please, go on."

She sighed and continued, "We finished lunch just as the storm began rocking the boat back and forth, so I went to my cabin, as did that secretary with the bad attitude. Alphonse—my late husband—put on a windbreaker and went up to the cockpit, but Valère and Agathe stayed down below, at the dining room table. As I dressed for bed, I could hear them arguing, but not what they were saying."

"Did they often argue?"

"No," she replied. "It was unusual, I suppose."

Verlaque asked, "The report stated that your late husband and Agathe Barbier also argued earlier that day. Do you know what about?"

Mme Pelloquin made a tsk-tsk sound and waved her hand in the air. "No idea. It could have been anything. They were probably arguing about Valère: Valère the tortured writer. Valère the literary darling."

Verlaque ignored the woman's poorly concealed jealousy and asked, "You didn't see or hear anyone go up on deck after Agathe did?"

"No, and we were rocking so much I actually didn't fall asleep. She wasn't up there very long when Alphonse came running down the ladder, calling for help."

"When was the last time you saw Valère Barbier?"

She paused and answered, "It must have been at my husband's funeral in 2001."

"You've had no reason to see M Barbier since then?"

She said, "Why would I? We had nothing in common after my husband died."

Verlaque wondered why an esteemed publisher

would marry such a woman. Pelloquin had published not only Barbier but also other great
novelists of that generation. Why marry a woman
who openly claims not to care about that world?
But Ursule Genoux had referred to Alphonse
Pelloquin as an opportunist.

"Agathe's death was not my husband's fault,"
Mme Pelloquin said. "Alphonse was a fine sailor,
Judge . . . Judge . . . what did you say your name
was?"

"Verlaque. Thank you, Mme Pelloquin,"
Verlaque said. "You've been . . . very helpful. I'll
see myself out."

Verlaque walked down the five flights of stairs.
On the third floor, an apartment door opened
and an elderly woman looked out. Verlaque said
hello, and she quickly closed the door. "Welcome
to the 16th arrondissement," he whispered. He
looked at his watch and saw that he was ahead
of schedule. Marine would still be at the Sèvres
museum. He walked out onto the narrow cobbled
street, only a stone's throw away from the busy
Trocadéro.

He'd take a taxi to Le Hibou in Saint-Germain,
where he could sit outside and smoke a cigar.
It was an overpriced café popular amongst Left
Bank literati and one where the people watching
merited the five-euro espresso.

While walking toward the taxi stand at
Trocadéro, he thought Mme Genoux's assessment

of Mme Pelloquin was very appropriate. Was the secretary also correct in her mistrust of Alphonse Pelloquin?

Marine quickly walked across the pont de Sèvres, rushing to get to her favorite museum. It was cool on the bridge; a breeze wafted up from the Seine, and she forced herself to stop. She leaned on the railing and gazed at the river: a dozen or so houseboats were tied to the shore near the museum, and she wondered what life was like in a floating house in a city on the water. Was it a paradise, but cheaper than an apartment in central Paris? Or was it a nightmare, full of mildew and who knows what floating by your bedroom window? On this warm summer day, she leaned toward the former opinion—today houseboat living looked magnificent. The boats were a few minutes away from a Métro stop, and they had communal gardens and parking, a rarity in the city. She imagined the owners having barbecues and parties on the river, like in a Renoir painting. The men mustached, the women with parasols.

A few minutes later she was inside the museum. She had called ahead, using her still-existent professor's ID, which allowed her to set up an appointment to look at Agathe Barbier's archives. But before that, she quickly took a turn around the museum's vast rooms filled with ceramics from throughout the ages: Italian Renaissance majolica to delicate, hand-painted seventeenth-century Sèvres porcelain coffee services to contemporary clay sculptures like Agathe Barbier's. In one of the last rooms, Marine looked at a white Picasso vase with a fawn-like face drawn in dark-blue glaze and handles like ears. In the middle of the room was one of Barbier's giant terra-cotta pots; it seemed to guard the Picasso plates and vases that were displayed behind glass. Marine remembered reading that the two had worked near each other in Vallauris, and she wondered how well they had known each other. Marine looked at her watch and turned around to make her way back to where she had seen signs for the archives.

Luckily, Verlaque snagged the last available seat on Le Hibou's terrace, an end table convenient for a cigar smoker, as he had only one neighboring table, to his right, where two young women discussed a recent translation of Rainer Maria Rilke's poetry while chain-smoking Marlboros. He smiled and lit his Predilecto, a gift from Fabrice and Julien via Cuba, and was thankful that at least in Paris discussions like the one on his right still occurred.

He ordered an amber-colored Belgian beer and sat back and watched the crowd. It was a little after five, and their TGV was at seven. He and Marine could have dinner on the train—

the microwaved risotto wasn't bad, he'd had it before—and be in Aix by ten.

The women to his right finished their coffees and signaled to the waiter for the bill. They were not a foot from their table when a man Verlaque's age quickly sat down with a sigh, relieved to get a spot. He glanced at Verlaque, and Verlaque pointed to his cigar and shrugged, as if to ask permission to smoke. "*Pas de problème*," the man replied, smiling. Verlaque said *merci* and then looked at the man again. "Charles-Henri?" he asked.

"Antoine!"

"I should have guessed I'd see you here," Verlaque said. They shook hands and laughed. He hadn't seen Charles-Henri Lagarde in years. A dinner party in Paris, he thought, perhaps at his brother's apartment. "How have you been?"

"*Impeccable!*" Lagarde replied, with a hint of forced enthusiasm, thought Verlaque.

"And you?"

"Married!" Verlaque said, holding up his left hand where his gold wedding band shone in the sun.

"Congratulations," Lagarde replied. "And good luck. I'm divorced, three kids, two Parisian mortgages now instead of one. Who's the bride?"

"Marine Bonnet," Verlaque replied. "She's a law professor in Aix-en-Provence."

"*Une Aixoise?*"

"Born and bred."

Lagarde whistled. "Is it true that the Aixoise buy the most lingerie in France?" he said with a wink.

Verlaque smiled. He remembered now why he had enjoyed meeting Charles-Henri but never bothered to keep in touch. He said, "Congratulations on your new book. I read a glowing review in *Le Monde*."

"And missed, I hope, the devastating one in *Les Echos*," replied Lagarde. "But thank you."

Verlaque tried to remember the book; he thought it was historical fiction, not a genre he usually read. He was about to say something about it when he saw that Lagarde seemed more interested in a woman in a miniskirt at the next table.

After a few seconds, his acquaintance asked, "Doesn't Valère Barbier live in Aix now?"

Verlaque nodded and finished his beer. "Yes, he lives in the country, not far from Aix. Are you friends?"

"Sure, we've met a few times." He glanced again at the woman, and then added unnecessarily, "At book launches and awards ceremonies."

They chatted for a few more minutes while Verlaque waited for the bill. He texted Marine that he was running late and would meet her at the station. When Verlaque got up to leave, he shook Charles-Henri's hand and said with genuine emotion how nice it had been to bump into him. For although Lagarde had reminded him of all that was wrong with his real-estate-mogul brother and his friends (and why Verlaque rarely saw Sébastien), Charles-Henri Lagarde had just given him the most insightful information about Agathe Barbier of the day.

Chapter Seventeen

New York City,
September 22, 2010

Valère had grown tired and asked Justin to tell him about himself—his family, his studies, his year in Paris—before excusing himself to go to the restroom. Justin drank three glasses of water as he waited for Valère to return. He also hurriedly texted his boss, who replied that the famous writer's interest in an underling was a good sign. Justin sighed at her use of the word "underling."

"Please, M Barbier," Justin said when Valère returned. He wanted to hear more of Valère's story, which was sounding increasingly like a confessional. But of what? "Let's get back to your story before the dessert arrives."

"I told the cheese guy to come back here with that trolley," Valère said. He poured them each a glass of wine.

Bon. Michèle Baudouin was now out of her coma but still not well enough to return to the house and certainly not well enough, to my dismay, to go back to her own place in Paris. Sandrine seemed to have no interest in returning home, either, and I enjoyed her company so I let her stay. There seemed to be no harm in it, and we had both grown attached to Léa, who would show up at the door to help us with the thousand-piece puzzle of Paris we had started. Just after dinner that night Judge Verlaque called me—it sounded like he was on a train—and asked if he could see me the following day. Had he been up in Paris? Sandrine asked, looking worried but trying to hide it. We were both tired and agreed that it would be lights-out soon, when—it must have been about ten thirty—we heard a car on the drive. We looked at each other, puzzled, put on the porch light, and went outside.

The passenger leaned his head out the window and asked, "Can you loan me seventy euros for the taxi fare?"

"I guess I have no choice," I replied, opening the car door. I could hear Sandrine mumbling, complaining that there was a shuttle service from both the TGV station and the Marseille airport that cost next to nothing and went to downtown Aix.

"We got lost twice," my guest complained. He huffed and tilted his head in the direction of the cabbie, who was busy getting the luggage out of the trunk. "The driver doesn't speak French, so I had to go to the village bar to ask for directions. He's Eastern European, I think."

I paid the cabbie and thanked him in Polish. It was a lucky guess—I love Poland and have been there many times—as he beamed and shook my hand, taking my hand in both of his. "*Red Earth*," he said in accented English, pumping my arm up and down. "Amazing book!"

"Thank you," I said again in Polish—my Polish is limited.

"Really amazing!" he said, getting back into the taxi. He drove off, waving out the window until he got past the Pauliks' farm.

Our guest lazily—because that's how he does everything—looked at his bag, wondering how it was going to get from the ground into the house. I smiled and said, "You can come in, but we were just going to bed." I made no move to pick up his bag, nor did Sandrine. "Sandrine," I said, "I'd like you to meet Agathe's son, Erwan. Erwan, this is my housekeeper, Sandrine."

To jump back a little, Agathe graduated in 1969 and was immediately hired as an apprentice to a master potter in the South of France, Georges Bonfand. Those four years, while Agathe worked in Vallauris, almost killed me. I thought there was no way I could leave a paper like *Le Monde* to work for some crap outfit like *Nice-Matin*, but looking back on it, I should have followed her down there. What? No, Justin, the TGV didn't exist yet. It was an overnight train ride from Paris to Nice in those days.

I was insanely jealous and knew that Agathe was hanging around with the crème de la crème, including Picasso. The village of Vallauris was *the* epicenter of contemporary ceramics, which is why Picasso worked there, painting fawns on plates and chasing young girls, including Agathe. The old fart was in his seventies, but that didn't stop him. Knowing how many creative people were hanging around the côte d'Azur motivated me—albeit in a jealous, highly self-destructive way—to begin my first novel. It was published in 1971, as you know, when I was twenty-nine years old, but I still kept working on proofs while I was at *Le Monde*, as I think that book sold about ten copies.

Then disaster struck. Agathe wrote to me in February of '72 and informed me that she was pregnant—not by me, of course, as I had hardly been down there—and was keeping the baby. Hilarious, Justin. No, Picasso wasn't the father. Georges Bonfand was. He agreed to help financially but preferred not to be present in the baby's life, as he was already in his sixties.

Somehow our relationship held together, and Agathe and the baby—Erwan, named after her grandfather—moved back to Paris in 1973. She opened a ceramics studio in Batignolles, and we got married that year too.

So that night, when Erwan got his butt out of the car, I was hit with a wall of emotions. Not all of them good. "*Bonsoir*," Sandrine said curtly, her hands on her hips. She had, in two minutes, figured him out. Erwan mumbled something and they shook hands. I have no doubt that Sandrine's handshake was firmer than Erwan's; in fact, judging from the look on his face, she gave him a death squeeze. It impressed me, especially when Sandrine and I were moving furniture around, how strong she was. "M Barbier, the guest room at the end of the hall upstairs is already made up," she said.

"That's great. Thank you, Sandrine," I replied. "You heard her, Erwan—up you go. We can get caught up tomorrow. And next time, call and let me know you're coming."

"My phone doesn't work anymore," Erwan answered.

"Haven't paid the bill in a while?" I asked.

Erwan shrugged and said, "Bit short on cash."

I followed him into the house; he was tall, like his mother, but oddly not as strong. He slouched, whereas Agathe had always held herself straight, even a bit rigidly. But Erwan had her dark wiry hair and strong features: high cheekbones, a Roman nose, and full lips.

Now, before I look like an uncaring stepfather, let me fill you in on Erwan Le Flahec. Erwan hasn't had it easy, with his biological father ignoring him, his stepfather too self-obsessed to give him much attention, and his mother dying young. But you can do the math, Justin, and see that Erwan does not act his age, nor has he ever done so. He drifted from job to job until he became unemployable, and now lives in Agathe's old studio in Batignolles, which she willed to him. I send him money every month, and Agathe, about a year before she died, made provisions for him to be paid a monthly allowance in the event of her death. The old studio is big enough to be split in two, so Erwan could make some money by renting part of it, but that is too much work for him, and he likes his privacy, he says. Can you imagine having a thousand square feet of free lodging in central New York or Paris? And being unemployed to boot? The only times I ever argued with Agathe were over Erwan. I wish I could have let it go, but my working-class upbringing did not allow me to ignore his spoiled behavior. Remembering Agathe, I did pause by Erwan's bedroom door and wish him a good sleep, before going into my own room.

I read for about an hour, to distract myself, and then turned off the light. It was quiet outside, and I smiled knowing that Hélène Paulik might spray the vines before the sun rose; that would send Erwan straight back to Paris on the next TGV. I giggled thinking that had I known Erwan was coming I could have arranged it with Hélène.

That night I tossed and turned, as is my usual sleep pattern, worrying about important things—Erwan, for example—and silly ones, like the fact that Sandrine and I had forgotten to move the potted succulents into the sun as we said we should. My therapist says that my biggest problem with Erwan is guilt. It's true that the day Agathe died we had had too much to drink, at lunch on the boat, and argued over Erwan. He had enrolled in some kind of expensive private business school, and Agathe was going to foot the bill. We didn't argue about the money, because by that time we had lots. It was the principle of the thing: yet another doomed project of Erwan's. I saw how each time he gave up or failed at something, it would crush Agathe. My publisher and his wife seemed to be having their own fight, up on deck, and who knows where Ursule, my secretary, was. She'd worked for me for years. She was discreet and faithful, but after Agathe's death she withdrew and seemed to blame me. She stayed on for a while after the accident, but by the time she resigned it felt like she hated me. Looking back on it, with the help of therapy, I see I probably took her for granted. I always paid her well, extremely well by French standards, well enough that she could buy an apartment in a nice neighborhood. But there's always more than just money—isn't there, Justin? I assumed that because I paid her well, she could, and would, always be available. That's one reason why I was trying to be considerate to Sandrine. Sandrine didn't have Ursule Genoux's refinement, but she was smart. No, quick. That's a better word. And one day, perhaps, she could stop cleaning my house and be my secretary. That was my plan, anyway.

I must have finally stopped thinking about all these people and drifted off, because the next thing I remember was being woken up by a breeze that blew over my right ear. I swatted at it, thinking it was a mosquito or a fly. I rolled over and tried to get back to sleep. The breeze now blew over my left ear. I was about to roll over again when I heard whispering. I lay there as still as I could and heard the whisper again. Was it my name? I opened my eyes but couldn't see anything; there was only a sliver of a moon and the room was quite dark. "Valère," the voice sounded again, and the breeze was closer to my face now. I closed my eyes, hoping it was a dream, too afraid to move. "Valère," it said, and I felt warmth on my neck, warm and moist air, from someone breathing.

"Bugger this!" I yelled and reached up into the night air with my right hand, ready to grab at whatever beast was breathing on me. A hand suddenly grabbed my own, with a grip stronger than mine could ever be. "Let go!" I yelled, struggling to sit up. "Get the hell out of my house!"

"Valère!" the voice called out. A woman's voice.

"Agathe!" I answered. Was I dreaming? Why was Agathe at my bedside? "Let go of me!" But the hand held mine even tighter.

"Stop it, Valère!"

"I'm sorry, Agathe!" I called out. I may have been weeping by this point.

The hand suddenly let go, and my head fell back on the pillow. I was drenched in sweat. A light came on, the bedside light. I kept my eyes closed.

"M Barbier."

I opened my eyes and turned my head. It was Sandrine. "I'm so sorry," she said. "I called you by your Christian name. But you were screaming in your sleep."

"Thank Christ," I said, closing my eyes again. "I thought you were . . . I'm not sure . . ."

Sandrine stayed respectfully quiet. Who knows what she thought.

"The breeze . . ." I muttered.

"I couldn't find the light switch," Sandrine said. She was now laughing. "That damn lamp! The switch is a mile down on the cord!"

I started laughing too, my eyes still closed. "You need to fix it for me, Sandrine. Do you do minor electrical repairs?"

She laughed. "That is beyond my capacity, M Barbier."

I rubbed my eyes and tried to sit up, but was too exhausted. "Stay still," she ordered. "I'll get you a glass of water."

"Erwan," I said. "I must have woken him up too."

"I'll go and check," Sandrine said. She got up from beside the bed—she had been kneeling on the cold tile floor—and left the room. I heard her knock on Erwan's door then call his name. In a few seconds, she was back. "We have a problem, M Barbier," she said from the doorway. "Your stepson is gone."

I lifted my head and looked at Sandrine, shocked by her announcement. I sunk my head back into the pillow, knowing that I wouldn't sleep anymore that night. But there was something about Sandrine's appearance that bothered me.

Chapter Eighteen

Aix-en-Provence,
Saturday, July 10, 2010

Marine loved taking her mother out for lunch. Her parents rarely dined in restaurants, and in fact Marine knew that Florence Bonnet really didn't care about food. She was now retired, but when Marine was growing up her mother had poured all her energy into her teaching and research at Aix's university. Marine was proud of her working mother, and used to show off Florence's articles to her friends. It didn't matter that the articles were published in little-read, albeit important, theological journals across the world. She loved seeing her mother's name, Dr. Florence Bonnet, in print, and knew that she herself had a doctorate in part thanks to her upbringing, in which books and ideas and learning were the most important things in life.

When Marine started teaching and became independent, she found that there were other things that made life worth living too. Good food, and sharing it with friends, was one of them. Her mother didn't have the reflex to dine out, so in return for indulging her caprice Marine would subtly pay the bill once they had finished eating. Sometimes their lunches didn't happen every week; Florence was still busy editing articles for a theological journal and singing in the renowned choir at Saint-Jean-de-Malte.

That day Marine chose a traditional brasserie close to the Rotonde. The classics—duck confit, steak tartare—were done well enough, without surprises, and the waiters were professional and discreet. She ordered two glasses of champagne, her mother fussing and protesting until she had her first sip. Marine smiled, watching Florence slowly relax and relish the sparkling wine. "*Maman*," Marine began, "I met Valère Barbier the other day."

Florence Bonnet looked up from her glass. "You don't say?"

Marine nodded. "He lives in an old house next to the Pauliks, in Puyloubier."

"La Bastide Blanche," Florence stated.

"Yes, how did you know?"

"Philomène."

Marine laughed. Philomène Joubert lived across the courtyard from Marine's old apartment, and was a fixture in downtown Aix, riding her aged bicycle with goggles and a knit hat no matter what the weather. She was also, along with Père Jean-Luc, the church's choir director.

"So what's he like, the Great Man?" Florence asked.

"Very affable," Marine replied. "Friendly, interesting, and smart. Just as I hoped he would be. Antoine has already taken him to his cigar club."

"How's Barbier sleeping?" Florence asked, draining her champagne and setting it down on the table with a thump.

Marine gave her mother a surprised look. "What do you mean, *Maman*?"

"The *bastide* is haunted—everyone knows it. Philomène was going on and on about the house the other night before practice. Some of the younger choir members were quite frightened!"

Marine tried not to burst out laughing. She could easily imagine Philomène Joubert holding forth in the ancient church. Perhaps only candles had been lit that night, the perfect setting for ghost stories. "So what's Philomène's story?" Marine asked.

"I can see from your expression that you think it's a lot of hocus-pocus," Florence said. "But there may be some truth in the ghost stories. There usually is."

"But, *Maman*, that's pure superstition, the kind of thing you normally fight against."

Florence shrugged. "It's an old house, and old houses have souls and histories." Marine looked at her mother aghast. Florence continued, "That's

229

one of the reasons your father and I bought a new house in 1964. Other than the fact that we wanted central heating."

"And it was close to the university," Marine added.

"Exactly."

"So, not really because of the house having an old soul you'd have to deal with," Marine pointed out.

"Well, I suppose not," Florence said. She paused, looking up at the restaurant's art deco ceiling, then went on. "But, in the case of La Bastide Blanche, there are just too many unexplainable circumstances."

Marine smiled, happy to see her mother so relaxed. "Go on."

Florence leaned forward. "What are you doing after lunch?"

"I was going to write."

"Let's take a quick detour to the university library."

"*Maman*!"

"It won't take long," Florence said. "We could verify Philomène's story, right?"

Marine nodded. "Okay, then perhaps we should just order a main dish to make it quicker."

Florence looked surprised, then disappointed. "*Quoi? Pas une entrée, ni dessert?*"

Marine smiled; perhaps she was slowly turning her mother into an epicurean.

· · ·

Bruno Paulik knocked on Verlaque's office door. "Come in," Verlaque said, moving a pile of papers aside with the back of his hand. "Coffee?"

"Can't," Paulik answered. "I have to go to the Bastide Blanche."

"*Now* what's happened?"

"Valère Barbier's stepson is missing."

"I didn't know his stepson was visiting," Verlaque said.

"He arrived late last night," Paulik said. "Hélène and I saw the taxi drive up around ten thirty, as we were going to bed. He came in on the seven o'clock TGV from Paris."

"Odd, Marine and I were on the same train," Verlaque said, standing up. "I'll come too, and on the way there I'll fill you in on what I learned in Paris. Why is Barbier worried? Maybe his stepson went on a hike or back to Paris?"

Paulik said, "Barbier and his housekeeper found a ransom note in the living room this morning."

They were able to get to Puyloubier in twenty minutes. Officer Goulin drove the commissioner, thrilled to be out of the office for the morning. The judge followed the police car in his vintage Porsche.

Valère and Sandrine were standing on the *bastide*'s front steps when they arrived. "Thank

231

you for getting here so quickly," Valère said as Verlaque, Paulik, and Sophie Goulin approached.

"We didn't touch the note," Sandrine said.

"We found it lying on the coffee table," Barbier explained as they walked in the house. "It was Sandrine's idea not to touch it."

"That was very smart," Paulik said.

Sophie Goulin took a set of tweezers from her kit, picked up the handwritten note, and held it before Paulik. " 'We have Erwan,' " he read aloud. " 'If you want him alive, please follow further instructions.' "

"The spelling is atrocious," Valère said.

"What happened last night?" Paulik asked. "Try not to leave anything out, even if it seems unimportant."

"M Barbier had a bad dream around three thirty," Sandrine said.

"But before that," Paulik said. "When did Erwan arrive?"

"Ten thirty or so," Valère said, looking at Sandrine for confirmation. "In a taxi from the Aix TGV station."

"Seventy euro fare," Sandrine added, crossing her arms.

"We went immediately to bed," Valère continued. "Sandrine had made up one of the guest rooms."

"And none of you heard anything?"

"Just M Barbier yelling in his sleep, like I

said," Sandrine said. "I ran into his room and woke him up."

"I was worried that I had also woken up Erwan, so Sandrine went to check on him and found he was gone."

"Did you check the house then?" Verlaque asked.

"Of course," Valère answered. "We checked all the rooms, upstairs and down. And neither of us saw the note on the table. I'm sure it wasn't there."

"Yes," Sandrine said. "I would have seen it. I had just cleaned the living room."

"I turned on the outdoor lights," Valère continued. "And nothing seemed unusual outside, so I went back to bed. I figured that Erwan must have walked into the village and hitchhiked into Aix, or called a taxi. I checked my desk drawer, where I keep cash, and money was missing."

"Whoever left this note must have come back, in the early morning, to deliver it," Paulik said. "Was the door locked?"

Valère and Sandrine exchanged looks. "That's the problem," Sandrine said. "We both thought the other had locked it." She looked out the window and could see Sophie Goulin now outside, walking slowly around the grounds, her head down.

Paulik said, "Whoever has Erwan will call you.

Make sure your cell phone is on and charged. In the meantime, Judge Verlaque and I will take your statements, separately, in the kitchen and your office, if that's a good place."

Valère shrugged. "Yes, that's fine. This kid . . . nothing but problems."

"Is there a chance it's a hoax?" Verlaque asked.

Valère shook his head. "He does get angry quickly, which is why I assumed he had left. I wasn't very welcoming. But he's never done anything this extreme."

"He did say last night that he was out of money," Sandrine said.

"Really?" Verlaque asked.

Valère looked at him. "To arrange a fake kidnapping would take ingenuity and energy, neither of which Erwan has."

"Maybe he has some Parisian friends who helped him?" Sandrine suggested.

"Mlle Matton may be right," Paulik said.

Valère shook his head. "I still don't see it . . . but I may be wrong."

Verlaque took the visibly tired and shaken Valère into the office, while Paulik and Sandrine (who was still complaining about the taxi fare) went into the kitchen.

"You have a beautiful office," Verlaque said sincerely, looking around at the mix of French and Italian furniture and the ancient built-in bookcases. Two large windows gave onto the pebbled terrace and its row of plane trees, which in turn framed the rolling hills covered in vineyards and olive trees.

"Yeah, the office every great writer has," Valère said with noticeable sarcasm. "On the desk a Gae Aulenti *Pipistrello* lamp purchased at a Drouot auction; first editions of Proust and Philip Roth on the bookshelf; and in the corner an Eames chair that once belonged to Le Corbusier."

Verlaque looked at Valère, reading his moroseness as guilt over Erwan's disappearance. "I was in Paris yesterday," Verlaque began, "and met Ursule Genoux and, later, Monica Pelloquin."

"Lucky you," Valère replied. He now seemed bored, and looked out the window.

Verlaque crossed his legs and also looked out at the vast view, the vines a sea of bright green. Barbier now seemed like the famous writer he had expected to meet—spoiled and indifferent—not the charming and talkative one he had taken to the cigar club.

Valère turned to Verlaque and asked, his voice now almost menacing, "Why in the world were you talking to *them?*"

Relieved that Valère had finally asked the question he should have a few moments before, Verlaque replied, "The inquiry into the death of your late wife has been reopened."

"Well, it was never really closed, since they never found her body—did they?" Valère asked, as if the police were at fault and Verlaque was somehow involved in their incompetence.

"That's correct," Verlaque said.

"So what's going on?"

"New evidence has come to light," Verlaque lied.

"Like what?" Valère demanded, leaning forward to lessen the space between him and the judge.

"I'm not at liberty to say," Verlaque said. "It's too early to tell."

"And what did Ursule and Monica have to say?"

"What they told me yesterday matches what they reported to the Cannes police back in 1988."

Valère grunted. "Of course it would."

"After I met with them, I ran into Charles-Henri Lagarde, on the terrace of Le Hibou."

"He practically lives at Le Hibou," Valère replied. "He sits there all afternoon hoping to meet writers and actors more important than himself."

Verlaque smiled. This was the kind of talk he had expected from a famous man: petty and gossipy. "I met Charles-Henri once, at a party, years ago," he continued, noting that Valère hadn't asked how he knew Lagarde. "And yesterday he told me that Alphonse Pelloquin also frequented Le Hibou."

"See, what did I tell you? Lagarde is a poof too. That's why his wife left him."

Verlaque ignored the homophobic comment. He was now not amused by, but disappointed in, Barbier. Besides, the way Lagarde was checking out the women at the café made Verlaque even surer of the stupidity and inaccuracy of such slander.

Valère again looked out the window. He asked, almost into the air, "And what do I care that Alphonse used to go to Le Hibou?"

Verlaque replied, "I'm not sure. This may not be news to you, but Lagarde told me he frequently saw your publisher at Le Hibou in the company of your late wife, Agathe."

Marine waited while her mother spoke with the university's head librarian. Léopold Crépillon adored Florence Bonnet, with whom he, too, sang in the choir. Marine smiled as she listened to them; she was too far away to hear the conversation but close enough to get a sense of the excitement they shared when in each other's company. Marine could hear Léopold clicking on the computer, the printer starting up, and then more excited chatter. When Marine finished writing a long e-mail to her editor in Paris, she realized that thirty minutes had gone by.

"You needn't have hid," Florence said when she found Marine.

"I wasn't hiding," Marine lied. Léopold was in his late forties or early fifties and still lived with his mother; the presence of any handsome woman under the age of sixty made him very nervous, and so Marine found an empty desk at the far end of the history stacks and read her e-mails on her cell phone. "I was just keeping my distance. I think I make Léopold break out into a sweat." Some of Marine's female colleagues referred to Léopold Crépillon as Le Creep, but Marine thought he was harmless. He just needed to bathe more often, another reason she kept her distance.

"Well, well," Florence replied, huffing. She held up a few slips of white paper marked with call numbers. "Léopold has given us some great places to start. He's always so useful." They divided up Léopold's suggestions between them and went looking for the books in the stacks. Marine could hear her mother making excited sounds a few rows down. "*Ciel!*" Florence loudly whispered after about ten minutes. "This is a real find!"

Marine took the two books that she thought might be useful back to the desk and pulled up a second chair. Florence joined her, her face flushed with excitement. "*Poverty and Charity in Aix-en-Provence, 1640–1789*," she quickly said, holding up a slim green-bound volume for Marine to see. "Let's start with this one."

Marine read the table of contents. "This looks great," she said.

"Good old Léopold," Florence said. "He also gave me this, which I've been saving for you." She beamed as she passed Marine a few photocopied pages, some of which Léopold had marked in red.

"Wow," Marine said as she began reading. "It's part of a late medieval census, listing the owners of the bigger properties in and around Aix, including La Bastide Blanche."

"Léopold marked La Bastide with a red *X*," Florence said.

"Was Léopold at the choir practice when Philomène told you about the *bastide*'s . . . legends?"

Florence nodded. "But he already knew all about it," she said. "His great-aunts used to tell him ghost stories when he was a boy. The stories about La Bastide Blanche were his favorites."

"Charming."

"Yes, well, when you were small your father and I agreed that stories that frighten children aren't necessarily the best bedtime reading."

"*Merci, Maman.*"

"Léopold even told me who to begin with," Florence said as she took a selection of colored pens and lined them up on the wooden desk. "Count Hugues de Besse," she said, whispering. She took the cap off the green pen and marked two Xs beside his name, which appeared on the first page of the photocopied list. "Born 1688, died 1760," she said. "He's our man."

"But what did he do?" Marine whispered.

Florence looked around and waited until a young undergraduate who was walking by, his arms full of books, passed out of earshot. "Léopold told me the Count had a huge appetite . . ."

Marine rolled her eyes. "I assume you're not saying he was a gourmet?"

Florence hissed. "Sexual appetite."

"What does that have to do with ghosts?"

"The ghosts of murdered babies," Florence whispered.

"Are you serious?"

Florence nodded. "Hugues de Besse fathered dozens of illegitimate children," she replied. "The babies were killed and buried beneath the house. That's the story, anyway."

"Let me guess," Marine said. "And the mothers were young, unmarried servants?"

"Exactly. The ghosts are the babies and their weeping mothers . . ."

Marine closed her eyes, trying to imagine the names and faces of those girls, if even for a moment. "It's just a story," she said. "Perhaps with bits of truth behind it."

"Without proof, that's all it is," Florence said. "Let's get to work."

They worked silently for over an hour, both taking notes and marking pages with tiny colored Post-its, which Marine always carried in her purse. Florence saw the Post-its and beamed with pride. "Once an academic . . . ," she said. She held out her hand and put it on top of Marine's. "This is so much fun."

Marine smiled and was about to reply when she saw that her mother already had her head buried in another book. Marine continued reading, pausing after a few minutes to read aloud, " 'Eighty percent of Aix's population in the seventeenth century worked to support the remaining twenty percent of wealthy clergy, civil servants, and nobility.' "

"Yes, they would have been farmers, artisans, food sellers, servants," Florence replied.

"Et les porteurs de chaise."

"Ah, yes, the men who carried the sedan chairs. Many noble Aixois couldn't afford a carriage and horses, but they could afford to pay two unlucky souls to carry them around the muddy streets." Marine smiled and nodded. She knew what the *porteurs* did. Her mother was in professor mode. There was no chance for her to add to the conversation.

Marine read on, saying, "Listen to this, *Maman.* In the medieval neighborhood, some families lived with anywhere from eight to forty people under the same roof."

Florence nodded. "The wages were so low that even if both parents worked they still couldn't afford to feed their children. Especially if there were an emergency."

"Like the plague," Marine replied. "Or famine."

"Or even another child," Florence added. "So they relied on charity houses, in Aix's case not run by religious institutions but privately funded."

"Their way to salvation," Marine said.

"Look," Florence said, showing Marine a page from the green book she had found in the stacks. "The hospital called Saint-Eutrope was founded by a merchant, Michel Jualme, in 1600. Later, in 1629, a foundation was set up for repentant prostitutes, although the text proudly states that Aix had many fewer prostitutes than Marseille." Marine sniggered and Florence continued, "And La Charité, a hospital for orphans, opened soon after."

"Then these charities would have been in existence during Hugues de Besse's time," Marine said.

"But neither the babies nor their mothers were sent there," Florence said. "The problems at the *bastide* were kept a secret."

Marine said, "I just read that most of the children weren't in fact orphans but *enfants trouvés*—abandoned by their families because there were already too many children and not enough money to feed them. What a terrible choice to have to make."

Florence put her pen down and stretched, something Marine had seen her do hundreds of times. "Why don't you come for dinner tonight?" Florence asked.

Marine wasn't sure whether the invitation extended to Antoine, who at any rate had just sent her a text saying that he would be home late. "I'd love to," she answered.

"Of course Antoine can come . . . ," Florence quickly added but without much enthusiasm.

"He's working late," Marine said.

"So it will just be the three of us. Your father can cook, and I'll tan both your hides at Scrabble."

Chapter Nineteen

New York City,
September 22, 2010

"What was so odd about Sandrine's appearance that night?" Justin asked.

Valère waved a hand in the air. "In a bit."

"Okay. I can wait. So, what were Agathe and Alphonse doing hanging out at Le Hibou? Alphonse sounds like such a jerk! What in the world were they meeting about? There must be an explanation."

Valère leaned back, enjoying the young editor's enthusiasm and the fact that he had believed every word so far. If anything, Valère congratulated himself, he was a master storyteller.

Valère continued, "You can imagine my shock at being told that Agathe and Alphonse had little tête-à-têtes at Le Hibou. And why was I being so cranky with Judge Verlaque?"

Justin grinned.

"Yes, I saw the face you were making when I told you the story. Well, Justin, that's how I used to behave when I was famous. I know I'm still famous, but I'm talking about back in the day—

in the eighties and nineties—when I'd hang out with rock stars and actors. It still sneaks up on me sometimes, that horrible behavior, mostly when I'm overstressed or overtired. I have no idea what Antoine Verlaque thought; I'm sure my shitty behavior affected our newly forming friendship, and for that I was sorry. But at the moment all I could think of was Agathe and Alphonse Pelloquin."

"But that Verlaque guy *was* trying to pin you into a corner," Justin said, pouring some wine into Valère's glass. "What did you say?"

I told the judge that I had no idea why Agathe would meet with Alphonse; they had nothing in common. Absolutely nothing. Agathe was an artist, and Alphonse was a shark. That's one of the reasons why I chose him as my publisher, early on in my career. To be honest, I really didn't care about literary integrity. I just wanted to sell books.

I asked the judge, "Why are you worried who Agathe drank martinis with, anyway?"

Verlaque replied, "I told you: I'm reexamining her death."

"No good will come of it," I said. "She's dead. She fell off a sailboat during a storm. That's all." Verlaque was about to say something when the house phone rang. I almost jumped out of my skin. Sandrine came running into my office wringing her hands. The commissioner was right behind her, and he said to me, nodding toward the phone, "This might be it."

I gulped, picked up the receiver, and quickly put it on speaker phone. "*Âllo*," I said. I tried to stop my voice from cracking.

A male voice said, "M Barbier, please listen carefully. We have your son."

"Stepson," I cut in.

"Shut up. To ensure his safety, please bring fifty thousand euros, in a duffel bag, to the chapel in Puyloubier."

"But that will take time—" I tried to say more, but he immediately cut me off.

"We will give you two days to get the cash together. Be at the chapel on Sunday at midnight. Alone. Please walk. No cars. Do you understand?"

"And then what?" I asked. "Will Erwan be there? How do I know he's all right?"

We heard a muffling sound, and Erwan came on the phone. "Valère," he said. "Please do what they say. I'm sorry . . . I just went outside to look at the stars and have a ciggie . . ."

There was more muffling, and the other voice came back on the phone. "We will see you at the chapel. Alone." Before I could ask any more questions, the line went dead.

"How did they get the house number?" Paulik asked.

"I'm afraid I've been careless," Sandrine quickly said, her voice trembling. "I've given it out in the village as the cell reception is lousy here."

"We have two days," Verlaque said as he paced the room. "Did you recognize the voice?"

"Certainly not," I replied. "He seemed to be trying to hide a southern accent. It popped up now and again."

"They were obviously watching the house," Paulik said. "But how did they know that Erwan is your stepson? He could have been just a casual visitor, stepping outside to look at the stars, as he said."

I held up my hand. "I still don't think Erwan is behind this."

"The whole village knows of M Barbier's wealth and fame," Sandrine said. "It's no secret." She paced back and forth, and I winced when I took a good look at her clothing: tight, stretchy faux-leopard-skin pants with a red tube top and matching high heels. I pictured her the night before, at my bedside. That's when it clicked: When she came into my bedroom to calm me down, she had been fully dressed, just like that. Not in her pajamas.

"So they would know he has a stepson," Verlaque said. "And it would be easy enough to find a photograph of Erwan on the Internet. But how did anyone in the village know that

Erwan was here? Unless, like the commissioner suggested, they were watching the house."

"Wait," I said. "He stopped at the bar to ask for directions."

"Who?" Verlaque asked.

"Erwan," I continued. "The cabbie was Polish and didn't speak French."

I saw the judge look at the commissioner, who nodded. The judge asked, "How would they know the Parisian asking for directions is your stepson?"

"I took Erwan to an awards ceremony last year, and a few weeks later there was a photo spread in *Paris Match*. I felt sorry for him, and anyway I had no one to go with." Sandrine threw me a look of disappointment. Once again, I was alienating my new friends. And what would they think if, or when, they found out . . .

Valère's hands had slowly slid off the table and were now resting in his lap. Justin saw the fatigue on the writer's face. How different Valère Barbier was now, compared to the jovial man who had come bouncing into the restaurant a few hours before. Justin snuck a look at his watch; it wasn't yet eleven, and he knew there was still much more story to be unraveled. He had to get Valère to talk more. "Sandrine," Justin said, pouring them both water, "do you think she had been out that night?"

Valère said, "Of course. She couldn't have changed that quickly. But even if she was deceiving me, I still needed her as a friend. I felt guilty. We had been arguing, too. Stupid things, like the house renovations."

"Leopard-patterned wallpaper?"

Justin's comment evoked a laugh from Valère, which is what he had hoped for. "She wanted to change the kitchen," Valère said, pushing his water aside and pouring them each more wine. "I thought it was perfect, except for the old gas oven. There was a little shallow round stone sink, which Sandrine said I should take out and replace with a double stainless steel job. The walls were rough-hewn stone, and some former occupant or servant had fastened thick wooden shelves to one of them, supported by simple metal brackets. One of the first things I had done was to put a selection of Agathe's smaller earthenware bowls on them, along with some big Riedel wineglasses. I saw Sandrine eyeing the shelves, imagining oak cupboards in their place. But we agreed that the outside of the *bastide*, and the views, were perfect. We'd had long discussions about that." Valère smiled and took out his cell phone. "I'll show you some photos."

"I love this one," Justin said, looking at Valère's phone.

Valère nodded. "A few months before I moved in, an acquaintance in Paris advised me to get a gardening team out to the *bastide* and install a drip system. It was excellent advice, because when I arrived in late spring the gardens were thriving, and the grass was still green. In a photograph taken in springtime, the field between my house and Hélène's vineyard was full of wildflowers."

"Look at that emerald-green lawn," Justin said. "It's practically Technicolor. And so is that purple flower. Lavender?"

"Yes, it was in full bloom when all the shenanigans began. That photo was taken from the pool, looking back up at the house."

"Purple, then silver from the olive trees, then the bright green grass and pebbled terrace, and finally—"

"The house."

"Those skinny green trees," Justin said, seeing Valère turn glum again. "Van Gogh was crazy about them."

"Cypresses," Valère said. "In Provence they are a symbol of welcome. But I've always seen them more as guardians, erect soldiers guarding a house. Although in my opinion the cypresses of La Bastide Blanche were doing a piss-poor job."

Chapter Twenty

Aix-en-Provence,
Saturday, July 10, 2010

Marine held the door open as she waited for Charlotte to climb the four flights of stairs to their apartment. "*Coucou, chérie,*" she said when Charlotte got to the landing. She gave her goddaughter the *bise*.

"*Coucou,* Marine," Charlotte replied, not even out of breath. She was thin, like Sylvie, but taller, and, like her mother, a natural athlete.

"I'm so lucky," Marine said, closing the door after Charlotte. "That makes three visits we've had together this week."

Charlotte sighed. "I'm sorry about that, Marine."

"Oh, I wasn't complaining!" Marine said, embarrassed that Charlotte had taken it the wrong way. But in truth both Marine and Verlaque wondered why Sylvie had needed to send Charlotte over so many times that week. Sylvie did have a busy professional and social life, but she was utterly dedicated to Charlotte, and one night out a week was usually her limit—that is, if Charlotte was at home in Aix and not with her grandparents in the Alps.

"*Maman* spent too much time in the bathroom again," Charlotte said, flopping down on the sofa.

Marine sat down beside her and said, "So I guess she isn't getting dressed up for a faculty meeting at the Beaux-Arts." She realized that it was Saturday she had lost track of the days—and that Sylvie no doubt had a date.

Charlotte laughed. "No, I guess not! Whoever this guy is, he'd better be nice!"

"I'm sure he is," Marine replied. "You know, sweetie, your *maman* has been a single woman for a long time, and she's young. There might be a day when she finds a man to share her, and your, life with."

"I know, I know," Charlotte replied. "She's already told me all that. Can we play cards now?"

Marine hugged her goddaughter—who smelled of the warm sun mixed with a tiny bit of little-girl sweat. She got out the *Sept familles* card set she kept in the console. "We'll play one game," Marine said, "and then after you beat me, you can help me prepare a salad to have with the dinner."

"Okay," Charlotte said. "When's Antoine coming home?"

"He'll be late. But my parents are coming over. They're thrilled to see you again." Marine leaned toward Charlotte and whispered, "My mother's very smart and nice, but she's not a very good cook, so I invited them here."

Charlotte laughed. "What are we having?"

"Ceviche," Marine replied, shuffling the cards.

"Huh? That's not French."

"Correct. It's Mexican, or South American perhaps." Marine began dealing, hoping that Charlotte wouldn't ask any more questions about the meal.

"What's in it?"

"Well," Marine began. "I may as well be frank with you. Raw, cold fish that sort of cooks itself as it marinates in lime juice. I made it this morning and now it's in the fridge. And there are red onions, olives, and avocados in it too."

Charlotte lifted her right hand and brought it up to her throat. She made a gagging sound, and Marine fell back onto the sofa in a fit of laughter. "I also bought a package of gnocchi for you," she said after her godchild recovered. She reached out to give Charlotte a squeeze. "I can make it with butter and Gruyère."

Charlotte hugged Marine and thanked her, then, licking her lips, picked up her hand and deftly began arranging her cards.

It was the kind of restaurant Verlaque loved. One Michelin star—enough for it to have great food and fine service, but not three, which often meant stuffiness and ten-euro espressos at the end of the meal. The restaurant, part of a five-star hotel, was on a mountain road with views of olive orchards that spilled south all the way to far-off Grasse. He hesitated when asked if he would like to dine inside or out, until he saw that the terrace was set with sturdy yet delicate reproduction Louis XVI chairs and linen-covered tables. No plastic in sight. *"Sur la terrasse, s'il vous plaît,"* he said. *"Et un verre de Fonseca Bin No. 27."*

He sat down and tried to enjoy the view, but his stomach was turning somersaults. Whether this was because of nervousness or excitement, he wasn't sure. A waiter brought the port, a brilliant ruby red, and as Verlaque took his first sip—plums, chocolate, and berries all at once—he wondered why he didn't drink it more often. He closed his eyes.

"You look like you're enjoying that," a voice said.

He opened his eyes and quickly got up. *"Salut,"* he said.

"Hello, Antoine," Chantal Sennat said, giving him the *bise.* "It's been a long time." She sat down, and a waiter appeared. "A glass of champagne, please," she said. Looking at Verlaque, she added, "So you came, after all. I hope you remembered the dossier."

"It's in the car," Verlaque replied.

"What made you change your mind?"

"Don't be coy, Chantal. I thought it right that

we see each other. We did spend two years of our lives together."

"Which I've never regretted," she said. A flute of champagne was placed in front of her and she made a toast. *"To Daniel de Rudder, professeur extraordinaire."*

Verlaque smiled. "Cheers."

The waiter reappeared with a rectangular-shaped plate that he placed between them. "Savory *macarons* compliments of the chef," he said. "Enjoy."

"You chose a nice out-of-the-way restaurant," Chantal said after the waiter walked away.

"I don't like Cannes."

She smiled. "Neither do I. So did you find anything interesting in Agathe Barbier's file?"

"Nothing much," he said, lying. "I think Rudder's old age has affected his judgment. Plus, he feels guilty about that case."

"No wonder," Chantal said, "with Agathe Barbier's body having never been found."

Verlaque was about to take a bite of a *macaron* and stopped. "It's a big sea."

"What if she made herself disappear?" Chantal asked.

"Why would she want to do that?"

Chantal shrugged. "Sick of being married?" Her dark-blue eyes gleamed at Verlaque.

The waiter came to the table, seeing that their glasses were empty. "Another aperitif?" he asked.

• • •

Le Bar des Sports looked like most village bars in Provence. It was lit by fluorescent lights that gave the bar a bright bluish-white glow. The television mounted on the wall behind the bar—it was Le Bar des Sports, after all—was permanently on. The countertop might have once been zinc or wood but was now Formica with an edge of scuffed and stained pine. Four imitation-leather stools lined the bar, each a different color, and one missing the footrest. The floor had been retiled in the seventies, in beige-and-white checks, the cheapest tile sold at the hardware store. The sole object decorating the stucco walls was a calendar from the volunteer fire department, dated 2008.

Paulik took a breath before he opened the door. He came to the Bar des Sports once or twice a year, usually after a village event, and would quickly drink a pastis, chat, and leave. In the daylight, the bar wasn't as depressing, as the fluorescent lights weren't on, and one could stand outside on the sidewalk with a drink, pretending it was a pretty terrace. Paulik thought about all the books glorifying life in Provence, and how they usually left out the village bars: Le Bar des Sports, La Boule d'Or, Le Bar des Touristes, or Paulik's personal favorite name, Le Bar du XXème Siècle.

"*Salut*," Paulik said when he got to the bar. He

smiled and nodded to two men standing to his right, both probably in their seventies and both missing about the same number of teeth.

"*Bonsoir*, Bruno," the barman said. "How have you been?"

"Excellent, thank you," Paulik replied, amazed that the barman remembered his name. "And you?"

"Fine. Things have calmed down now."

Paulik looked around. There were the two old guys at the bar, and at a corner table was a guy, perhaps in his thirties, fast asleep. "Right," he said, remembering. "The World Cup."

"It was great fun, except for Les Bleus," the barman said, wiping down the Formica. "But at least the Spaniards beat the Dutch."

"Bloody Orangemen," muttered one of the old guys.

The barman asked, "What can I get you?"

"*Un Ricard, s'il te plaît*," Paulik said, relieved that a pastis could be drunk quickly. He was about to reach into a bowl of peanuts but pulled back his hand, realizing that the two old men had probably been eating the peanuts all night, and hadn't washed their hands in hours. He wondered how he could bring up the subject of Valère Barbier, and Erwan's appearance in the bar the other night, without raising too much suspicion.

"Here you go," the barman said, leaning his

hands on the counter. "How are things going with your famous neighbor?"

Paulik laughed, relieved that he hadn't needed to start the conversation. "M Barbier is very low-key," he said. "He seems to be a thoroughly good guy."

"That's the word around here," the barman said. "No late-night parties or orgies with his famous girlfriends, eh, Gaston?" The barman laughed and tugged at one of the old men's shirts.

"He's hardly had any guests," Paulik went on, taking a sip of his pastis. "Except a fellow writer, and now his son from Paris. He's in his early forties, named Erwan. He arrived the other night. Apparently he and his taxi driver got lost. Lost in Puyloubier!"

Gaston laughed. "They came in asking for directions, they did."

The barman said, "Was that Valère Barbier's son? The stuck-up Parisian?"

"Is he stuck-up?" Paulik asked. "I've never met him."

The barman made a grunting noise and began pouring another beer for Gaston's friend.

"He made it quite clear that he didn't like the looks of this bar, or of us, he did," Gaston said.

"Who else was here besides you two?" Paulik asked, taking a sip of his pastis.

"Who wants to know?" the barman asked, folding his arms across his chest.

Paulik said, "I'll be frank with you. There's been a spot of trouble at the *bastide*, involving Erwan. I need to know who saw him arrive in the village last night."

Gaston looked down into his beer, and his friend pretended to be very interested in the Michael Jackson video that was playing on the television. The young man in the corner still seemed to be asleep.

"Sorry," the barman finally said. "Can't help you there. People were in and out of here all night."

Paulik nodded and drained his pastis. "Thanks anyway." He laid two euros on the counter and left, discouraged that he hadn't handled the situation as well as he could have. His Range Rover was parked in front of the bar, and as he unlocked the front door a squealing noise sounded behind him. He turned around and saw Thomas pull up on his pizza scooter. "Hey, Thomas," he said, walking toward him.

Thomas took off his helmet and shook the commissioner's hand. "*Bonsoir*," he said, opening the red box behind his seat and taking out a pizza.

"Bar delivery?" Paulik asked.

"Old Gaston and his buddy. Gaston's greatniece bought him his first cell phone, but I think the only calls he makes are to us and to her."

Paulik laughed and grabbed a menu out of the box, pretending to read it. "Thomas," he said, keeping his eyes on the menu. "Pretend we're talking about pizzas, okay?"

"Got it."

"Did you deliver any pizzas here last night?"

"Yeah, late," Thomas answered. "It was after ten."

"Bingo," Paulik replied. "Who was in the bar?"

"Gaston and his buddy and the barman, of course, and the guy who usually sleeps at the corner table and two thugs, I think they're brothers or cousins. Pioger is their name."

"Who are they?"

"You don't want to know," Thomas answered. "Or maybe you do, given your day job. They're bad news. Sometimes I deliver pizza to their place. They live in a shabby apartment above the old hardware store."

Paulik handed Thomas the menu and patted him on the back. "Thanks, mate."

After dinner Marine received a text message from Sylvie, asking if Charlotte could spend the night. Marine answered in the affirmative and went to the linen closet to get sheets. If they bought a house in the country, they would have more room for guests, she thought as she set up a bed for Charlotte on the living room sofa. She gave Charlotte a new toothbrush and a clean T-shirt and tucked her in. "Would you like me to close the living room curtains?" she asked after she kissed Charlotte on the forehead.

"No, thank you," Charlotte answered. "If I lift up my head a little bit, I can see the lights on the cathedral steeple."

"I love that view too," Marine said as she turned off the lights. A house in the country wouldn't have that view, only darkness. Marine had never lived in the country and even as a child had preferred being in town. She went into the bathroom, showered, and brushed her teeth, putting on a new, sheer nightgown that she had bought on the first day of the July sales. Walking into the bedroom, she did a pirouette.

Verlaque was in bed, reading. He'd arrived home, in a sour mood, just after her parents left. Marine cleared her throat, but he did not look up. "Antoine," she said, getting into bed. "Why are you so cranky this evening?"

"Is Sylvie out again?" he asked.

Marine, who usually liked to defend her best friend, agreed. "Sylvie's absences are beginning to bother me too," she whispered. "I'll try to talk to her tomorrow."

"No idea who's she seeing?"

"Nope," Marine replied. "She was at the international photography conference in Arles last week. Perhaps she met someone there. That's where she met Charlotte's father."

"And he has no idea about Charlotte, right?"

"He was married, with ten- and twelve-year-olds, and living in Berlin," Marine answered. "So Sylvie never told him. She didn't want to upset his marriage."

Verlaque snorted.

"Don't throw stones," Marine said.

"You're right."

"Your meeting went late this evening."

Verlaque coughed. "It was a waste of time. How was the Sèvres museum, by the way? I was so busy on the train we really didn't get to talk."

"Agathe Barbier's letters were more interesting than I thought they'd be," Marine answered. She had detected an intentional switch in the conversation but decided to let it go. "Not so much in what they said but in how they were written. She really was a beautiful letter writer."

"Those were the days," Verlaque said. "I remember my grandmother Emmeline spending a good part of her day writing letters. It's a practiced art that's been lost."

"I still have the letters you wrote me," Marine said, kissing Verlaque. She rubbed his stomach, and he kissed her.

"I spent about an hour writing that first postcard to you," he said.

"From Rome."

"Yes, I remember the exact café where I

wrote it. You were such a good catch, and I so desperately wanted to impress you."

Marine smiled but secretly wished he had said something other than wanting to impress her. What, she wasn't sure. She couldn't put it into words.

Verlaque continued, "I didn't want to say anything in front of Charlotte, but Valère's stepson showed up late last night from Paris and was promptly kidnapped. There was a ransom note and a phone call this morning asking for fifty thousand euros."

Marine sat up. "What?" Verlaque filled her in on the details. "Did the stepson set this up?" Marine asked. "They've never gotten along very well."

"How do you know?"

"*Paris Match*," Marine answered. "At the doctor's office."

Verlaque laughed. "Bruno and I asked Valère the same thing, but he was adamant that Erwan isn't capable of carrying out such an organized plan. Valère was a wreck."

"I should think so, the poor man."

"He looked like a recovering drug addict or alcoholic who hasn't been allowed to drink for two weeks," Verlaque said. "He was sweating and had the shakes. He admitted he hasn't been sleeping."

"More ghost stories?"

"Yes. They're more frequent and of a more disturbing nature."

"Do you believe him?"

"Something is making him wake up in the middle of the night," Verlaque said. "Even his housekeeper said so."

"Sandrine?" Marine asked. "She's a weird bird. Weird in a good way, though."

Verlaque held up a battered copy of *Rebecca*. "It was one of Emmeline's favorites. When the first VCRs came to France, my grandfather bought one for the Normandy house, and Emmeline would let us stay up late to watch the Hitchcock film."

"I've never read it. Can you give me the condensed version?" Marine asked as she lay on her side, propped up on her elbow.

Verlaque began: "A wealthy widow, Maxim, marries a young woman, who upon arrival at his estate, Manderley, is tortured by pranks perpetrated by the housekeeper, Mrs. Danvers, more famously known as Danny, who will do anything to get the young wife out of the house and drive the couple apart."

"What was Danny's motive?"

"Love," Verlaque said. "Or obsession. You're never really sure. She was in love with Maxim's dead wife."

"Rebecca."

"Exactly."

Marine took the book from him and asked, "Are you thinking that Sandrine is behind the late-night frights?"

"I don't know," Verlaque slowly answered. "Sandrine began living in the house almost the day he moved in, which is—"

"Odd," Marine cut in.

"Yes. Valère's lawyer is her uncle," Verlaque said. "I'm going to call him tomorrow. Physically, Sandrine doesn't resemble Danny at all, but Ursule Genoux certainly does."

"Valère's secretary?"

"Yes, tall and gaunt, with not a hint of emotion in her voice. A very sad woman."

"But she's in Paris, while Sandrine is in the house."

"Yes, it would be difficulty to play those kinds of tricks from the 8th arrondissement."

"I read something interesting about Ursule in Agathe's letters," Marine said. "Ursule was recommended for employment by her younger sister, who was an old friend of Agathe's. All three of them went to Les Loges for high school, and the sister, Célestine Parent, is now the school's director."

"That's quite a coincidence," Verlaque said. "Which campus, Saint-Germain-en-Laye or Saint-Denis?"

"Saint-Germain," Marine replied. "The letter mentioned a 'stressful' event and that Ursule was smart and a fast typist and needed employment. Agathe must have answered in the affirmative—her reply wasn't there—but Ursule was then hired as Valère's secretary, right?"

"Yes, Ursule began in the late seventies—1979 I think," Verlaque said. "She's exactly the kind of woman you'd expect to be a famous wealthy man's secretary. If Valère's spoiled and uncooperative behavior today is any indication of what he was like in the days when he was hanging out with the Rolling Stones and Norman Mailer, then Ursule Genoux could have handled it." He put *Rebecca* back on his nightstand and sighed.

"You're a little out of sorts this evening. Is this case getting to you?" Marine asked.

"I drove to Cannes this evening," Verlaque quickly said. "To deliver the Agathe Barbier files."

"Oh, that explains why you got home so late. Was the traffic bad? Is that why you're upset?"

"I gave the files to the examining magistrate, and then we had dinner in the hills."

"And I assume it wasn't a good time?" Marine asked.

"It was just like old times," Verlaque replied. "But I'm so happy I'm married to you."

"Oh, I'd forgotten," Marine said, looking down at her hands. "The new judge there is Chantal Sennat. Your old college flame."

Verlaque nodded. "It was a mistake to have gone," he said. "But I wanted to tell you."

Chapter Twenty-one

New York City,
September 22, 2010

That evening Michèle returned from the hospital. Sandrine managed to get Tinker Bell started and drove off in a huff, saying she was going to stay at her sister Josy's place. Sandrine had been a ball of nervous energy all day, walking around the house biting her nails and rubbing her hands together. Several times I asked her what was wrong, but she just mumbled to herself and kept pacing.

I told her she could have a few days off—she deserved it, with all that had been going on at the house. I was relieved not to have the two women there at the same time, but I still thought Sandrine had nothing to do with Michèle's fall. Michèle had had too much to drink and lost her balance, and because of the drink, she imagined someone had pushed her.

Michèle was in surprisingly good form. But, then again, she always had an excess of energy. I made cheese-and-ham omelets, and we ate in the kitchen. Her face was still bruised, and I was fascinated by the one on her forehead, which had the same shape as France. "Stare much?" she asked as she gobbled up her dinner. "Wow, you don't get a simple good omelet in a hospital. Thank you, Barbier." She pushed her plate aside and lit a cigar.

"Can you smoke?" I asked.

She looked at me like I was a stupid boy. In other words, the way she always looked at me. "Of course," she said. "But I'm laying off the booze."

"Right," I answered, clearing away the plates and going to get my own cigar. "I'll make us herbal tea."

"We are like two old fogies," she said, watching me pour water into the kettle. "I always knew we'd end up together."

"What do you mean?"

"Relax," she said, laughing. "I only meant that I knew that we'd still be friends when we were old."

"As fate would have it," I said. "We grew up on the same street, and here we are."

"But you have the Bastide Blanche."

"Do you want it?" I asked. "You keep saying how much you've always loved the fresco in the stairway. I'm thinking of selling."

"You don't say," she said, blowing smoke out of her mouth. She didn't ask me why I wanted to sell the house so soon, and it wasn't until days later that I realized that was odd. She shrugged and said, "I'm not so sure I want it now. You know me and my instant urges. They quickly wear off. Besides, I have a house in Cuba. And there's an Italian island near Tunisia that's awfully hip right now."

I put the teapot on the table between us and got two mugs out of the cupboard. With all that had been happening in the house these past days, I had been ignoring my friend on the wall, the lady in the pink dress. I sat down and looked at Michèle. "Where exactly did you first see the fresco?" I asked.

"Oh, I can't remember," she answered, twisting one of the oversized rings she likes to wear. "In some magazine perhaps."

"Michèle, why are you here?"

Her rings made a clunking sound as she smacked her hands on the table. "I told you the other night, before my *accident*."

"All you did was try to threaten me into writing a book with you, based on some phony piece of evidence you claim to have, which Sandrine may have overheard."

"It's not phony," Michèle said, reaching into her gaudy Louis Vuitton purse. She carefully pulled out a manila envelope and handed it to me. Opening it, I pulled out some faded pieces of paper, typed on a typewriter. As soon as I saw it, I knew exactly what it was.

"Where did you get this?" I demanded.

"It doesn't matter—does it?" she said, grinning, grabbing the pages back from me before I had a chance to do anything. I know, Justin, I wasn't fast enough.

"So tell me about your project."

"We'd write a book, a great book."

"I'm retired."

"A writer never retires," she insisted.

"I've retired from fiction," I replied. "If I write anything, it will be nonfiction."

"Your memoirs?" she snorted. "Like some film star or professional athlete."

"It's a great genre."

"It's voyeurism."

"That's funny coming from you," I said. "You've made millions selling love stories."

"Tens of millions," she corrected. "But I haven't written a serious literary book. One that will be read in schools, like yours are."

"Who's stopping you?" I asked, draining my tea.

"Valère, you know I can't do it alone. I have the ideas," she said, tapping the side of her head, "but not the poetry. I need you for that."

I tapped my own head, mimicking her. "It's all dried up."

"I don't believe that," she said. "You're just being lazy."

"What's in it for me?"

"Your name would be up in lights again," she answered.

"We'd be coauthors?"

"Why not?" she asked. "A joint venture between lifelong friends."

"It's one of your crazier ideas," I said, getting up and taking my mug with me. I let my cigar burn itself out. "Well, this lazy boy is going to bed." I was so tired I didn't even care if the ghosts were rattling around that night. I was sure I'd sleep through any noise they could make. Let them keep Michèle up.

I walked across the kitchen, toward the door. Michèle stayed sitting at the table. "Or if you prefer," she said, twisting to face me, "you could be a silent partner. A ghostwriter. Sleep tight, Valère." She then winked, relishing the power she had over me.

Chapter Twenty-two

Verlaque ordered a *café crème* and took a soft croissant out of the basket and bit into it, brushing aside the crumbs with a paper napkin. He saw Bruno Paulik walk in through the Café Mazarin's swinging doors and waved.

"*Salut*," Verlaque said, standing up and shaking the *commissaire*'s hand. "Thanks for coming in on a Saturday."

"Good morning," Paulik said. He ordered the same coffee as Verlaque and sat down.

"Croissant?" Verlaque asked. He tipped the basket in the direction of Paulik.

"No thanks. I ate with the girls this morning."

Verlaque looked confused. "But you can eat a croissant, surely?"

"I'm trying to be careful." Paulik laughed and rubbed his stomach. "I ran into Valère this morning at the mailbox. He's thinking of selling the *bastide*."

"He's only just moved in."

"Yes, it seems too soon," Paulik said. "Hélène

and I were talking . . . What if someone is trying to scare Valère into doing just that?"

Verlaque nodded, thinking of the book on his bedside table. "I thought of that too. Any ideas? Sandrine?"

"I don't see what she has to gain," Paulik said.

"True. She'd be out of a job, for one."

"And yesterday she seemed genuinely frazzled."

"I agree," Verlaque said. "All the same, I'm going to call her uncle when I get to the office. What do we really know about Sandrine Matton?"

Paulik shrugged. "Go ahead," he said. "But I think she's harmless. Just high-strung. Hélène has a cousin like that."

"You *think?*" Verlaque said, smiling. "You can't use hunches in this line of work, remember?"

"But you do become good at knowing when someone is telling the truth," Paulik answered. "Although I suppose one can always be tricked."

Verlaque finished his croissant and made a neat pile of crumbs with the back of his hand. "The vines on Valère's land might be worth almost as much as the house. Are there winemakers who'd want them?"

"Like Hélène?" Paulik asked, visibly irritated. "No local vintner could afford to buy the place. Including us."

"Erwan's kidnapping—any leads?"

"The only kidnapping case in Aix happened over ten years ago," Paulik said. "And the three guys responsible are still in jail, but I've assigned two officers to search the records for criminals living between Aix and the Var. I went into our village bar last night and found out who was in there the night before: two old guys, the barman, a guy who everyone says sits in the corner and sleeps—I can verify that's what he was doing last night—and two brothers or cousins named Pioger. Although it's not clear if the Piogers were there when Erwan walked in."

"Pioger?" Verlaque asked. "Jean-Claude Auvieux told me about them. They're cousins and bad news. Live above an old store—"

"The hardware store."

"That's it. Let's start with them—shall we?" Verlaque said, reaching into his pocket for his wallet. "I'll get your coffee."

"Thanks," Paulik said, getting up. "My turn next time."

"One last question," Verlaque asked. "Which bar? Des Touristes? La Boule d'Or?"

"Bar des Sports," Paulik answered.

"Drats," Verlaque said. "I was hoping it was Le Bar du XXème Siècle. It's my favorite local bar name."

When Verlaque got to his office, he picked up the telephone and called Guillaume Matton on his cell phone. "*Âllo*," Matton replied.

"*Bonjour*, Maître Matton," Verlaque began.

"This is Antoine Verlaque, the examining magistrate in Aix-en-Provence. Thank you for taking the call."

"I hope there's nothing wrong with Valère," Matton said. "I haven't heard from him in a while."

"M Barbier is fine. But his stepson, Erwan, has disappeared. A ransom note and a phone call have been received."

"What? Is he okay?"

"So far," Verlaque replied. "They called yesterday, and Erwan was allowed to speak to M Barbier."

"Bloody hell, that Erwan," Matton replied. "How much are they asking for?"

"Fifty thousand euros."

Verlaque could hear the lawyer breathing. "That's not much," Matton finally said.

"No, it isn't," Verlaque replied.

"Amateur job?"

"Possibly. Has anything like this ever happened before to M Barbier?"

Matton replied, "No. I feel partly responsible. I encouraged Valère to buy that house, and I suppose it has left him rather . . . exposed. In a big city one is more easily hidden. At least I can be assured that my niece Sandrine is there with him."

"She has been a big help to M Barbier," Verlaque said.

"Excellent, as I'm the one who recommended her. At least I did that right. I was concerned about Sandrine going to work in Puyloubier, so I'm glad she's been a help to Valère."

"Concerned?" Verlaque asked. "Why?"

The lawyer paused again, then said, "An old flame of hers lives in Puyloubier—of all the villages in Provence."

"Really?" Verlaque asked.

"I adore Sandrine," Matton continued, "but she has always had bad taste in men and a hard time letting go."

"What's the ex's name?" He picked up a pencil and poised it above a notepad, but he already knew what the name would be.

"Pioger," Matton answered. "Hervé, I believe. Tell Sandrine to stay away from him. You're a judge—she might listen to you. I may be an experienced lawyer, but to her I'm just a fancy city uncle who's clueless."

Sylvie, after much hemming and hawing, had agreed to meet Marine at Le Mazarin for lunch. As she walked down rue Fabrot, Marine realized she was ten minutes early. As a splurge—she rarely bought makeup but was a sucker for face creams and lipstick—she walked through the automated doors into the air-conditioned Sephora. The blast of cold forced her to hug her chest, but she knew that in a few minutes she'd be used to the artificial temperature. Looking up at the vaulted stone ceiling, Marine smiled. This particular branch of Sephora was special, and she had been coming here for years. The gothic vaults above her head dated from the fourteenth century; the shop, in a former life, had been a chapel in the couvent des Grands-Carmes. The soaring ceiling permitted it to have a mezzanine, where she had often played Lego at the children's table with Charlotte, while Sylvie strolled around filling her metal shopping basket with creams and scents. The head of a carved angel, with a ghostlike face and hollowed-out eyes, watched the shoppers: *A medieval security guard,* thought Marine, and she selected a pale-pink lipstick. She thought of the histories and secrets—women's— that these old walls hid and protected. Even now, the mostly female shoppers and employees each had their secrets, their joys and their pains. She was making her way to the *caissier* when a young employee, dressed in Sephora's black-and-white uniform, tugged gently on Marine's arm. "Excuse me, mademoiselle," the girl said.

Marine swung around, agitated at first as she didn't want or need assistance, but she saw that the girl was still in her teens, so she smiled. "Yes?" Marine asked.

"I just have to tell you that if your hair was redder, and you weren't so tall, you'd be a twin for Isabelle Huppert."

Marine beamed at the compliment and thanked the sales associate.

"And with your beautiful fair and freckled skin," the girl continued, "don't forget to wear sunscreen."

Marine once more thanked the girl—knowing that it was not a sales pitch but instead kind advice. She paid for her lipstick and walked out into the midday heat. She turned right onto the cours Mirabeau and zigzagged through the hordes of locals and tourists to the Mazarin, just a few doors down.

"*Salut*, Marine," Frédéric said as she walked through the café's swinging front doors. It wasn't air-conditioned in the café, but it was several degrees cooler inside than outside on the crowded terrace. "Sylvie's upstairs already," he continued, before shouting an order for three glasses of rosé to the barman.

"Thanks, Frédéric!" Marine said as she quickly walked up the carpeted steps.

Sylvie raised her left eyebrow when Marine sat down at their table. She saw the small black-and-red Sephora bag and asked, "Shopping?"

"Lipstick," Marine said.

"Let's see."

Marine took out the lipstick and put some on.

"Subtle," Sylvie said. "Very you. Good choice."

Another waiter came and took their order. Both women chose salads because of the heat. "How dull," Marine said, smiling, to the waiter as she handed him back the menu, "to order a salad in a restaurant."

The waiter nodded and left, and Sylvie said, "Is the Lego table still upstairs?"

"I didn't go up there," Marine said. "I hope so."

"I've been thinking a lot about when Charlotte was little," Sylvie said, resting her elbows on the table and holding her chin in her hands.

"About Charlotte," Marine said. "I've been concerned—"

Sylvie held up her hand. "I know, I know. I've been unfair, keeping you—and Antoine—in the dark, not explaining what's going on."

"You have been gone an awful lot," Marine said. "But I want you to know that I love spending time with Charlotte, and that I trust you. I know you must have a good reason."

Sylvie reached across the table and squeezed Marine's hand. "I'm so lucky to have you," she said. "I'm feeling very blessed right now." The waiter came back and placed the *salades niçoises* before the women.

Marine picked up her fork. "Go on."

"You see, at the Arles photo symposium—"

"I knew it," Marine said. "You met someone."

"Re-met."

Marine stared at Sylvie. "You don't mean to say . . .?"

279

"Yes," Sylvie said. "And I'm over the moon—crazy, crazy, crazy in love. And so is he."

"But Wolfgang is married."

Sylvie shook her head. "Divorced, three years ago. When we had that affair, Wolfgang wasn't happy with his wife, but their two kids were still small. Now, the kids are out of the house, one studying engineering at a university in Cologne and the younger studying to become a midwife in Copenhagen, so they amicably divorced. He said he worried for two years about contacting me, then told himself that he'd leave it to chance if we'd meet each other again."

Marine smiled and didn't say aloud that of course they'd meet again, as both were successful European photographers. Marine had seen Wolfgang's work at exhibitions in Paris, and she thought it odd that they hadn't "run into each other" sooner. "Does he know . . . ?"

"I'm going to tell him this afternoon."

"Sylvie!"

"I promise!"

"And Charlotte?"

"I'd like you to be there with me," Sylvie said, "when I tell her."

"I don't think that's necessary . . ."

"Please, Marine. I'd be an emotional wreck. You know I would."

Marine remembered one of the first times she had been invited to Sylvie's, before Charlotte was born. Sylvie had answered her apartment door weeping. A cat was stuck at the top of one of the tall pine trees outside Sylvie's balcony and was too far to reach. He had been crying for two days, keeping everyone who shared the courtyard awake and distressed. They paced around the terrace, Sylvie crying and Marine calling to the cat, and ended up calling the fire department.

"All right," Marine said. "When?"

"Tonight?"

"I'll come over before dinner," Marine said.

Chapter Twenty-three

No matter how many times he drove his battered green Range Rover down the route nationale 7 toward Puyloubier, Bruno Paulik never tired of the view. He loved it in every season, but especially now, in summer, when the neon-green vine leaves contrasted with the red earth so loved by Cézanne. In fall, the vines would turn color: first yellow, then orange, then red, but a darker, richer red than the soil. Mont Sainte-Victoire loomed ahead, with its bright-white limestone, getting bigger and bigger the farther Paulik drove from Aix. When they first visited their farm, before buying it, Léa had held her hands over her eyes and exclaimed, "The mountain is going to fall on us!"

Paulik parked in front of the narrow village house he knew to be Gaston's. Its freshly painted green front door was shaded by a magnificent wisteria that bloomed for a few weeks in early spring, and the clean white lace curtains hanging in the front windows signaled that there was a woman in the house. He knocked, using the brass knocker, and a moment later the door opened, revealing Gaston wearing a cook's apron. "*Ah, monsieur le Commissaire,*" Gaston said, stepping aside. "*Entrez.*"

Paulik nodded and walked in, not at all surprised that Gaston knew his occupation. The news that Paulik was a police officer had probably been known throughout the village before he and Hélène had even signed the deed to their property. That, too, explained why the Pioger cousins had lain low and why Paulik had not known of their existence before Thomas told him about them.

"Something smells good," Paulik said, making his way down the narrow hallway to the back of the house, where he imagined the kitchen was. Village houses like these normally had similar floor plans.

"*Lapin,*" Gaston replied, gesturing for Paulik to sit at the polished wooden table.

Paulik thought he might find Gaston's wife in the spotless kitchen, but then remembered that Gaston was wearing the apron. "Are you cooking the rabbit with white wine?" Paulik asked.

"And olives. It was the way my dear Mathilde cooked it."

"You're a widower?"

Gaston nodded. "Mathilde died four years ago.

But does that mean I should live in filth and not eat properly?"

"I should say not," Paulik agreed.

"Not like old Marcel," Gaston went on, walking toward an antique hutch. Paulik smiled; he loved the way some elderly people, like his parents, referred to others the same age as "old." "He lives like a pig."

"Is that your buddy down at the bar?"

Gaston nodded, opening the cupboard. "*Un petit verre*?"

"That would be nice, thank you," Paulik replied. He looked around at the kitchen, every bit as clean and tidy as the front of the house had been, and he realized that Gaston frequented the Bar des Sports not because he was depressed, or an alcoholic, but for companionship.

With trembling but big hands, Gaston took out an unlabeled bottle and two small liquor glasses. He walked over to the table and set them down, winking. "A little elixir."

"Perfect," Paulik said, picking up the bottle and looking at the clear liquid. "You made it."

"Of course," Gaston replied. "Mathilde used to, but now that she's—" He stopped himself and poured out the alcohol.

"What did you do before retirement?"

"I worked on the rails."

"And how long have you been retired?" Paulik asked.

"Since 1979."

Paulik coughed, surprised that the still virile man in front of him was much older than he thought. "Are you serious? I was in middle school then!"

"In those days, if you worked for the SNCF you retired at fifty-five. I'm now eighty-six."

"Congratulations," Paulik said, holding up the dainty crystal glass, toasting Gaston partly on his long retirement but also because the old man looked like he was in his early seventies. Paulik took a sip and then looked at Gaston. "This is delicious." He took another and said, smelling the liquor, "I can't place the flavor. There's a bit of cinnamon in it . . ."

"*Angélique*," Gaston replied.

"Ah," Paulik said, setting the fragile glass down carefully. "My daughter loves that flower. She said to me the other day that all flowers should be white."

"There's lots of it around here, but Mathilde came from Haute-Provence, where there's even more. She called this the monks' liquor."

"And you're from Puyloubier?"

Gaston nodded. "Born in this house."

"I'd like to ask you a few questions about Puyloubier."

"Ah, I thought so."

Paulik went on, "Specifically regarding La Bastide Blanche."

Gaston whistled. "When we were kids at the village school we used to sing a song about the *bastide. Le fou qui va à la Bastide Blanche, va avoir une vie de turbulence!*"

"Was the house already closed up back then?"

"Oh yes. Once, when I was about six or seven, I decided I'd go up there and see the place for myself," Gaston said. "I got halfway up the lane to the *bastide* when my mother caught up with me. It was the only time she ever laid a hand on me." He rubbed his behind for effect. "I can still feel it."

"What exactly happened at the *bastide*?" Paulik asked.

Gaston grimaced and twisted the cork back into the bottle. "Not for me to say . . ."

Trying a different tack, Paulik said, "I could go and ask Marcel . . ."

"That old fart?" Gaston cried out, pulling the cork out of the bottle and refilling their glasses. "I'd trust him as much as the plague."

Paulik smiled; it had been years since he heard that expression. He sipped his angelica liquor and waited. Gaston took a sip and began, "The *bastide* was built in 1660, by a nobleman by the name of de Besse. He died just a few years after it was completed, and it was passed on to his son, who raised his own family there, two sons and three daughters, I believe. His oldest son in turn inherited the estate in the early

1700s—Hugues de Besse. Le Monstre Hugues."

"*Ah bon?*"

"You've no doubt heard all about the Marquis de Sade, and the goings-on in his château up in Lacoste?"

Paulik nodded. "I grew up on a farm in Ansouis."

"That's just down the road from Lacoste," Gaston said. "Hugues was worse than Sade. Or so they say."

"But he's long dead," Paulik said. "Why was the house locked up, and everyone afraid of it, even your mother?"

"Ghosts," Gaston replied frankly. "The crying ghosts of the poor girls—servants from Aix and around here—who were Hugues's sex slaves, their unwanted babies buried in the basement."

Paulik grimaced. "Does everyone around here know about the ghosts?" He thought of the Pioger cousins, and anyone else who might have wanted to frighten Valère.

"Oh, sure, everyone knows. At least, everyone over twenty years of age and locally born. But now Puyloubier is what they're calling a bedroom community for Aix. There are a lot of foreigners." He looked at Paulik and raised an eyebrow. Paulik knew that he, too, even though Provençal by birth, was being included in that group.

"Not everyone's afraid of the house," Paulik went on. "The new owner told me that when he bought it, the rooms had been tagged by local teens."

Gaston shrugged. "They're young and silly."

Paulik took his last sip, enjoying the sensation of the alcohol's warmth passing through his body. "You know, my daughter, Léa, who's eleven, definitely felt something in the house, but it wasn't fear."

Gaston nodded. "There are some locals who have said the same thing. When I was in high school, a gang of my classmates used to go up to the *bastide* and try to scare each other. There was this sweet girl, Jeanne, who later became a nun—I haven't seen her in years. She used to go with them. They broke in one night and ran from room to room for about ten minutes, then left, having worked themselves into a frenzy. But once outside, they noticed Jeanne wasn't with them. Two of the guys volunteered to go back in—they bragged about this for weeks after, they did—to look for Jeanne. They found her in the attic, sitting on the floor, motionless. They claimed it took them a good ten minutes to get her to hear them and stand up. Afterward, she told everyone that she wasn't frightened but warm, more like, and secure. That's the way she described it. Warm."

"You never went up there?"

"No, sir," Gaston replied. "Not after the licking I got. I had more sense than that."

Chapter Twenty-four

Aix-en-Provence,
Sunday, July 11, 2010

Officers Goulin and Schoelcher parked an unmarked car in front of the boarded-up hardware store in Puyloubier. The store, once one of the hubs of the village, along with the *boulangerie*, *boucherie*, and *cave coopérative*, looked like it had been closed for some time. It still had its wood storefront, including peeling wooden shutters that would have been closed when it wasn't open. Verlaque had briefed the officers on the Pioger cousins, but since they didn't have a warrant, they were to simply watch the apartment's front door and wait for signs of either Didier or Hervé. Photographs of the cousins had been easy to obtain, since both had criminal records.

"We can't stay here too long," Sophie said to her partner, Jules. "It's one thing to stake out an apartment in Aix, where people are always coming and going, but here . . . we're in a village. Everyone must know each other."

Jules shrugged, keeping his eyes on the

sidewalk on either side of their car. "Maybe not," he answered. "Villages like Puyloubier have a lot of tourists in the summer and newcomers who commute into Aix every day." He spread out a map on the dash, to make it look like they, too, were tourists.

"Some local will probably ask us if we need help finding something," Sophie said.

"I doubt it," Jules replied. "We're not in Alsace."

Sophie smiled but didn't reply. Jules Schoelcher was Alsatian, and when he first arrived on the force, fellow officers had teased him over his ironed jeans and meticulousness. "Look," Sophie said. "That old guy on the other side of the street. He's slowing down in front of the apartment's front door."

"There can't be two apartments upstairs," Jules said. "It looks too small."

"He has a key," Sophie said. She tilted her head to see well. "He's going in—"

"Let's wait five minutes."

After three, Sophie looked at her watch and said, "I'm uneasy about this."

"You're right," Jules said, opening his door. "We can't leave that old guy up there. Let's go."

"We're from the Green Party," Sophie whispered as they crossed the street. "I have a clipboard prepared, with fake signatures."

"Got ya."

The old man had left the street door unlocked, and the officers bounded up the stairs. Jules Schoelcher knocked on the door. They heard moaning and exchanged looks.

"Let's go in," Sophie said.

"*Âllo!*" Jules called out, opening the unlocked door as he did. "Are you all right?"

They walked into a living room furnished with relics from the 1970s, including faded wallpaper patterned in orange and yellow plaid. "*Oh mon dieu,*" moaned the voice, and they continued on into the kitchen, where the old man sat at a Formica table, his head in his hands.

"Sir," Sophie Goulin said, approaching the man and putting her hand on his left shoulder. "Are you all right?"

"They've cleared out," he answered, looking up at her. "And they owe me three months' back rent."

Sophie and Jules exchanged looks. "The Pioger cousins?" Jules asked.

"*Mais oui!*" the old man answered angrily, as if Jules should have known who rented his apartment.

"Perhaps we can help you, Monsieur . . .?"

"Cheneau," he replied. "Marcel Cheneau."

"You're sure they've left?" Sophie asked, glancing around the filthy kitchen.

"Their clothes and papers are all gone," Cheneau replied. "And their fancy stereo." He

291

looked up at Sophie and asked, "And who are you, anyway?"

"Police officers," Sophie replied. "From Aix."

"Did you know the Piogers left me high and dry? How did you know that before me?"

"We've been sent by the examining magistrate in Aix," Jules replied, sitting down at the table, "on another matter. A kidnapping at the Bastide Blanche."

Marcel Cheneau looked at Schoelcher, wide-eyed. "You don't say? And you think the Piogers did it?"

"We're not sure," Jules replied. "When did you see them last?"

Cheneau shrugged. "Maybe two days ago, down at the bar. I was there with my buddy, Gaston. We had a few beers and then ordered a pizza."

Sophie asked, "Did a Parisian come into the bar, asking for directions to the *bastide*?"

"The commissioner already asked that question," Cheneau replied. "Yesterday, in the bar. Yes was my answer. I didn't want to make a fuss—"

"Do you want to get your rent money?" Jules asked.

Cheneau sighed. "Yeah, they were there. And they left pretty quickly, too, after they saw that fancy Parisian."

"Do you have any idea where they might have

gone?" Sophie asked. "Don't worry, M Cheneau. We'll protect you."

Cheneau nodded and mumbled, "I think so. La Riviera."

"On the coast?" Jules asked.

"No no," Marcel replied, shaking his head. "A hunting lodge in the woods. It's called the Riviera because, well, it has a view of a creek out back."

It was almost noon, just before Sunday lunch, at the *cave coopérative* in Rians—their busiest time. They would close promptly at twelve thirty and not reopen until Tuesday. The license plates in the parking lot revealed a variety that was only found in summer: cars from the Netherlands and Germany, even a right-hand-drive English convertible, were parked beside cars and small vans from both the Bouches-du-Rhône and the Var—the two departments Rians straddled. Three other cars, Citroëns, all dark gray, were parked side by side at the far end of the lot. Bruno Paulik spread a detailed map of the area on the hood of one, flattening it out with the side of his hand.

Paulik pointed out a thin white road and said, "The hunting shack is eight kilometers northeast of Rians, off the D70. M Cheneau said it isn't indicated, but that exactly 2.2 kilometers north of Esparron there's a bend in the road, and immediately after, on the right, is a dirt track and a sign marked '*privé*' nailed to an old olive tree.

The shack is about a kilometer down the track."

"There's only one way in?" an officer asked.

"According to M Cheneau," Sophie replied, "yes."

"Let's park our cars up and down the D70 to avoid suspicion," Paulik continued. "We will meet at the olive tree and go up the track in pairs. Those of you in uniform can encircle the shack, and Officer Goulin and I will approach it, pretending to be lost hikers." Sophie Goulin looked down at her shorts, glad that she had chosen them instead of pants. It was already over 30°C, and in shorts she looked more like a hiker. She looked at her boss, who wore sunglasses and a large straw hat, and tried not to smile. She hardly recognized Bruno Paulik like that, so she knew the Pioger cousins wouldn't either.

Ten minutes later the cars were parked, scattered along the narrow road. Jules Schoelcher was to stay at the olive tree, phone at the ready in case he had to alert the others. He sat on a rock and got out a map, pretending to read it, while the others went into the woods. If anyone stopped to speak to him, he would reply with a German accent—easy enough for someone born in Colmar and who still spoke German with his parents—and say he was looking to get to Gréoux-les-Bains by the back roads. He'd tell them he had borrowed the car from a friend in Marseille.

Sophie's heart was pounding as she walked up the dirt road beside her boss. She had read the files on the Pioger cousins and knew that they were violent and unpredictable. She tried not to get distracted by the woods; she grew up in the country, and knew that lizards made a surprising amount of noise as they darted back and forth between the plants.

They had been walking for about twenty minutes when the shack came into view. "Keep going," Paulik whispered as they continued, albeit slower now. She tried not to smile at the name La Riviera—obviously a joke—for the wooden shack had a corrugated metal roof and leaned to one side, looking as if a sneeze could knock it over. She tried her best to resemble a lost hiker—someone who had no idea what lurked within the building ahead. An innocent. She realized the commissioner must be thinking the same thing as he reached out and took her hand, holding it as if she was his lover or wife.

The door of the shack suddenly opened and a man stepped out, clearly agitated. "What's going on?" he yelled across the twenty or so yards that separated them. "What do you want?"

Paulik let go of Sophie's hand. "I'm sorry to disturb," he replied. "We were just out walking."

"You get lost," the man said. "Now. This is private property."

"Not thinking of selling, are you?" Paulik

asked, walking slowly toward the man, whom he now recognized as Hervé Pioger. He heard a muffled sound coming from inside the shack.

Pioger came closer. "Are you deaf?" he asked.

"It's just that we've been trying to buy property around here for months," Paulik said. "And this place looks like it could use some TLC." He walked closer, until he was about a meter away.

"It's not for sale," Pioger said, holding up his hand. "Go now."

"Let's go, sweetie," Sophie said, walking beside Paulik and pulling on his hand. She could see the sweat gleaming on Pioger's forehead, his mouth gaping. She could also smell the liquorice odor of pastis.

"Honey, you know how much we love this area," Paulik said, looking at his partner.

"Do as your sweetie says," Pioger said.

Paulik saw from the corner of his eye that everything was in place. "All right," he said, putting his hand up. "We're so sorry to disturb."

At that cue, the other officers barged in the back door Marcel Cheneau had told Sophie and Jules about. "Mighty useful when our hunting shack used to get raided by the local gendarmes," he had said.

Out of instinct, Hervé Pioger swung back around toward La Riviera's door, and Paulik lunged forward, tackling him to the ground. Sophie pulled her gun from the back of her shorts and pointed it at Pioger's head. "Don't move." She could hear one of her colleagues yell, "To the ground, now!" and she breathed a sigh of relief. Sophie quickly thought about her neighbor, a hairdresser with whom she loved having a glass of wine sometimes after work, while their kids played together. What could she tell her of her workday? Nothing, only the vaguest of details, more often having to do with her fellow officers—how Jules had made her laugh while they were driving, how another officer was getting married the next weekend—than with their operations. Her neighbor had the opposite problem: her clients spilled out their most personal hopes and fears while she cut their hair. She couldn't tell Sophie what kind of conversations went on, only the very light ones. But she could talk about her work: the haircuts, the dyes, the blow-drying.

"Finally!" a voice hollered from inside the shack.

"You can take him off our hands!" Hervé Pioger yelled at Paulik, his head pressed sideways against the ground in front of the door.

Sophie and Paulik exchanged looks as a man in his late thirties or early forties walked out the door, accompanied by one of the officers, who held his arm. "I'm perfectly fine!" he said, shrugging off the officer's hand. "I'd like to press charges—"

"Shut up!" Hervé Pioger hollered.

"We'll deal with that, M Le Flahec," Paulik said. Another officer came out of the shack with Didier Pioger, handcuffed, while Sophie got Hervé upright and handcuffed him. Paulik said, "We need to take you to the hospital for a checkup—"

"I said I was all right," Erwan insisted.

"A doctor will verify that," Paulik said. "You were held against your will." He looked at Erwan Le Flahec, trying to read his expression. Paulik still wasn't sure if the kidnapping had been set up by Le Flahec himself.

Sophie called Jules and told him to bring one of the cars, and two of the other officers had already left, running back to get the remaining two cars. She turned to Erwan and said, "We'll take you to the clinic, and then you can go home and get cleaned up and sleep, before you come in for questioning tomorrow."

"If you say so," Erwan slowly replied. His eyes closed and his body swayed before he slumped forward, Sophie catching him in her arms.

Chapter Twenty-five

New York City,
September 22, 2010

Much to my relief, Sandrine wasn't at La Riviera with the Pioger cousins, and Erwan said that she had never been there," Valère explained. "I believed him. Bruno Paulik called me right away, as soon as they found Erwan, and Erwan arrived at the house a few hours after his hospital visit. He looked exhausted, and was irritable, but that's understandable. I felt lost without Sandrine, now that I had two guests in the house, and I was worried about her."

"But where *was* Sandrine?" Justin asked.

"I tried to call Matton in Paris, but there was no answer, so I hung up without leaving a message. I didn't want to worry Guillaume unnecessarily. Luckily, the village market was that morning, and Hélène and Léa offered to go shopping for me."

Justin shifted in his chair, frowning.

"Do you mind not fidgeting?" Valère asked. "The details are important."

"Sorry. Go on."

• • •

I pulled out Agathe's dog-eared Ali-Bab cookbook and got to work making a soup; we could have it with fresh bread and goat's cheese. When Léa returned from the market, she sat at the kitchen table, doing puzzles in some kind of activity book, while I cooked. Michèle was down by the pool, yelling into her cell phone at her Japanese publisher or a film rights lawyer in Los Angeles, and Erwan was upstairs sleeping. "I wonder what the blind lady is having for dinner," Léa said as she watched me cutting leeks. "*Maman* and I saw her today, near the market, walking down the sidewalk, guided by her white cane."

"Blind people get used to doing all sorts of things that we can't imagine they can do," I replied. "I'm sure she's cooking something healthy and good to eat."

"I hope Erwan is going to be all right," she continued.

I had forgotten how kids could change topics so easily. I said, "He just needs about fourteen hours' sleep."

"My papa once slept fourteen hours," Léa said. "He stayed up two entire nights all night because of work."

"*Âllo!*" came a voice from the front hall. It was Bruno Paulik, who had come to pick up Léa.

"Come in, Bruno," I answered. "We're in the kitchen."

Paulik walked in and bent down to give Léa a kiss. "Time to come home, Léa," he said.

"Léa has been very good company this afternoon," I said.

"Glad to hear it. We like her company too," Paulik said, winking at his daughter.

"On your way through the garden, would you mind telling Michèle that dinner will soon be ready?" I asked.

"No problem," Paulik answered. "Does she always yell into the phone like that?"

"Yep."

"We could hear her from our place."

"Sorry about that," I said.

"Any news from Sandrine?" Paulik asked, stopping at the kitchen door on his way out.

"Nothing," I answered. "That reminds me—I'm going to try calling her uncle in Paris again. I've been having trouble getting through to his cell phone."

"Let me know what you find out," Paulik said. There was no antagonism in his voice, but I knew that the commissioner suspected Sandrine of setting up Erwan's kidnapping and pushing Michèle down the stairs. I had to agree that it didn't look good. It was a total surprise to me that Sandrine had dated, and still felt something for, Hervé P. Is that why she came to work for me? To

301

be close to him? And now she had disappeared.

"Is Sandrine okay?" Léa asked, looking up at her father. "I like her."

"She's fine. I'm sure of it," I too-quickly answered. Léa gave me one of those "I don't believe you" looks that eleven-year-olds are particularly good at.

The evening didn't improve, with Michèle pestering me about writing the book with her. She had made one of the most miraculous recoveries I have ever seen. We went upstairs just before eleven, and I checked on Erwan, who was fast asleep. This time I left his bedroom door, and mine, open. I wasn't taking any chances. And now for my dream, Justin. A warning here. I've never been one to recount my dreams. I had a friend in university who, every morning, as we groggily sat around our kitchen table, would come charging into the kitchen and tell us his dream, in every boring detail. We were sure his dreams were made up, as they miraculously always involved one or two of his favorite actors—he was their chum, and they did all kinds of fun things together—and the dream ended happily. That's not how dreams work, at least not mine.

As I crawled into bed, I realized that I had forgotten to call Guillaume Matton. I wrote myself a reminder on a Post-it and stuck it to the lamp beside my bed. I'd call him first thing in the morning. The wind had picked up, and I closed the windows, preferring a stuffy room to the howling and groaning wind. The shutters lightly banged against the stone walls, even though they were latched. Sleep didn't come straightaway, as I was overexcited from the day's events. And so I lay there, hypersensitive to the noises and my bodily sensations. At times like this I become a hypochondriac. I counted my heartbeats, partly to try to fall asleep but mostly because I was convinced they were irregular and I was dying. My head began pounding: an aneurysm, obviously. My stomach turned, and I imagined a tumor. What I was doing was fighting sleep, because whenever I closed my eyes, I saw a sea—not the blue-green Mediterranean but a dark, gray, turbulent sea. As the hours passed, exhaustion took over, and I must have fallen asleep. And this is what I dreamed:

I walked along an expanse of beach, not sandy, like the Atlantic beaches here, but rocky, as they are in Provence. I was barefoot, and the stones hurt my feet, but I kept walking. I looked back now and again, and the Bastide Blanche was there, on a hill overlooking the sea, its shutters closed. Lifeless. The scene before me was bleak: sea and sky the same misty gray, the waves turbulent, the wind howling. Nothing on the horizon, no sign of life, and I had stared at the sea for some time when a bobbing black image appeared; a moment more, and it was Agathe. She wasn't swimming but trying to climb over the waves. I couldn't see her face, but I knew it was her. And I could sense her anxiety, and fear, as she tried to jump over each wave and get closer to me. She was crying, and her sobs rang out over the beach. As she got closer I could sense her panic, as she kept looking over her shoulder. Behind her, another bobbing mass appeared, in a sort of bright-red cloak; it was chasing her. I tried to run into the water, but the waves held me back—pushed me back, even. Nor could I call out; I was suddenly mute. The howling continued, as did the crying, and then Agathe suddenly disappeared, as did her pursuer. I awoke and sat up, out of breath.

I fell back to sleep as the sun was coming up, and must have slept for a few dreamless hours, for when I went downstairs it was already after eleven, and Michèle and Erwan were sitting at the kitchen table in silence. Erwan was holding his head in his two hands, and Michèle was looking out the window, lost in thought. When I walked in, Michèle turned her head to look at me. "Well," she said, "glad someone could sleep."

I rubbed my eyes, walked over to the espresso machine, and switched it on. "I finally fell asleep early this morning," I said.

Erwan looked up. "So it kept you up too?"

"What kept me up?" I asked. "I first fell asleep after three, but had a terrible dream."

"Did you hear crying in your dream?" Michèle asked.

I nodded, my mouth dry.

"That wasn't a dream," Erwan said. "We heard the crying too. A woman crying."

"It sounded like more than one to me," Michèle countered.

Erwan said, "Possibly—"

"The howling wind." I suggested.

Michèle laughed. "I'm almost seventy years of age, and I think I know the difference."

My cell phone began to ring. I walked over to where I'd set it down, next to the espresso machine, and picked it up. It was Guillaume Matton.

"Matton," I said, taking the phone into the larger salon. "I've been trying to call you."

"I thought you may have," he replied. "Yesterday I took the Métro for the first time in years, and got pickpocketed. They stole my cell phone, but not my wallet, thankfully. That was in my briefcase."

"Bad luck," I said. I almost added that I didn't miss the hustle, bustle, and violence of the city, but more things had been happening down here than I imagined happened in Matton's secure and boring 8th arrondissement.

"I thought I should let you know that I now have a new phone, same number," Matton said. "And if you could pass the news on to Sandrine;

she may have been trying to call me as well."

"I wanted to talk to you about her," I said.

"About Hervé Pioger?" Matton asked. "I told the judge that as far as I know, they don't see each other anymore. But she may still be sweet on him."

"Well, they can't see each other as he's in detention right now," I replied. "Kidnapping." Matton whistled, and I told him about Erwan's capture and rescue. "The problem is," I went on, "I can't find Sandrine. She seemed upset, or out of sorts, and has been gone for two days. Do you suppose she's with Josy? Could you give me Josy's phone number?"

Matton was silent for a few seconds, long enough for me to become nervous. He finally said, "Josy's dead. She died in a car accident three years ago."

Chapter Twenty-six

Paris and Aix-en-Provence, Monday, July 12, 2010

Marine looked out the train's window, thinking about Sylvie and Charlotte and the new person in their lives. Charlotte had taken the news calmly, but when Marine had hugged her afterward she could almost feel the girl's heart pounding. Earlier, when Marine asked Sylvie how Wolfgang had taken the news that he had an eleven-year-old daughter, Sylvie bit her upper lip and quickly lit a cigarette. "Other than throwing a glass across the room, and yelling at me for about ten minutes, I think he took it rather well."

Marine had arranged to meet Sylvie at the hotel where Wolfgang was staying, to go tell Charlotte the news. Verlaque had walked her over there, after they'd picked up some groceries, and by chance they ran into Sylvie and Wolfgang on their way back to the hotel, where the latter was planning to wait out Charlotte's briefing. They made small talk, as locals and tourists walked past them chatting and laughing and taking photographs of Aix's buildings, enjoying the summer dusk and mild evening temperature. Wolfgang was staying at a newly built hotel attached to Aix's Roman springs. "There's parking. It's downtown. There's a swimming pool," he had dryly answered, in perfect French with a thick German accent, when Marine had asked if he liked it. "But the spa—it doesn't interest me. I can think of nothing more boring."

Verlaque had laughed, and agreed, and spontaneously invited Wolfgang over for a drink while the women spoke to Charlotte. Wolfgang shook Verlaque's hand, saying he would gladly accept. Marine and Sylvie beamed, both grateful for Antoine's thoughtfulness.

When Marine returned from Sylvie's, the men were sitting upstairs on the candlelit terrace, a bottle of wine between them on the table. Another bottle, empty, sat on the floor. They both got up and greeted Marine, waiting to sit down again until she was seated. Verlaque poured her a glass of honey-colored wine, and she took a sip before speaking. "It went well, I think," she said. "Charlotte was quiet, a bit overcome by emotions, but when I left she was happy and laughing, excited even."

"I can't imagine how she's feeling," Wolfgang said. "She and Sylvie have been a team for eleven years, and now I come along—"

"Hey, dude, it will be fine," Verlaque said, reaching over and squeezing Wolfgang's shoulder.

Marine looked at her husband and squeezed her hands together to stop herself from laughing; the words "hey, dude" had never before come out of his mouth. She assumed he was a bit drunk.

Wolfgang sipped some wine. "Eleven is such an important age," he began, watching the wine swirl in his glass. "Carl Jung said he became conscious at eleven. He compared it to walking out of a fog. 'I knew who I was,' he said of that moment." At that instant Marine liked, even loved, Wolfgang, and she knew that not only would everything be fine but that he would now be permanently in their lives.

She saw the water-treatment plant from the train's window. One of the round tanks had a gigantic eye painted on its side. This was Marine's cue that they would soon be in Paris. She was thankful for France's high-speed trains and their wonderful efficiency, as this was her second trip to Paris in a week. She began to gather her things. Pulling out her map for one last look, she studied her route: take the RER A train to the end of the line, west of Paris at Saint-Germain-en-Laye, then a taxi to the town's ancient forest where the private girls' school Les Loges was located.

"If I remember correctly," Marine said, walking along Les Loges' covered arcade, "Napoléon founded this school, and the one in Saint-Denis."

"Exactly," replied her old friend Nathalie Garcia. "In 1810—for girls whose fathers, officers and knights of the Legion of Honor, were killed while fighting. Nowadays, descendants of those men are welcome at Les Loges, provided they have the grades, mind you." Nathalie Garcia had studied law with Marine in Paris and, like her, had forsaken a life in the courts for one in education. She was now assistant director of the school.

"It's an idyllic spot," Marine said, looking around the vast Cour d'honneur.

Nathalie nodded. "This courtyard is normally noisy—full of laughing girls in blue uniforms. They'll be back at the end of August. I'm around for another two weeks, organizing the new media room, and then I'll take a short vacation myself. Now, tell me, what is it, exactly, you're looking for? Your e-mail intrigued me."

"The records for Agathe Barbier," Marine replied. "Née Le Flahec. She was a student here in the early 1960s."

"I know," Nathalie said. "Are you researching the history of French ceramics these days?"

Marine laughed. "Not exactly."

"Well, you are the second person to ask to look at Agathe Barbier's records this month. But I suppose that's not unusual, given how well known she became."

"Who was the other person?"

"An art history scholar," Nathalie replied. "The head librarian assisted her."

Nathalie opened a door and motioned for Marine to go ahead. "The archives are up here," Nathalie said, following Marine. "Turn left at the top of the stairs. We've just renovated." To Marine's relief, Nathalie, always discreet, didn't ask any more questions about her research.

They walked through a large room lined with bookshelves. Marine pictured girls reading at the long tables that ran down its center.

Nathalie used a key to open yet another door. "This is it," she said, motioning Marine into a much smaller room, full of filing cabinets and glass-fronted bookcases. "The director would like to know more precisely why you're here," Nathalie said, once she'd closed the door behind her.

Marine tried not to grimace. So she wasn't off the hook.

Nathalie continued, "Our records concerning former students are not normally open to the public, as you can imagine."

Marine set her purse down on a wooden desk and took a letter from it. "The inquest into the death of Agathe Barbier has been reopened by the examining magistrate in Cannes," she said. "This is a letter from her colleague in Aix."

"Our *directrice* was a classmate of Agathe Barbier's," Nathalie said. She read the letter and handed it back to Marine, pointing at Verlaque's signature. "You're married to him."

Marine felt herself blushing. "Yes, for a year now."

"I read the announcement in *Le Monde*. Congratulations."

"Thank you."

"I'll get the dossier and let you get to work. I'll be in the media room across the hall when you're finished. I won't ask what you're looking for."

"It's only a hunch," Marine said. "I'm not sure myself. What will you say?" She knew that Nathalie would have to immediately report to the *directrice*.

"Why don't you tell me?"

"Could you tell the *directrice* that I'm writing a biography of Mme Barbier?"

Marine had been reading the young Agathe Le Flahec's file for over an hour when she came upon something interesting. She sat up in her chair and retied her ponytail, something she always did when excited. She then leaned forward, holding the document in her trembling hands.

When she had read through Agathe's correspondence at the Musée de Sèvres, Marine had been impressed, and surprised, by the quality of the artist's prose. Of course, Agathe Le Flahec had gone to a rigorous school, and had been

312

raised during a time when people still wrote letters, and wrote them well. Agathe died long before the Internet and instant messaging killed the art of letter writing. But her prose was even better than Marine had expected. It was poetry. Marine opened her notebook to where she had jotted down the important dates concerning Agathe and Valère Barbier. Agathe died in the summer of 1988. And two years later Valère Barbier drastically switched his genre from literary fiction to romance. Was it, as he claimed at the time, because he was heartbroken? Or had someone else helped him pen his many award-winning books? Marine thought especially of his short stories published in 1980, in her mother's favorite volume, *Tales from Brittany*. Agathe was *bretonne*, not Valère.

Marine grabbed her phone and smirked, realizing that she was about to use modern technology—a cell phone and the Internet— to look up facts. She scrolled through the results, looking for articles about Valère Barbier published around 1990, after the release of his first romance, *Another Day*. She found several, including a lengthy one in *Paris Match* explaining the writer's sudden genre switch and gushing over the new book. Most of the articles she came across were of the same ilk, even with the same wording, as if they had been forwarded by Barbier's publicity team, which they probably were: he was heartbroken, and in his books now wanted to try to explain love, not philosophical or moral issues. After about half an hour she found an article dating from March 1991 in the satirical paper *Le Canard enchaîné*—a favorite of her father's, much to her mother's exasperation. It included a cartoon that depicted Valère Barbier lying on a chaise longue, eating from a box of chocolates, while writing, with a plume pen, what was obviously a romance. Behind him, his framed Prix Goncourt for *Red Earth* was hanging crookedly on the wall.

The cartoon was followed by an article by Jean-Yves Bastou that suggested Barbier no longer wrote literary fiction because he couldn't. The journalist hinted that Barbier may have had help writing his earlier fiction, although he made no reference to Agathe. Marine next looked up Bastou and found a few more articles written by him, more often dealing with rock music than literature. She then came across his obituary. He'd died of a heart attack in May 2002, at sixty-three years of age.

Surely, Marine thought, she wasn't the only person to have read Agathe's lovely prose and seen the connection? She switched off her phone and looked at the document on the desk, a creative writing prize won by Agathe Le Flahec in 1964, her last year at the school. The essay's title, "A Chance Meeting on the rue du Faubourg," was also that of Valère Barbier's first book, published in 1973.

Once again, Marine found herself following Nathalie Garcia through the halls of Les Loges. "I want to thank you, Nathalie," Marine said.

"I hope your trip to Saint-Germain wasn't wasted."

"No," Marine said, hugging her purse. "Although I didn't find anything earth-shattering," she lied.

"The *directrice* won't keep you long," Nathalie went on. "She knows you have a train to catch." Marine looked around her at the framed photographs of former students, teachers, and directors. A painting of a queen caught her attention, and Nathalie stopped before it. "Anne of Austria," she said. "She founded the convent here in 1644."

Marine nodded, and they walked on through the silent halls. She almost felt like she was going to meet the mother superior, and her hands began to sweat. A door opened and a short, plump woman in her seventies walked toward them, smiling. She had curly white hair and wore round tortoiseshell glasses. A secretary, thought Marine. The woman held out her hand. "Welcome to our school," she said. "I'm Célestine Parent, the *directrice*."

"How do you do," Marine said, shaking her

hand. "Thank you so much for letting me use the archives."

"Please," she said, gesturing toward the door. "Come into my office. That will be all, Mlle Garcia."

Nathalie nodded and turned away, and Marine followed the *directrice* into her office. She may look harmless, thought Marine, but Mme Parent certainly spoke with authority. "So," Mme Parent said, walking around her mahogany desk and sitting down. "You're writing a biography of Agathe Le Flahec?"

"Yes," Marine said, lying. "And I have this funny theory that those who excel in making beautiful pots can be wonderful writers. Poets, even."

Mme Parent nodded, smiling.

"I was hoping to include passages of Mme Barbier's own writing in the book. You know, diary entries and the like."

"Interesting," Mme Parent said, sitting back. Marine saw the *directrice*'s shoulders fall, relaxed. "I went to school with Agathe."

"*Ah bon?*" Marine said, pretending not to have known.

"From 1961 to 1964," Mme Parent continued. "We were good friends. I adored her."

"So you must know Valère Barbier," Marine offered.

"Barely," Mme Parent answered.

Marine smiled and tried to sound chatty. "Oh, I'm only asking because he's such a celebrity."

"You can say that, yes. Valère Barbier is a celebrity."

"So I take it you and Mme Barbier didn't stay in touch after her marriage?" Marine asked. "I'm only asking for research purposes. The biography is in its early stages, and I'm trying to figure out who knew Agathe Barbier, and when."

"I wouldn't be much help," Mme Parent said. "After 1964, that is."

"I saw from the school records that you became *directrice* in January of 1990," Marine said. "Did a journalist named Jean-Yves Bastou contact you around that time? I know it was long ago . . ."

Mme Parent folded her arms across her chest. "I don't remember that name," she said. "But you're not the only one who has asked to check our records. Agathe went on to become renowned in her field, as have many other Les Loges students."

"Yes, Nathalie told me that just a few weeks ago someone else asked to see Mme Barbier's records."

Mme Parent nodded. "A scholar. I was held up in meetings all day so wasn't available to greet her."

Marine said, "I didn't find much in the file. I was a bit surprised." It occurred to Marine that the scholar, whoever she was, may have taken some of the documents.

Mme Parent flinched, and a look of worry quickly raced across her face. "Agathe may have kept a great deal," she said, shrugging. "After her death . . . who knows. Her widower may have disposed of everything or given it to her son."

"Did you read her essay about the rue du Faubourg?" Marine asked.

"About a hundred times," Mme Parent answered, smiling for the first time. "We'd proof-read each other's essays. But mine were never as good."

"Don't you find it odd—"

"I'll admit it's a strange coincidence," Mme Parent said. "I've always assumed that Agathe suggested the title to her husband. I don't know if you had time to read it, but the story has nothing in common with the book."

Marine said, "I couldn't read it. The story wasn't in the file. Only a mention of the prize it received."

Mme Parent's face whitened. "You must be mistaken. The story is there. Those files are kept under lock and key in our archives." Mme Parent stood up, and Marine looked at her watch.

"I have to catch the TGV soon," Marine said. "Thank you for your time." But she saw that the *directrice* had not heard a word she'd said.

Chapter Twenty-seven

Aix-en-Provence,
Monday, July 12, 2010

"She's lying or keeping something back," Marine said over the sound of running water. Finished brushing her teeth, she tapped her toothbrush on the edge of the sink, walked into their bedroom, and slid into bed beside Verlaque.

"What do you think Mme Parent is covering up?" Verlaque asked, removing his reading glasses and setting them and his book on the bedside table.

Marine bit her lip. "I don't know if she's protecting Agathe or her sister. By the way, she didn't mention that her sister was Valère's secretary for years. And I didn't bring it up. There seems to be this weird silence."

Verlaque said, "You're right, that's very odd."

"Mme Parent didn't speak well of Valère."

Verlaque turned to face his wife. "He and Agathe did argue that day, on the boat," he said. He crossed his arms and looked at his beloved Pierre Soulages, the painting's textured blackness dominating the room. "But Valère speaks so kindly of Agathe, with real love in his eyes."

"Now you're the one who sounds like a Hollywood movie," Marine said. "A schmaltzy love story."

Verlaque laughed. "Touché," he said. "But I still think that Pelloquin may have purposely left all that equipment snarled on the boat. I'm going to call Daniel de Rudder tomorrow morning."

"I just don't know," Marine said, as if she hadn't heard her husband. "Mme Parent's protecting Ursule and Agathe. And despite the fact that you've become chums with Valère, I don't think he's trustworthy. He's a phony for one thing. Right?"

"That's your opinion," Verlaque said. "I still can't believe that Valère didn't write those wonderful books."

Marine sighed. "I can't either. Once you fall in love with a book, it's hard to separate it from the author. But right now, *cher Monsieur le Juge*, my instincts point to Agathe." She switched off the bedside lamp, then curled up beside her husband.

The next morning, Verlaque walked down rue Gaston de Saporta, taking a roundabout route to the Palais de Justice because he felt like getting a strong espresso from the coffee roaster's on place Richelme. He knew he would probably end up in a few tourists' photographs: walking under the Gothic arch of the tall, square clock tower, a man

320

of medium height, wearing a mustard-colored linen suit with a blue shirt—wide shouldered and ample bellied, with messy, thick gray-and-black hair, and crooked nose. That's all they would know about the stranger in their photograph, once they got back to Kansas or Amsterdam or Tokyo.

He slowed down in front of the town hall and, hands in his pockets, looked up at its facade. A voice behind him said, "*Monsieur, s'il vous plaît.*" He turned around and saw a young couple, perhaps in their early twenties.

"You'd like me to take your photograph?" Verlaque asked in English.

"Oh yes, please," the woman answered, smiling and offering her phone.

"Italian?" Verlaque asked.

"Venetian," the man said, sticking his chest out in such a way that Verlaque almost laughed out loud.

"How lucky," Verlaque replied. The couple stood in front of the honey-colored town hall, and Verlaque took two photographs. They thanked him and walked on, probably on their way to the cathedral. He turned around and again looked at the facade of the three-story town hall, lit up in the morning sun. He could see why the Italians—no, Venetians—wanted their picture taken there. It was at once majestic and intimate. Above the wide entryway, where on Saturdays newly married couples streamed out after their obligatory state wedding, were medallions bearing not the usual three inscriptions, but five. Verlaque had never noticed them before. *Liberté*, *égalité*, and *fraternité* were joined by two newcomers: *générosité* and *probité*. These two additions were more personal than the other three. Generosity was one of Verlaque's own favorite traits, inherited from his paternal grand-parents Charles and Emmeline. Their homes in Paris and Normandy were always open to family, neighbors, friends, and colleagues. "If I was down to my last shilling, I'd still throw a party," Emmeline used to say to her grandsons in her educated London accent. Verlaque realized that generosity was something important to all his friends, for those who were stingy, or "mean" as Emmeline used to say, were soon struck from his list of acquaintances. A colleague once told him about a Christmas he had spent in America. Friends of friends were throwing a party. They were well off and living in a big house whose mortgage, bragged the husband, was paid off, but written on the invitations was "BYOB." The colleague kept the invitation as a souvenir, and when he got back passed the letter around the Palais de Justice. His Aixois coworkers tried to guess what the acronym could possibly mean. "Bring your own bottle!" the young law clerk had to explain. "Bottle of what?" a secretary asked. People looked at each other, bewildered. "Wine or whatever," he went on. "I didn't know what it meant, either, and arrived bearing only flowers and expensive Parisian chocolates. So I went to the kitchen and poured myself a glass of tap water. I refused to drink alcohol that night. For the first time in my life, I was at a party where I drank water."

Verlaque smiled, fondly remembering the young clerk, who had since moved to another city. He looked up at *probité*, thinking of his conversation with Marine the previous evening. Honesty was Marine's paramount trait. She was the most honest person he had ever met. He walked on, his hands in his pockets, thinking of Barbier. The snapshots of him with his arms around actresses and rock stars. The numerous television appearances. Verlaque walked into the coffee-roasting house and said hello to the three women who had worked there as long as he could remember. He leaned against the counter and ordered an Italian, thinking about Valère as he watched one of the women make his coffee and simultaneously load the dishwasher. *How could Valère have faked his way all that time? Why hadn't the journalists and critics caught on?* Verlaque thanked the woman for his coffee and, tapping a sugar packet on the counter and then opening it, poured half in. Two men at the opposite end of the counter joked with the women, their voices and laughter loud, ringing out over the piercing noise of the grinder. Verlaque then realized that Barbier always laughed and joked in the same way. It was one of the reasons he was so loved, and such a popular guest on literary talk shows. The nation's favorite writer was a cutup, a joker. What a good way to disguise the fact that you weren't as profound as you sounded in your books.

Fifteen minutes later Verlaque was at his desk, having firmly closed the door to his office. He picked up the telephone and called Daniel de Rudder. "I hope it isn't too early," Verlaque said.

"Are you joking?" Rudder asked. "I've been up for hours. What else am I supposed to do? So, what have you come up with?"

"I had a good look at the photographs of the boat, taken by the police just after Agathe's disappearance."

"And?"

"The mess . . . From all accounts, Pelloquin was a good sailor, maniacally so, and a good sailor doesn't leave the bow in that kind of state."

"Hmm."

Verlaque could tell that Rudder was smiling on the other end of the phone. "The anchor wasn't even in the well, which means Pelloquin may have set Agathe up—"

"Or . . ."

"Or wanted someone else to trip?" Verlaque

324

winced, embarrassed to sound unsure to his former teacher.

"Did you go through the records?" Rudder asked.

"Certainly," Verlaque said. "Everyone on board had a clean history. As you know, Agathe and Valère Barbier argued that day, and so did Agathe and Pelloquin. But that doesn't tell us much. My wife was in Paris yesterday, at Les Loges—"

"Oh really?" Rudder asked. He began to cough, and Verlaque waited until the coughing subsided.

"Yes, an old schoolmate of hers is now assistant director. Marine, my wife, looked at Agathe's records and had a very informative meeting with the current *directrice*."

"And?"

"A few oddities," Verlaque said. "Agathe was a talented writer, and won an award for an essay with the same title as Valère Barbier's first novel."

"*Rue Faubourg*?"

"Exactly."

"She gave him the title, most likely."

"That's what I think," Verlaque said. "But my wife thinks otherwise."

"Hogwash—although . . . if Agathe did help write the books, that would give Valère Barbier a nice motive for killing her."

"Or Alphonse Pelloquin," Verlaque said. "He must have made millions off of Barbier's books.

Speaking of Pelloquin, I have an acquaintance who saw Alphonse and Agathe together in a café in the 6th more than once."

"Now you're getting warm. Do you not find it interesting that her body was never found, despite the fact that she fell off the boat relatively close to Nice? I think you should—" Rudder began to cough again, and Verlaque held the telephone away from his ear.

"Are you all right?" Verlaque asked once the noise had stopped.

He heard some shuffling noises and a woman came on the telephone. "Judge Verlaque?" she asked. "I'm Daphné de Rudder. I know that my father-in-law has been calling you."

"Yes. Is Daniel okay?"

"Yes, yes," she said. "He just needs to rest right now. He was up far too early this morning." Verlaque could hear Rudder arguing in the background.

"I understand," Verlaque said. "And thank you for taking such good care of Daniel." As he hung up, someone knocked on the door. "Come in."

Bruno Paulik walked in, shook hands, went to the bright-red espresso machine, and turned it on. "Coffee?" Paulik asked.

Verlaque shook his head. "I've had two already. Do you think it odd that Agathe Barbier's body was never recovered?"

Paulik shrugged. "Not really. Anything can

happen in the sea. There are sharks out there."

"Nice. But then an arm or a leg would turn up, no?"

"Now you're the one being morbid. Are you thinking she planned her accident and is still wandering around?" The espresso machine's red light went out, signaling it was ready, and Paulik made coffee. "Are you sure?" he asked, holding up his demitasse.

"Okay, go ahead and make me one," Verlaque said, smiling.

"You're a pushover." Paulik made another espresso. "Faking a death has always seemed far too unreal to me," he said, handing Verlaque a demitasse and sitting down across from him. "It can hardly be worth all the fuss. Why?"

"Revenge. She's frightening Valère. Trying to drive him mad."

"But for what?"

Verlaque filled Paulik in on Marine's discovery. "Plus, my old law professor seems to think that Agathe may have staged her own death."

Paulik listened with an open mouth. "This is beginning to sound like a novel."

"Exactly," Verlaque said, thinking of *Rebecca*.

"But what if," Paulik suggested, "Valère Barbier is simply imagining these ghosts? What if it's just an old house making weird noises at night, and Valère really did write those great books all on his own?" He put his right hand on his heart. "Because I'm having a very hard time believing otherwise. *An Honorable Man? The Receptionist? Red Earth?* Not written by our national hero? What if Agathe Barbier did simply fall off a boat?"

"For an opera lover, you really are very unimaginative."

Verlaque ran into their apartment and emptied his pockets, setting his wallet and cell phone on the kitchen counter. It was still warm out, nearly 30°C, he suspected, and on the walk home he had thought about how good a shower would feel. But he was too excited. "Marine!" he hollered.

"What?" she called from the mezzanine. "You're making so much noise down there!"

"Come down!" he cried.

"Oh, brother," Marine mumbled, turning off her laptop. She had been staring at the same sentence for over half an hour; it was time to stop. She could hear her husband opening the refrigerator and banging the kitchen cupboards.

"White?" he called as she walked down the metal staircase she had always thought too contemporary and masculine for such an old apartment.

"Yes, please," she said, walking into the kitchen and hugging Verlaque. "You're warm."

"And sweaty," he said. "Sorry. I'm going to dive into the shower before dinner. Too bad we can't fit a lap pool on the terrace. But first," he said, pouring them each a glass of white burgundy, "I want to talk about Valère."

"*Santé*," Marine said, tapping her glass to her husband's then taking a sip. "Did you speak to Daniel de Rudder?"

"Yes, and he's put an idea in my head," Verlaque said. "I think Agathe is still alive."

Marine tried not to laugh. She walked around their small but efficient kitchen and sipped more wine. "And she's trying to frighten Valère?"

"Exactly."

"There's a problem with that theory," she said.

"What?"

"Erwan. She'd want to be with her son, no?"

"Maybe Erwan knows. Perhaps they see each other secretly."

"For twenty-two years? And," Marine said, her face getting flushed from the heat and wine, "if Agathe wrote the great books, wouldn't she still be writing, or at least making pots?"

Verlaque grinned. "That's why I ran up the stairs and put my shower on hold."

"You ran up four flights of stairs?"

"I paused on the second-floor landing. Just be quiet and listen."

"You're such a jerk," Marine said, laughing.

"Claude Petitjean."

"I gave it back to Sylvie," Marine asked.

"Sorry."

"I'll buy it—don't worry. Did you read *Le Monde*'s literary section last weekend?"

Marine set her empty glass on the counter and stared at her husband.

Verlaque continued: "Petitjean has published five books, the first four were critically acclaimed but little read, and now this one—"

"A huge success," Marine cut in, "despite the author refusing to do interviews or even release his or her photograph. Claude can be either male or female."

"And guess when Claude Petitjean's first novel was published?"

"Just after Agathe's death?" Marine asked.

"In 1990."

Verlaque's cell phone began to ring. He picked it up and looked at the caller. "*Merde*. It's Jacob from the club. He never calls. Do you mind if I answer?"

"Go ahead. Tell him I say hello. I'll start preparing dinner."

Verlaque picked up the phone and took it into the living room. Marine opened the refrigerator and took out a bunch of arugula she'd bought at the market that morning. Digging into the back of the fridge, she found a bag of pine nuts, a chunk of Parmesan they'd brought back from their most recent trip to Liguria, and some herbed pancetta from her butcher. She'd make linguini, using these ingredients cooked in chicken broth.

Ten minutes later Verlaque came back into the kitchen and set his phone back on the counter, plugging it in to charge.

Marine was pacing back and forth. "Something kept bothering me when I was reading the Petitjean."

Verlaque opened the fridge, grabbed the wine, and refilled their glasses. "Oh yeah?"

"Do you remember me telling you what it was about?"

Verlaque nodded. "Two kids who grew up on the same street in Paris get back in touch in their seventies." He looked at Marine. "Of course . . . It reminded you of Valère and—"

"Michèle Baudouin."

Verlaque walked over to Marine and wrapped his arms around her, kissing her forehead. "I hope we're wrong about this. I don't like impostors."

"I agree." Marine turned to stir the pasta. "Why did Jacob call?" she wondered. "If you don't mind my asking."

"They're moving to London."

"Really? Why?"

"Lower taxes," Verlaque replied.

Marine sighed. "The older I get, the more socialist I become."

"That's the opposite of what Churchill said naturally happens to us with age," Verlaque said. "But I agree."

Verlaque's answer surprised Marine, but she

was too hungry to talk politics. "He called to tell you about the move?"

"Yes, and to tell me that he's selling his house," Verlaque said. "And he'd rather not go through an agent. We have first dibs."

As Antoine Verlaque and Marine Bonnet were eating dinner on the terrace and celebrating the idea of living in Jacob's house with a bottle of champagne that went surprisingly well with the pasta, Bruno Paulik was sitting in Gaston Bressey's brightly lit kitchen. He had run into Gaston while buying bread and joked that he was an orphan that night, as his wife and daughter were eating in Aix with his wife's sister. Gaston immediately invited Paulik to dinner, adding that, given the warm weather, he would make pasta with salmon. Paulik gladly accepted and bought an apple tart from the *boulangère*, one with a fine crust and thinly sliced apples arranged in a pinwheel pattern. Paulik went home to have a quick shower, wishing as he did that they had the money to build a swimming pool, and arrived at Gaston's at eight o'clock sharp, with the tart and a bottle of chilled rosé cradled in his arms.

Paulik had to sit at an angle, as his legs would not fit under the small wooden table. He watched Gaston cook as he sipped Hélène's rosé—she sold so much she could hardly keep up with the demand. Gaston was bent over the counter, cutting leeks, and Paulik imagined the counters here were several inches lower than at his house. Gaston's wife must have been barely five feet tall. The old man took his time, slowly stirring chopped leeks and garlic in butter and olive oil while they chatted. Paulik asked Gaston about the village over the years, and his job working for the SNCF. Gaston replied with insight and thoughtfulness. *Much the way he cooked*, thought Paulik. Gaston carefully removed thyme leaves from their woody stalks and added them to the leeks. Paulik could smell it from where he was sitting: lemon thyme, which grew in low bunches along the driveway.

"It must be hard seeing all these newcomers in the village," Paulik said as he munched on crispy radishes dipped in *fleur de sel* that Gaston had poured in a small saucer. Since earlier that morning in Verlaque's office, Paulik could think of nothing but their conversation about Agathe and Valère Barbier. He hoped to get some information from the old man that might put the idea of a still-alive Agathe out of his head.

Gaston shrugged. *"Le changement, c'est normal."* He put a small cast-iron frying pan on the gas stove and watched as it heated up. Unscrewing the lid of an old jam jar, he poured in a handful of pine nuts and gently stirred them in the dry, hot pan with a wooden spoon. Paulik stopped eating the radishes, saving his appetite for dinner.

When the pine nuts were toasted a medium brown, Gaston took them off the heat and set the pan aside. Paulik asked, trying to sound casual, "Are there any unusual newcomers to the village?" Gaston turned around, frowning, and Paulik immediately regretted his transparent question.

"What do you mean?" Gaston asked, still holding the wooden spoon in his hand. "Have you come here just to ask police questions?"

"*Non, je suis désolé, Gaston*," Paulik said. "Let me explain a bit." Paulik told Gaston about the mystery of Agathe Barbier's death, and the old man listened as he cooked.

"Dinner soon," Gaston said a few minutes later, as he drained the pasta and added several large tablespoons of crème fraîche to the leeks. He set the spoon down in the sink and turned to face Paulik. "I've seen the girl, Sandrine, in the village dozens of times," Gaston began, "but a few days ago I saw her talking with one of the Pioger cousins. They saw me and quickly walked down an alleyway together, as if they didn't want anyone noticing them."

Paulik asked, "Can you remember exactly when that was?"

Gaston scratched his head. "That's a little difficult for someone my age."

"Fair enough," Paulik said.

"But yesterday I saw something even odder."

"Really?"

Gaston leaned down and turned off the burner. "It was late last night, and I couldn't sleep, so I came downstairs and made some chamomile tea. It happens about once a week. I looked out the kitchen window, the one right beside you."

Paulik looked out the window and saw the backs of the *maisons du village* on the street parallel to Gaston's. "And?"

"The lights came on upstairs," Gaston said, walking over to where Paulik was sitting. "In that one, up there," he said, pointing.

Paulik looked at Gaston, waiting for an explanation.

"Don't you think that odd, Commissioner? Why would a blind lady need to turn on the lights in the middle of the night?"

Chapter Twenty-eight

Aix-en-Provence,
Tuesday, July 13, 2010

Despite the heat—already formidable at 9:00 a.m.—Florence Bonnet insisted on riding her bicycle to the archdiocese, which was located just north of the place Bellegarde on a nondescript street lined with postwar-era apartment buildings. From there it ruled over the combined Aix and Arles parishes, but only those with business to conduct would ever find it, for only the address, cours de la Trinité, hinted at the function of the pale-pink building at the end of the residential street. Professeur Bonnet had been coming here for almost fifty years, since she was an undergraduate, and almost always by bicycle. There was never an available parking spot.

She, of course, knew the head archivist, who, unfortunately, had arrived at his position not thanks to talent and hard work, but via connections and politics. As she walked in, signed the guest registry, and continued down the hallway toward the archival rooms, she wondered how best to approach him. Tell him exactly what she was looking for? Tell him the bare minimum? She opened the door and a young woman—perhaps in her late twenties—looked up from the desk and smiled. Florence returned the smile, introduced herself, and asked for the head archivist. The woman shook her head. "He's gone for two weeks," she answered. "Vacation." Florence pursed her lips, forgetting that many workers now chose to take vacation at any time instead of during the traditional mid-August break.

"I see," Florence said.

"But I'd be happy to help you," the young woman quickly added. "All I've done this week is catalog."

"Have I seen you at the university, in the theology department?" Florence asked. In fact, she wasn't sure, as these days all the students looked the same to her and she was rarely on campus, unless she had a meeting to attend.

"Perhaps," the young woman answered, smiling. "I'm a graduate student. I've read some of your articles on Saint Augustine."

"Well, well," Florence said, flustered. "What is your name?"

"Elodie."

"Then let's get going, Elodie," Florence said. "We need the archives for the parish of Puyloubier."

"Easy."

"From 1688 to 1760."

Elodie's face lit up. "I can get those."

Florence smiled and said, "Excellent. My area of specialty is centuries earlier, as you know. Actually, the man I'm looking for, Count Hugues de Besse, was born in 1688, but let's begin with, say, twenty years after that date, until his death in 1760. The church in Puyloubier is Saint-Pons."

Elodie shook her head. "Not then. It was Sainte-Marie, which is still there, up behind the village. A few weeks ago I cataloged some old photographs of it. I'll go and get the right books and then join you. We can work here. As you can see, it's a quiet period of the year."

"Perhaps because no one knows that the building's air-conditioned," Florence said, setting her purse and carryall on a large wooden table. She reached into the fishnet bag and took out a light-blue cotton sweater, its lapels bordered by yellow embroidered daisies—a gift from Marine. Before putting it on, Florence glanced at the label and winced. She had often passed the boutique—one that specialized in fine knitwear—and she dreaded to guess what the sweater had cost her daughter. Shaking her head, she blamed it on Antoine Verlaque and his extravagant tastes. Marine had been raised to shop at Monoprix, and during the sales.

Minutes later Elodie reappeared, carrying three large, dark-green ledgers. Florence noticed, as the young woman carefully set the books down, that she wore white gloves. Elodie reached into her pocket and gave a pair to Florence. "We'll begin with these," Elodie said. "The top ledger begins in 1710, when your count was twenty-two. Is that okay?"

"Perfect."

Elodie sat down and opened the book. She looked at Professor Bonnet and softly asked, "Would you mind telling me a little bit about what we're looking for?"

A door opened and closed down a hallway, and Florence moved her chair closer to Elodie's. Whispering, she told the girl what she knew, and the gossip about the count that circulated, thanks to people like Philomène and Léopold. Elodie listened intently, trying not to grimace at certain parts of the story. "Before going downstairs to get these books, I looked up the name of the archbishop during this time," Elodie said, after Florence had finished.

"Excellent," Florence said. She looked at ledger's first pages and the delicate cursive handwriting that filled its columns. "This is fascinating."

"These are birth records from Sainte-Marie," Elodie said.

"But of course the Bastide Blanche births we're concerned with wouldn't have been recorded."

"What about a doctor's record?"

"No," Florence said, shaking her head. "They would have had a midwife."

"Oh, of course," Elodie said. "Or they might have even helped one another with the births."

"The poor girls."

"Court records?" Elodie asked. "If someone complained about the count? Surely someone did?"

"That would be my daughter's area of expertise," Florence said. "But I doubt any of the girls felt they could reveal what was going on in that house. So," she said, carefully turning a page, "I'm not sure what we are looking for, nor do I think that these record books will reveal anything."

"Letters? Diaries?"

Florence sat up straight and looked at Elodie. "Do you have such things?"

"Yes," she answered, pulling her chair out from behind the table. "I wasn't sure, at first, what you were looking for. The archbishop may have kept letters, and diaries, I can't remember offhand. They're downstairs. When I first started interning here, I was given the parishes of Sainte-Victoire to reorganize. That includes Puyloubier, of course. I'll be right back."

Elodie closed the library between noon and two o'clock, and they ate their lunch together, in a small kitchen downstairs. Mercifully, it, too, was air-conditioned. "We aren't supposed to let patrons stay during the lunch hour," Elodie said. "But I think given that you are a retired theology professor—"

"I don't want to get you in trouble!" Florence protested. But at the same time, she didn't want to have to eat outside in the heat.

"No, it will be fine. I'm usually the only person who uses this kitchen. Everyone seems to be away, or they eat in town at a restaurant."

After finishing her tuna sandwich, Florence took off her sandals and had a nap on an old leather sofa pushed against one of the kitchen walls, while Elodie read a novel. Florence envied Elodie's youth, especially the ability to be able to read all day. Her own mind wandered too much now.

Florence looked up at the clock. It was almost four. They hadn't found any diaries kept by the archbishop, Jean-Baptiste de Brancas, but they did find a stack of letters. "Anything?" she asked Elodie, who was reading, her head held in her hands.

"Not yet, and I'm almost through my half," she answered, yawning. "The handwriting is hard to read, and the letters are very official."

"You have the right to say that they're boring," Florence said.

"They're boring."

Florence laughed and bent her head back down and continued to read. Only letters addressed to the archbishop had been saved. His letters were now either lost or in another archives, perhaps in Paris or the Vatican. She certainly wasn't willing to spend more time on this than she had today, and she regretted not having brought along a silk scarf to protect her neck and throat from the air-conditioning. Her head began to ache.

"Bastide B.," Elodie said aloud.

"Pardon?"

"This is a letter from a priest, Père Guy Bernard, from Sainte-Marie in Puyloubier," Elodie continued. "It looks like Père Guy is complaining about '*des problèmes*' at the Bastide B. It's hard to read his writing." With a gloved hand, Elodie passed the letter to Florence. "There's more at the bottom. Can you read it?"

Florence took the letter and leaned forward, trying to ignore her pulsating headache. " '*Avec les bonnes*,'" Florence read aloud. "Servant girls. He calls them '*les filles rondes*.'"

"Round?" Elodie asked. "Pregnant?"

Florence nodded. "And as the parish priest, Père Guy would be frequently at the *bastide*."

Elodie began to read the next letter. "This is a letter from the cardinal," she said. "He mentions, near the bottom, '*Je regrette de ne pas pouvoir vous aider avec les problèmes à la Bastide B.*'

The date is hard to read, but it looks like it says July of 1742."

"The cardinal cannot help with the problems," Florence said. "Can't or won't?"

Elodie read on, and once she finished the letter said, "The cardinal says, at the end, that he would like to remind the archbishop of the count's generosity."

Florence slammed the wooden table with the palm of her right hand. "Now we need to look at those ledgers again."

"To look up the count's donations?" Elodie asked.

"Exactly. He bought himself out of *les problèmes*."

Verlaque awoke that morning with the first chirping of birds and, mercifully, cool air coming in through the open window. He looked at Marine, still asleep, her arms straight at her sides, her expression serene. As he pulled up the white sheet, to cover her shoulders, he heard his cell phone ring in the kitchen. He jumped out of bed and ran and picked up the phone. He was about to turn it off when he saw that the caller was Bruno Paulik. It was just before seven.

"Bruno, good morning," Verlaque answered.

"Sorry to call you so early," Paulik said. "But something's strange in Puyloubier."

"I'll say."

"There's a blind lady—a Parisian—who turns on the lights in her house every night."

Suddenly, the entryway of Ursule Genoux's apartment came into Verlaque's head. Happy yellow walls, with hats hanging on pegs. "And during the day, does she wear big sun hats?" he asked.

"Come to think of it, yes. Léa and Hélène see her a lot. Léa commented on the hats, as around here it's usually British women who wear them."

"Or women from northern France careful with their skin," Verlaque offered. "Ursule Genoux, her sister, or—"

"Agathe Barbier. I'll order a squad car put in front of the woman's house."

"Perfect. I have a day full of meetings in Marseille," Verlaque said, looking at his watch. "Marine and I are eating dinner in Puyloubier tonight. Marine's crazy about that place, especially the eccentric waitress. We'll swing by your house after, for a nightcap."

Chapter Twenty-nine

New York City,
September 23, 2010

The next day was one of the happiest and most terrifying of my life. First, for the good stuff. I can't remember a time when I felt as happy as I did when I heard Tinker Bell coming up the drive. I ran outside as Sandrine was parking the car. "Where were you?" I yelled as she got out and opened the back hatch, pulling out various bags.

"I told you!" she answered, walking over and giving me the *bise*.

"You most certainly did not."

"I most certainly did, M Barbier famous la-di-da writer. Don't you check your text messages?"

"All the time," I said. "And your uncle didn't know where you were either."

She closed the trunk and looked at me. "I told him too."

"No, apparently not."

She put her huge blue purse on Clochette's dented roof and dug around a bit, pulling out her cell phone. She turned it on and scrolled through her history. "*Merde!*"

"What?"

"It didn't send," she said. "I copied you both on the same message. I must have been out of range."

"So where were you?"

"In the Cévennes," she replied. "At a friend's old *cabanon*. She lets me use it whenever . . . I need to get away."

She began walking toward the house, and I grabbed one of the bags from her to help. I said, "I've been worried sick."

She turned and looked at me like I had just said the nicest thing in the world. "You were?"

"Of course."

As she walked into the house she stopped, looking around. "Do you remember that part in *The Sound of Music* when the mother superior tells Maria to go back to the captain's house and face her demons?"

"Vaguely," I replied, still pissed off. "Let's get a glass of wine and you can explain."

Sandrine marched on, ahead of me, toward the kitchen, her high-heeled sandals making an extraordinary amount of noise on the tile floors. All of a sudden I was thrilled to have her back in the house.

"Do you think there are demons here?" I asked, getting a bottle of white wine out of the fridge.

"No," she said, again looking around as if we were being overheard. "But there are ghosts. And . . . I just couldn't face . . ."

"The ghosts? And sad memories?"

"You know about Josy?" Sandrine whispered.

"Your uncle told me," I answered. "I'm so sorry, Sandrine."

She slumped down in a chair. "It's the only time when I'm down," she said. "I'm afraid I don't know how to deal with it . . . It's been three years, but it doesn't seem to get easier."

"It will," I said. "I promise."

She looked at me and her eyes welled up with tears. "I'm sorry, M Barbier. You've been through it too."

I nodded. "You could get professional help. I did."

"Huh?"

"A therapist," I explained.

She waved her hand in my face. "That's for rich city people. A few days in the Cévennes did the trick. Besides, who would I go to?"

I didn't understand at first, but then I realized she meant a therapist. "We'll find someone in Aix." Her face got a funny look. "The sessions can be paid for by the government health plan," I said. "Or if it's been too long since the accident, I'll pay. And I don't want any arguments. There is one more thing, though. That night I called out in my sleep—"

Sandrine began to whistle and look around the kitchen.

"Sandrine. Where were you that night? Were you seeing Hervé Pioger?"

She looked at me and began crying. "I sure know how to pick 'em, don't I? He wouldn't even see me. I kept knocking on his door . . . and the next day I bumped into him in the village, and he said such cruel things."

"Forget about him, Sandrine," I said, handing her a tissue. "It's better to be alone than with someone who isn't good for you, who'll bring you down. You're way above that kind of guy."

"Really?"

"I'm certain of it."

"A girl gets lonely, M Barbier," she said.

"I understand all about loneliness, Sandrine. I'm not judging you."

She sat up straight and lifted her glass. "I'm better already, thank you." She looked around and then asked, "Where is everyone? Erwan? Michèle?"

"You'll be happy to know that they both left," I replied. "For now, anyway. Erwan left, taking with him one of Agathe's smaller vases—"

"You let him?"

"I'm tired, Sandrine, and I wanted him out of here."

"He'll only sell it—"

"His mother made it," I answered. "He has a right to it." I skipped over the part about why I let the little bastard take the vase.

"And Michèle?"

"In the Luberon at some film producer's megamansion," I said. "She's coming back in a few days, to get the rest of her bags, and then leaving."

"Phew!" Sandrine said, lifting her glass again and touching it to mine.

We were taking our first sip as Léa walked in. "*Coucou!*" she called from the kitchen door. "Sandrine!" she called, running into her arms. "I knew you'd be back soon. But we didn't know where you were!"

"I'm sorry, *chérie*. Technical hitch. I was in the Cévennes, but now I'm back, and on my way here I swung into Aix and picked up something for you." Sandrine dug into one of the bags and pulled out a flat rectangular box, handing it to Léa.

Léa sat at the table and opened it. It was the photograph of me and Maria Callas, framed. I won't tell you about the frame. Let's just say it had lots of rhinestone hearts on it. "Thank you!" Léa said. She hugged it to her chest then carefully put it back in its box and set it on the counter, as I had challenged the girls to a game of Scrabble—them against me. We spent an enjoyable hour or so playing, Sandrine helping her team win by turning *on* into *déception* in a triple-word score using all their tiles. Well, it was Sandrine who thought of the word but Léa who correctly spelled it.

At eight Léa looked at the kitchen clock and said she had to go home for dinner. Sandrine said that she had found a risotto recipe in *La Provence* and asked Léa if she'd like to help. "That's the least we can do for creaming you at Scrabble, M Barbier," Sandrine said. I argued that it was a close game and they were lucky with their letters, while Léa telephoned her parents for permission to eat with us. Sandrine and Léa had left the finished game set up, pushing it to the edge of the table, teasing me. Sandrine flew around the kitchen, gathering ingredients for the risotto, and Léa helped stir the rice, a long and arduous task, and one that always made me glad not to be involved.

We finished eating around nine thirty and got out some flashlights and walked Léa home through the garden. Yes, Justin, I know this sounds like a detailed unemotional police report, but I'm trying to give you all the facts here. This Tennessee bourbon is very good, by the way. I would have gone for the traditional Armagnac.

When we got to the Pauliks' house, the lights were on and Léa opened the door, waved good-bye, and that was that. Sandrine said, "*Zut!* Léa forgot her photograph."

"We can bring it to her tomorrow," I said. Sandrine then insisted that we walk a little longer to work off the risotto. I was in such a good mood that I agreed. Besides, I had a cigar in my pocket and quite like smoking and strolling.

We made it all the way to the village—lifeless at that hour—and then walked home. It was only ten fifteen, and we were both suddenly exhausted. We said good night on the landing, and then the telephone rang. "*Âllo*," I answered rather gruffly. It was late and I don't like calls at night.

"*Âllo*, Valère," Bruno Paulik said. "I know you guys must be having fun, but it's time for Léa to come home. I can come up and get her."

My heart leapt to my mouth. I couldn't answer.

"Valère?" asked Paulik.

"She's at your place," I said. "We dropped her off an hour ago."

"Don't kid."

"I'm serious," I said. Sandrine heard the conversation and came out of her bedroom, her face white and her mouth open. Bruno said something to Hélène, and I could hear her shrieking. "Check her bedroom. She probably went straight to bed," I offered, as if I knew their child better than they did.

"She isn't in our house," Bruno said. "I'll be right there—"

He hung up before I could say anything. I turned to Sandrine, and she started to run down the stairs. "Maybe Léa's in the garden," I said, following her.

Sandrine ran through the downstairs rooms, calling Léa's name. I went into the kitchen and stared at the four walls, utterly unable to move or do anything of use. Sandrine came in and ran to the kitchen counter. "Léa's photograph is gone," she said.

I said, "Do you think she came back to fetch it?"

"Obviously," Sandrine said. "I'm sorry, M Barbier!" She got wide-eyed and began to scream. "But then where is she? This house! This ghost-filled house! I should have stayed away!"

"Sandrine, calm down!" I took her by the shoulders and thought she was going to cry, but she pulled herself together when we heard Bruno's 4x4 pull up in front of the house. I ran outside as Bruno came up the steps.

"Is she here?" he asked, panting.

"No," I said. "We've called her name throughout the house. We think she may have tried walking back here to get something she forgot in the kitchen."

"Let's search the garden," Bruno said, turning around to look at the olive trees and vineyards that separated our properties. The outdoor lights suddenly came on, lighting up the garden.

Sandrine then came out. "Do the lights help?" she asked.

"Yes," Bruno snapped. Suddenly a roar came across the vines, and a bright light shone in the vineyard. "Hélène," he said. "She's on the tractor."

Sandrine handed us flashlights. "Let's each take a row and walk toward your house." The *cagole* telling the police commissioner what to do.

I ran ahead, toward the swimming pool, without waiting. I felt sick to my stomach. Could she have fallen in? But when I got close I could see, thanks to the pool lights, that it was empty, just the blue-green water lapping gently at the tiled sides. "Thank God," I muttered, and turned on my flashlight to join the others.

There were four adults yelling Léa's name, and the sound of the tractor going up and down the rows, its light so powerful you had to look away when it came near you. I could see why Hélène thought to bring it out.

"We were watching a movie. Léa may have even called out to us, but we didn't hear," Bruno said to me when we met at the end of our respective rows. He held his bald head in his hands.

"I should have taken her into your house," I said, "and said a proper good evening to you and Hélène. It's my fault."

Bruno quickly said, "An old villager told me last night that the blind woman who's been renting a house isn't who she claims to be—"

"What?" I demanded.

Hélène climbed off the tractor. She bent down, as if looking at her vineyard; the grapes hung in huge clumps among the wide, bright-green leaves. I thought it odd that she was inspecting the vines; then I realized she was bent over because she was throwing up. Bruno ran to her and rubbed her back, and we stood there, not knowing what to do, staring and waiting for directions from Bruno. He's the police commissioner, after all. Bruno then looked up at us, his face lit by an orange glow. I could hear a rumbling sound coming from behind us. "The house!" he yelled as he got up and began to run.

Hélène followed, and Sandrine quickly caught up with her as I ran behind. It was only then that I saw that Hélène was wearing her nightgown and running shoes, and Sandrine was barefoot. She must have kicked off her high heels as we left the house. Women are stronger than us, Justin, especially in moments like this one. You need to know that and accept it. Agathe was certainly stronger than me.

The sky was lit up, the same orange-red that had lit up Bruno's face. The *bastide* was ablaze, flames curling from every window.

Chapter Thirty

Aix-en-Provence,
Tuesday, July 13, and
Wednesday, July 14, 2010

Antoine Verlaque saw the orange glow from the village. At first he thought it might be from fireworks in a neighboring village, and he looked at his phone to double-check the date. No, Bastille Day was tomorrow. Besides, the glow was coming from the north, below mont Sainte-Victoire, where there were only a few houses, like Bruno Paulik's and La Bastide Blanche. He joined Marine, who was waiting, standing beside the car, looking up at the sky.

"Our blind woman isn't at home," he said. "Will you look at that sky."

Marine said, "I almost ran up to the house to get you, but a bunch of people came out of the bar, looking at the sky and yelling. The barman rang the fire station on his cell phone. I'm worried, Antoine."

"Let's go to Valère's." They were about to get into the car when Verlaque's cell phone rang.

"*Merde*," he said, looking at the caller ID. "It's Rudder."

"Answer it," Marine said, running around to the driver's side of the car. "It may be important. I'll drive."

"Daniel," Verlaque said, holding the phone under his chin while he buckled up in the passenger seat.

"My daughter-in-law is outside," Rudder said. "So we don't have much time. Did you think about—"

"Yes," Verlaque replied. "Your theory that Agathe may still be alive is fascinating."

Rudder began to laugh, which turned into a cough. "Whatever are you talking about?"

"Your last words to me—"

"We got cut off by Nurse Ratched," Rudder said.

"But the theory fits, whether it's yours or not," Verlaque continued. "Claude Petitjean. Don't you see?"

"Claude Petitjean?"

"The writer." Verlaque looked at Marine and winked, but she had her eyes on the curving road.

Rudder yelled into the phone, "I know who you're talking about! Petitjean *is* a woman, but she's in her late forties, not late sixties. An ex-biology professor from Limoges. Lives in the countryside with her husband and twin kids, girl and boy, ten years of age. They've done one of those barn conversions."

Verlaque sighed. "How do you know?"

"Ratched loves her books," Rudder explained, his breathing raspy. "So I promised to find out a little bit about our mystery writer. My sources are infallible."

"I'm sure," Verlaque said. "But the last time we spoke, you pointed out the fact that Agathe's body never washed up."

"I was just thinking out loud," Rudder said. "What I was going to suggest is that you look more at Les Loges—" He began to cough, and Verlaque could hear a shuffling noise and a woman's voice. "My time's up," Rudder said, laughing and coughing at the same time. "Bad joke. Sorry."

As they got closer to the *bastide* the sky became brighter, but the field of vision immediately in front of the car became impaired by smoke. Verlaque quickly filled Marine in on his conversation with Rudder, but she had understood most of it by listening to them. "Even if Agathe didn't write the Petitjean books, she might still be alive," she said. "There's another woman to add to the list of suspects, also in her sixties or seventies."

Verlaque looked at Marine. "Michèle Baudouin."

"Yes. I've seen them together, and their relationship is beyond weird. A sort of love-hate thing, just like in the Petitjean book."

"What's in front of us now is more like *Rebecca*," Verlaque said as he leaned toward the windshield, trying to see the road.

"Is this how the book ends?" Marine asked, quickly looking at him. "A fire?"

"Yes, Danvers goes up in flames." They turned up the lane at the Pauliks' farmhouse, stopping the car on the edge of the road about halfway to the *bastide*. "This is as close as I want to get," Marine said, turning off the ignition.

"We can go on foot from here," Verlaque said, already half out of the car. They got to the front terrace just as Bruno Paulik arrived, frantic.

"Léa's in there!" Paulik shouted over the noise of sparks, the roaring fire, and distant sirens. His face was streaked with tears and sweat.

Verlaque took him by the elbows. "We can't go in, Bruno!"

"Bruno, the firefighters are on their way!" Marine shouted. "Let them do their job."

"Sod that!" Paulik hollered, throwing off Verlaque's grip and making for the front door, where black smoke was billowing out. Tearing off his T-shirt and holding it up to his face as a mask, he disappeared inside.

"Bruno!" Hélène yelled as she arrived alongside Sandrine. "No!"

"The back door," Sandrine said. "Let's go and open it. The fire may not be at the back of the house yet."

"The doorknob may be too hot to touch," Verlaque yelled.

"The barbecue gloves," Sandrine called back. "I'll get them and meet you back there!"

Valère Barbier arrived, out of breath, his hands on his knees to steady himself. "M Barbier," Marine said, going to him. "You need to sit down."

"I could never sit down," he replied, looking up at the house with tears in his eyes. "If Léa's in there—"

"She may not be," Marine replied.

"But Léa came back to the house to get a photograph she had forgotten," Valère said. "She obviously caught this woman in the act, working out her fright antics."

"Who do you mean, Valère?" Marine whispered.

"The blind lady—"

"You know about her?"

"Bruno just told me that the blind woman," Valère began, his voice shaking, "who's been living in the village . . . is behind all of this . . ."

The sirens got unbearably loud, then abruptly stopped, as two fire engines pulled up. "She must have chased Léa," he went on, seeming not to notice the trucks and the firefighters who were unrolling their hoses.

"Léa may have gotten away," Marine offered, her arm around the writer's shoulders.

Valère shrugged off Marine's arm. "Agathe!" he cried, looking up at the house. "Agathe!"

"Are there people inside?" the fire captain asked Verlaque as he got to the terrace.

"Possibly three," Verlaque replied, looking over at his wife. Was Agathe Barbier in the house? "Bruno Paulik, the police commissioner, has just gone in. His eleven-year-old daughter may be inside. And a woman . . . in her sixties."

The firefighters began to spray water into the windows, and two, in full gear, walked into the house wearing oxygen masks. "They'll find them," Marine said, consoling Valère.

Sandrine came back, panting. "The back door was wide open," she said. "I can't stand here and watch. I'm leaving. Good thing I have my keys in my pocket!"

"What?" Valère yelled. "Now?" She ran toward the carport, and seconds later they could hear Clochette whizzing down the driveway. "She's so unstable," Valère said, shaking his head.

"We all react to situations differently," Marine said, looking up at the blazing house and saying the Lord's Prayer in her head.

Verlaque yelled as the two firefighters came out of the house, supporting Bruno Paulik in their arms, an oxygen mask covering his face. "Is he okay?" Verlaque asked.

They laid Bruno on the ground. The younger one replied, "We found him at the top of the stairs, passed out."

"He was trying to get to the attic," Verlaque explained. "His daughter likes to play up there."

"Let's go," his partner said, and they went back into the house.

"Five minutes," their captain shouted. "The roof may collapse any minute."

Hélène came back and fell beside her husband. "He'll be all right," Verlaque said, kneeling beside her. "They've gone back in to find Léa."

Two minutes later the firefighters emerged, empty-handed, tearing off their masks. "We couldn't make it to the attic," one of them said.

Hélène sobbed, bent over, grabbing at the pebbles with her hands and dragging them across the terrace. Her body heaved. "My baby!" she screamed, her body writhing. She got up to run into the house, and Verlaque grabbed her.

"Hélène, she might not be in there," he said, holding her in his arms.

"We need to get farther back," the captain explained. "The roof is dangerously close to collapsing." As if it heard him, a rumbling noise roared through the house, accompanied by sparks and the sound of falling timbers. "There she goes," he said. "The wood beams are collapsing."

"It's all my fault," Valère said. "Who's behind all this? She must have known all along—"

"Known what?" Marine asked.

Valère mumbled, "I swear if Léa comes out of this all right, I'll confess—I swear to God . . ."

"Confess?" Marine asked. From far away a car horn sounded, getting louder and louder. "It's Sandrine."

A firefighter ran up to Sandrine's car, admonishing her for driving so close to the house. "Whatever!" Sandrine yelled as she jumped out of the car and ran around to the passenger side, opening the door. "Come on, sweetie pie," she gently said.

"*Maman!*"

"Léa!" Hélène yelled. Bruno ripped off the oxygen mask and slowly got to his feet, stumbling. "Easy there, Bruno," Verlaque said, running to help him stand up.

"Oh, thank God," Marine said, hugging Valère. They looked at the Pauliks, who were locked in a three-way embrace.

Sandrine ran up to them, and Valère hugged her. "You're a genius!" he said. "Where was she? The chapel?"

"Yep," Sandrine said. Marine looked down, noticing that she was barefoot. Sandrine continued, "I figured that Léa may have run there, out the back door, to get away. It was a lucky guess."

"Why didn't she just go home?" Marine asked.

"She told me in the car that she was worried

that the woman chasing her might guess that's where she would go," Sandrine said, "and catch up to her there."

"Smart kid," Valère said.

"And there was no sign of anyone else at the chapel?" Marine asked.

"Nope, but we didn't stick around long," Sandrine said. "That place gives me the willies. In fact, this whole countryside does. I can't wait to get back to downtown Aix."

Valère looked at his sidekick and smiled. For Sandrine to say that meant she was healed of her pain. No more running.

Marine realized that her husband was no longer standing beside her. She looked around and saw him by the swimming pool, talking on his phone. She walked down, partly to get farther away from the smoke, and partly to nudge him that it was time they headed home. "*Merci*, Charles-Henri," Verlaque said as he hung up the phone.

"Everything all right?" Marine asked. "It's late for a phone call."

"Charles-Henri stays up late. I asked him to do me a favor." He looked up at the *bastide*, now a smoking shell. "There's a woman in there—I'm certain of it."

Marine took him by the shoulders. "I think you're right," she said. "We'll know more tomorrow. Come on. Let's get home."

● ● ●

A mistral blew through Aix-en-Provence the next day, causing the temperature to drop almost ten degrees, much to everyone's relief, but also canceling the Bastille Day fireworks for most of the region. The fire at La Bastide Blanche was contained by early morning, but because of the wind the firefighters stood watch.

Bruno Paulik called Verlaque's cell phone just after ten, telling him that everyone was all right. Shaken, but all right. Léa and Hélène were still sleeping, cuddled together in the master bed. Paulik suggested that Verlaque and Marine come out to the house after lunch, as both the fire captain and the chief of the local gendarmes needed to question all who had been present. Valère and Sandrine had booked rooms in a roadside chain hotel near the highway, and would come at two o'clock as well. "They need clothes and toiletries," Bruno added, giving Verlaque their sizes and the name of their hotel.

"Right," Verlaque said, hanging up and taking a cappuccino to Marine. "Here you go," he said, handing Marine the coffee as she sat up in bed, fluffing the pillows behind her.

"Thank you," she said, taking the coffee and blowing on it. "You're an angel."

"Drink up. We need to hit Monoprix to buy clothes for Valère and Sandrine before lunch, then go out to Bruno's."

"Just give me a few seconds," Marine said sleepily.

"What a night," Verlaque said, sitting on the edge of the bed. "Everything happened so quickly."

"I know." Marine took a sip and said, "When you were paying the restaurant tab, Nathalie called. She's my old friend who works at Les Loges. She said it took her a few days to work up the courage to call me, as she's recently divorced and is terrified of losing her job. After my visit, Mme Parent, the director, ran up to the archives in a rage, screaming about their lack of care and gross ineptitude. The archivist was on holiday but had obviously done a shoddy job of checking the ID of this apparent scholar."

"Michèle Baudouin—"

"Yes," Marine said. "The archivist didn't recognize her, obviously. Mme Parent grabbed Agathe Barbier's file from some poor underling and opened it in a fury, throwing papers all over the room. Nathalie said it was obvious that something was missing."

"Agathe's prize-winning story."

"'A Chance Meeting on the rue du Faubourg,'" Marine said. "Ursule's proof that Agathe had more than just helped Valère. Mme Parent told me it had nothing in common with the book, but I think she was lying."

"Good thing we chose to eat in Puyloubier last

night," Verlaque said. "Although I don't feel that we—I—helped that much."

"We were there," Marine answered. "That's help enough."

"So Michèle must have this story with her," Verlaque said. "Wherever she is in the Luberon."

"Or it could have been left in the house—"

"In which case it's gone forever."

"Maybe that's a good thing," Marine suggested. "Now it's up to Valère to tell the truth."

"No more deception," Verlaque said. He thought of Valère deceiving Agathe, Ursule Genoux and Alphonse Pelloquin deceiving Daniel de Rudder, Michèle Baudouin deceiving Célestine Parent and the poor archivist, and he himself almost deceiving his beloved wife. It was only for a second, but it had scared him all the same.

Marine asked, "What did you ask Charles-Henri Lagarde to do for you last night?"

"It's just a hunch, but there's someone we forgot—someone who could gain from driving Valère Barbier insane. I asked Charles-Henri to do some asking around, since he knows everyone in the newspaper and publishing world."

"You can fill me in when we're at Monoprix," Marine said. She flung off the sheets then stopped. "Oh—my. Yes."

"You just thought of her too, didn't you?"

"Yes. It makes so much sense." She got out of the bed, opened a drawer, and began choosing

clothes. "Let's go. It's cooler today, thankfully."
She then began to laugh.

"What's up?" Verlaque asked. "Why are you laughing?"

"What on earth are we going to buy Sandrine to wear?"

Verlaque and Bonnet had just finished shopping and were walking to the parking garage when Verlaque's phone rang. It was Bruno Paulik. The *cigales* were making a racket, and the streets were busy with shoppers leaving the market, battling the wind, their bags full of tall leeks and even taller sunflowers. Marine put the Monoprix bags down beside a fountain and sat on its edge while Verlaque took the call.

"How are you all?" Verlaque asked.

"The girls went back to bed and are sleeping again," Paulik answered. "But the firefighters have been working all morning at the *bastide*. This mistral is badly timed. The fire chief and gendarme captain came by and had coffee with us, when Léa was still up. They found a body in the attic."

Verlaque sat beside Marine and held the phone between them so she could hear. "A woman?"

"Yes," Paulik replied. "Léa explained what happened last night. She went into the kitchen and grabbed the photograph, but on her way out she heard noises at the top of the stairs, and followed them all the way up to the attic. A woman was up there, dressed in some kind of long white gauzy dress, designed to frighten Valère, no doubt. Her face was exposed, and Léa recognized her as the blind woman from the village. Léa screamed, and the woman chased her. Léa ran out the back door, running all the way to the chapel without stopping. What she couldn't have known was that the woman tripped over the gown and hit her head on the stairs' wrought-iron banister. The fire chief said she was probably unconscious when the fire started."

"Are the gendarmes searching her rented house in Puyloubier?"

"Done. They uncovered her purse and ID, still sitting on the kitchen table."

"Who was it?"

"Monica Pelloquin," Paulik answered. "The publisher's wife."

Verlaque looked at Marine, and she nodded. "How did she sneak off to the *bastide*?" Verlaque asked. "I thought her house was being watched."

"It was supposed to be," Paulik answered. "But we were understaffed—there was a friendly match in Marseille last night, since Spain just won the World Cup."

"The soccer game," Verlaque cut in, sighing. "France against the UK."

"We had to send as many officers to Marseille as we could. The hooligans . . ."

"On both sides," Verlaque said.

Paulik asked, "Did you know about Mme Pelloquin? You don't sound surprised."

"I figured it out late last night," Verlaque said. "I kept thinking of her luminous pale skin, so someone who would wear a sun hat. Daniel de Rudder had me barking up the wrong tree, thinking it was Ursule Genoux or her sister. Plus it seemed to me that Mme Pelloquin had a lot to gain by exposing Valère as a literary fraud."

"I wouldn't say he's a fraud—"

Verlaque smiled. He, too, such a lover of Barbier's early books, wanted to defend him. They'd soon know how much Valère wrote and how much his late wife did. "A Parisian acquaintance did some calling around late last night and early this morning," he said. "It seems that press and literary folks are either night-hawks or early risers. Anyway, Mme Pelloquin had indeed approached a few newspaper and magazine editors with what she called 'the Valère Barbier scoop of the century.' She even talked to a film producer. She could have made a lot of money and found fame."

"Alphonse Pelloquin must have told her about Agathe's involvement."

"Yes, and Monica probably thought they were having an affair too. Agathe's dead; she couldn't get back at her. But she could attack Valère in her place."

Chapter Thirty-one

Aix-en-Provence, Wednesday, July 21, 2010

Marine held up her champagne. *"Santé,"* she said, tipping her glass toward her husband's.

"Cheers," Verlaque replied, as he always did when toasting, in English.

"It was very kind of Jacob and his wife to let us stay here for a few days while they're in London," Marine said, looking at the low rows of purple lavender that led to the swimming pool.

"It only makes sense," Verlaque said, "to stay in a place before you buy it. It's crazy that we have to make such rushed decisions when buying property, never being able to try it out beforehand, like a test drive."

Marine nodded. "When I bought my apartment in the Mazarin, two other prospective buyers were breathing down my neck. I had to decide and make an offer in about ten minutes. I've deliberated longer buying shoes."

Verlaque looked back at the long, low farmhouse that had been added onto throughout the centuries. "It's not as majestic as the Bastide Blanche," he said, turning back around.

"Thank goodness for that."

"It's probably not haunted, either."

"Do you really think?" Marine asked. "The *bastide*—"

"Yes," Verlaque answered. "But don't tell anyone."

"I do too," Marine said. "Even without Monica Pelloquin's tricks, there were too many mysterious things going on."

"And the objects disappearing and reappearing."

"Like you always misplacing your reading glasses."

"Very funny," Verlaque said.

"I'm sorry about Judge Rudder."

Verlaque looked up at the clear blue sky and smiled. "He lived a good long life. I'm glad I was able to fill him in before he died. He seemed relieved."

"Three dead," Marine said.

"Sadly, Ursule Genoux believed the only way to overcome her guilt was to take an overdose of sleeping pills."

"And with both Ursule and Alphonse Pelloquin dead, we'll never know for sure what happened on that boat."

"We know well enough," Verlaque said, "Célestine Parent knew quite a bit. Her visit to Aix yesterday turned out to be quite fruitful." He took a sip of champagne, loving the way the light bubbles slid from the back of his mouth down his throat. "Mme Parent said that Ursule told her she went out into the storm and called for help, hoping that Alphonse would come out. She hated him for keeping Agathe's literary talents hidden for so long. In the fog she wouldn't have been able to see that the tall person walking toward her, disguised by rain gear, was Agathe. Ursule pushed her overboard and only would have realized who it was when Agathe screamed. Agathe and Pelloquin had been arguing, probably about her ghostwriting. With Agathe dead, Pelloquin's problem was solved. Ursule told her sister that he came out onto the bow and, seeing Ursule's distress, realized right away what had happened. He lorded it over her, threatening to expose her to the police, so they both stayed quiet. Mme Parent was enraged that Agathe's essay was burned in the fire."

"It was her proof. And now Valère's cleverly left France. Where is he exactly?"

"Pantelleria," Verlaque answered, pulling the dripping bottle out of the ice bucket. He refilled their glasses and sat back. "He told me before he left that Michèle Baudouin had recommended the island. He's going to write his memoir from there, after he finds a new publisher."

"Sounds egotistical."

"He did make right with some things," Verlaque

said, shrugging. "He's talking about buying that old-fashioned shoe store on the rue Thiers for Sandrine to run."

"Are you kidding?" Marine asked. "I was just in there yesterday, buying sandals. I was so sad to hear they were closing. I bought a pair for Charlotte, too, who should be on a plane right now to Berlin." She took a sip of champagne and then looked over at her husband, who sat on a chaise longue, legs extended and eyes half-closed, slowly moving his right foot back and forth, a slight smile at the corners of his mouth. Usually, only Italy made him this relaxed. Jacob's house would be perfect for them. "You liked Valère—didn't you?"

"He was just the kind of person I always hoped the great writer would be," Verlaque said. "Smart, funny, kind, absentminded. A bit silly, even."

The noise of tires crunching on gravel caused Marine and Verlaque to turn around.

Verlaque slapped his forehead. "I invited the Pauliks," he said. "I forgot to tell you. Bruno mentioned that they would be in Aix this evening, running errands—"

Marine quickly got up and wrapped a sarong around her bathing suit.

"Hello!" Bruno Paulik called out as he came around the corner of the house, carrying a cooler. Hélène and Léa followed, each carrying a tote bag. "Not a bad place," he continued, grinning, as he looked up at the golden stone house, with its taupe-colored shutters, and the manicured gardens that led down to the pool.

"I think it will do for us," Verlaque said, shaking Paulik's hand and giving Hélène and Léa the *bise*.

"We brought food from Aix," Hélène said, gesturing to the cooler. "Two roasted chickens, a big potato salad, some fruit, and a few bottles of my new vermentino."

"And cheese and bread!" Léa exclaimed, holding up a bag.

"Wow, this place is straight out of *Architectural Digest*," Hélène said.

"Is it too posh?" Marine asked, wincing. She knew what her parents, especially her mother, would say when they saw it.

Hélène shook her head. "Not at all. It's chic and stylish."

"Léa and I would like to test the chic and stylish swimming pool," Bruno Paulik said, putting his arm around Léa.

"Go right ahead," Verlaque said. "There's an insanely big pool house down there, where you can change. I'll take you."

"Come into the house with me," Marine said to Hélène. "I'll show you around a bit."

Hélène whistled as they walked into the vast kitchen, redone by Jacob in stainless steel, Carrara marble, and pale ash cabinetry, with the farmhouse's original deep-red terra-cotta tiles on the floor. "*Terre cuite*," Hélène said, tapping her foot. "*Super belle*."

"My mother will tell me how hard terra-cotta is to keep up," Marine said, laughing.

"My mother would do the same," Hélène said, setting the cooler on the floor.

"How has Léa been?" Marine asked, opening the cupboards and looking for more wineglasses.

Hélène leaned against a counter, looking out a large bow window with views of the garden. "She's better now," she answered. "But at first she was really sad."

"Yes, that's understandable. That night . . . being chased . . ."

Hélène nodded. She smiled as she watched her daughter jump into the pool, followed by her husband who was pushed in by Antoine Verlaque. "But she was more *sad* than *upset*."

"Oh, really?"

Hélène turned to Marine. "We're worried about her," she said. "Léa told us she would miss her friends at the *bastide*."

"Valère and Sandrine," Marine began.

"No," Hélène said. "I mean, she said she'd miss them too, but she'd miss her secret friends. Léa's never been a child who had imaginary friends."

Marine got goose bumps on her arms, and shivered. "My bathing suit is damp," she explained when Hélène looked at her, concerned.

"We're thinking of taking Léa to a therapist," Hélène continued, "to help her deal with the trauma of that night. Gosh, even I need it. Bruno told me your mother has been researching the history of the *bastide*. Has she found anything interesting?"

"Nothing much," Marine replied.

"Well, whatever was going on in that house is now gone forever."

"Ashes to ashes," Marine said, setting down four large wineglasses.

Chapter Thirty-two

New York City, September 23, 2010

Justin had spent so much time worrying about the restaurant and what wines to order that he hadn't chosen a spot to smoke cigars after dinner. Instinctively, he ushered his guest toward the river, where there were bike lanes, trees, and views of Brooklyn. Thankfully, it was still warm out, despite being after midnight. Neither of them felt like going to an uptown cigar bar. They bought some sparkling water on the way.

"Is that Brooklyn?" Valère asked as they cut the Cuban cigars he'd removed from his jacket.

"Williamsburg," Justin replied, touching a newly purchased torch lighter to his cigar and slowly turning it, trying to get it just right.

"Maybe someday you can buy a house over there, eh? A brownstone?"

"In my dreams."

Valère sat back and took his first mouthful of smoke. "Chocolate."

"Gingerbread," Justin said, smoking.

"And earth," Valère said. "Always earth. That red earth of Cuba."

"Like Provence, right?"

Valère nodded. "In Pantelleria it's mostly rock. But from my new house I can see Tunisia. Did I tell you that? Always buy a house for the view—never because it's big or because you like the way it looks. What you see from inside, looking out, is more important. It makes the soul soar."

"You won't miss La Bastide?" Justin asked.

"No. All those bad memories—my own, and the past residents'—are gone now."

"You kind of breezed over that part," Justin said. "Hugues de Besse and the young girls."

"It's too terrible to even think about. Marine Bonnet and her mother took me out for tea one afternoon and told all about it. Those poor girls."

"And Agathe's essay?"

"It's gone too. Michèle told me she left Agathe's story behind at the *bastide*, hidden between her mattress and box spring, instead of taking it to Gordes. She'd given me until July 14 to make up my mind about working with her; if I said no, she was going to tell all to the press. But I'm not sure if she was telling the truth."

"Maybe it doesn't matter," Justin said, turning toward Valère. "It all depends on the kind of book you're planning to write."

"I told you," Valère said. "A memoir. Starting

with my childhood, schooling, first job at *Le Monde*, then writing."

"And what happened at La Bastide?"

"Undecided."

"I don't know how much of Michèle Baudouin's claim is true, but this book could be your chance to defend yourself."

Valère smoked, not speaking for a minute. "Are you saying I should confess?"

"I didn't say that," Justin said. "But, if, let's just say, Mme Baudouin still has that story, and if, let's just say, there's some truth to her accusation, and your late wife did help you write the early books, why not take the high road?"

"And beat her to it?"

"Exactly. Again, you're the only one who knows how much of her claim is true. And if you did confess, I'd back you up 100 percent."

"My career would be in shambles," Valère said. "Your company wouldn't make any money on this book."

"*Au contraire*," Justin said, smiling, pleased that he managed to remember a French phrase.

Valère stared at him. "Explain."

"Americans love confessionals," Justin said.

"The French don't!"

"But it's more than a confessional. It's a story of redemption."

"But if what Ursule claimed, and Michèle is claiming, is true, I'm a cheat. And a liar."

"Your romances! You've made millions of dollars on the power of your storytelling," Justin said. "You're loved as a storyteller, and readers will want to know everything about you, even if you have failed. In fact, it's better if you've slipped up. It makes you human, like them. And you'll no longer be a liar, because you'll be fessing up. Telling the truth."

Valère thought for a moment, smoking. "Redemption is trickier than justice—isn't it?" he said. "Redemption is beyond the law. We get there by our own methods and means—hopefully."

"I'd wager that with this book you'll lose some readers but gain many more."

Valère nodded. "And I'll wager, too," he said, gesturing toward the opposite bank, "that one day you will own one of those brownstones."

Justin laughed. "I'd be happy with a small village house in the South of France," he said. "Somewhere near the Pauliks."

"A young guy like you has no business in one of those dilapidated old houses," Valère said, waving a hand.

"Perhaps you're right," Justin chuckled. "Did the fire start because of the faulty wiring?"

"Yes, and lit the hot-water heater, which had a fuel leak, on fire."

"All those stacks of newspapers . . ."

"Poor Monica. I never liked her, but still . . ."

"Why did she do it?" Justin asked, shaking his head. "Was she trying to drive you mad?"

"Yes, as mad as she was," Valère replied. "She was mad with jealousy. I had always seen that side of her. But she was greedy, too, and could have made a lot of money by exposing me."

"How did she get up to Paris so quickly?"

"It's only a three-hour train ride," Valère answered. "She may have overheard either Antoine Verlaque and myself, or me and Sandrine, speaking of his planned trip to Paris. We now know Monica was hiding in the house even when we were all there. Or she may have just gotten lucky and been back in Paris exactly when Verlaque showed up."

"Ursule Genoux was obviously suffering," Justin said. "Was she in love with Agathe?"

"No no," Valère replied. "She loved her, yes, but not in the way you're implying. If Ursule had her doubts about Agathe's participation in writing my books, she never let on. That said, her sister must have shown her the documents in the archives at Les Loges. But I know for sure that Ursule was even more dedicated to Agathe than to me. So if Agathe didn't want anyone to know that she was *helping* me, then Ursule and Célestine would have respected that."

"The schoolgirl bond thing."

"Exactly."

"And Michèle?" Justin asked. "You told

Sandrine that she was in Gordes but was coming back."

"You're a good listener, despite your fidgeting. When I saw Michèle again, two days later, she didn't even seem to care about our joint project. The film producer in Gordes took out an option on three of Michèle's recent books, for a television series, so writing with a has-been like me was no longer interesting. Especially when the producer offered Michèle a minor role in the series."

"Wow. She could play herself."

Valère laughed. "Yes, no script needed."

"One last question before we get back to discussing your next book," Justin said. "Sandrine?"

"I bought her the shoe store. It really wasn't that expensive, and the family who owned it was thrilled. Sandrine sends me postcards, and once I decipher the spelling mistakes, I get little pieces of her life in Aix. She's actually making money on the store, for one, and Marine Bonnet stops by once a week to say hello. When we were trying to rid the house of ghosts, Sandrine told me we should tell the ghosts that their time on earth was up, and that they should go peacefully toward the light. I think it was sage advice, even if she did get it from a shoddy Web site. I like to think that when the house burned down, all its pain and sordid history went with it. My own included."

Valère reached into his jacket pocket and pulled out a black-and-white postcard: a somewhat out-of-focus photograph of a grand house.

"La Bastide Blanche?" Justin asked, looking closely at the postcard.

"Yes, Sandrine must have picked it up at the flea market," Valère replied. "I'll read you what she wrote on the back, as it's in French: '*When La Bastide caught on fire, I decided to let Josy go. Once we knew that Léa was safe, I suddenly felt lighter, relieved that there's no hell or final judgment. Josy's safe up there. And you, M Barbier, should think of Agathe like that too. Safe and perhaps looking down at you. Possibly laughing. But watching all the same.*'"

"That's really lovely," Justin said. "Did you lose everything in the fire?"

Valère stretched out his legs and reached into his pants pocket. He pulled out a linen handkerchief and Justin immediately knew what it was.

"Not this," he said with a smile.

Books are produced in the United States using U.S.-based materials

Books are printed using a revolutionary new process called THINKtech™ that lowers energy usage by 70% and increases overall quality

Books are durable and flexible because of Smyth-sewing

Paper is sourced using environmentally responsible foresting methods and the paper is acid-free

enter Point Large Print
500 Brooks Road / PO Box 1
rndike, ME 04986-0001 USA

(207) 568-3717

S & Canada:
00 929-9108
enterpointlargeprint.com